IF I HAD STAYED ON THE THOROUGHFARE THAT day, not taken the alley, I would never have met him. The thought of never knowing him bothers me, leaves me feeling restless and aching.

I sit, defeated, at the small dressing table and shuffle the deck of cards for the hundredth time. I cut the deck and mix it, my fingers now adept where seven days ago they fumbled through it. I close my eyes and draw a card at random.

FATE.

I always draw FATE.

ALSO BY
KIERSTEN WHITE

THE CHAOS OF STARS

MIND GAMES

PERFECT LIES

PARANORMALCY

SUPERNATURALLY

ENDLESSLY

ILLUSIONS
of FATE

KIERSTEN WHITE

HARPER TEEN
An Imprint of HarperCollinsPublishers

HarperTeen is an imprint of HarperCollins Publishers.

Illusions of Fate
Copyright © 2014 by Kiersten Brazier
All rights reserved. Printed in the United States of America.

Library of Congress Cataloging-in-Publication Data
White, Kiersten.
  Illusions of fate / Kiersten White. — First edition.
    pages cm
  ISBN 978-0-06-213590-2 (pbk.)
  [1. Schools—Fiction. 2. Magic—Fiction. 3. Love—Fiction. 4. Fantasy.] I. Title.
PZ7.W583764Ill 2014   2014010021
[Fic]—dc23   CIP
                                                                AC

Typography by Torborg Davern
15 16 17 18 19   CG/RRDH   10 9 8 7 6 5 4 3 2 1
❖
First paperback edition, 2015

To everyone who goes looking for magic and finds it was always inside them, after all.

One

Dear Mama,

I am most certainly not dead. Thank you for your tender concern. I will try to write more often so you don't have to worry so between letters. (Because a week's silence surely means I have fallen prey to a wasting illness or been murdered in these boring, gray streets.)

School is going well. I am excelling in all of my classes. (Apparently, some things never change, and girls are not challenged in Albion in the same way they weren't on Melei.) My professors are all intelligent and kind. (Kind of horrible.) None *stand out.* (I refuse to mention *him* by name, no matter how many obviously "subtle" questions you ask.) *The other students are also quite focused on their schooling, and none of us has much time for socializing. Boys and girls attend separate classes as well, so no, I have not met many interesting young men.* (I am neither courting nor being courted. Please stop hoping.)

Tell Aunt Li'ne thank you for the mittens. They are very much appreciated in this cold, damp climate I am so unused to. And please tell the sun hello and I miss her very much! I also miss you, of course. (I do. Very much.)

All my love,

Jessamin

Reading over the letter to my mother, I am so absorbed in my head with adding the true statements to my written words that I fail to pay attention to the street. I cannot decide which shocks me more—nearly being run over by the horse-drawn cart, or the fluid stream of cursing in my native tongue that is being directed at me.

I look up, cheeks burning, and meet a pair of black eyes that, combined with the familiarity of the language, hit me with a longing for Melei so deep and painful I can scarcely draw a breath.

The man pauses, obviously surprised to see how dark of skin and eyes I am in spite of my school uniform. And so I take the opportunity to insult his manhood, his lineage, and his horse in a single, well-crafted turn of phrase I haven't used since my friend Kelen taught it to me when I was fourteen.

He smiles.

I smile back.

Brushing his hand through the air in another gesture so achingly familiar it brings tears to my eyes, he clicks his tongue and the cart moves on, our near-collision forgotten.

He's made me crave heat. The sun's anemic rays pull more warmth from me than they offer. I hate Albion, the whole gray country. I hate Avebury, a city just as gray, teeming with people but coldly lifeless.

No. Homesickness does me no good. Wiping under my eyes, I straighten my shoulders and march toward the hotel. I only have a couple of hours before my shift to do my reading for tomorrow's classes, and I will not be anything less than the best. I cannot afford it.

I cut away from the main thoroughfare and find myself in a narrow alley. It's old, the lines not quite vertical as they lean ever so gradually overhead.

"What's wrong, chickie bird?"

I startle, my eyes whipped down from where they traced the line of the sky. A man with the thick build, intricate tattoos, and accompanying ripe scent of a dockworker stands directly in front of me.

"Nothing." I flash a tight, dismissive smile honed these last few months of learning to blend in. "Just passing through."

"Nah, don't do that." He steps to the side as I do, and his

mass blocks me from walking by. "Come have a drink with me, yeah? Make you feel all better."

"I have somewhere to be."

His smile broadens, blue eyes nearly lost in the tanned squint lines of his face. "You ain't from 'round here, are you? An island rat, that's what you are." He reaches out with a meaty hand to touch my hair, black as night and waterfall straight, where I have it pulled into a bun at the base of my neck.

"Excuse me." I back up but he follows, leaning in closer. "Let me by."

"I've heard stories about island rats. You can tell me if they're true."

I lift onto my toes to sprint away when a hand comes down on my shoulder.

"There you are, darling. So sorry I'm late."

I don't know this voice, a low tenor with the clipped, stylish vowels of the classes I only see when delivering orders to their expensive hotel rooms.

I stiffen under his fingers, which are light but steady on my shoulder. Now there are two of them to deal with. I slide my hand into my satchel, gripping the handle of the paring knife I borrowed from the kitchen and keep with me all the time. The gentleman's fingers tighten.

"Not necessary," he whispers.

I turn to look at him—a low, round hat is pulled over his forehead, obscuring his eyes. His lips are sly and twisted into a smile over teeth far finer than my dockworker friend's. This man is a porcelain doll compared to the brute blocking my path.

He's taller than me but lean, all angles in his suit that reeks of money.

Apparently, the dockworker has the same assessment. "This your girl? I don't think she is."

"I would never accuse you of thinking, my good man." The gentleman lifts his silver-topped cane, tapping it once in the middle of the dockworker's forehead. "I shouldn't worry it'll be a problem for you to give up the practice of thinking entirely."

The dockworker blinks once—twice—so slowly I notice his stubby blond eyelashes, and then he moves to the side like he has forgotten how to walk on land.

"Good day, then." The gentleman steers me forward with his fingertips, and I've barely time to process what happened before we're out of the alley and back onto the main street.

"Well." I clear my throat, embarrassed. I look down the walkway instead of at the gentleman, not wanting to see in his eyes whether he did that out of the goodness of his heart or if he expects something in return. This is Albion, after all. "Thank you for your help. Good-bye."

"I'd like to walk you home, if it isn't too much trouble. Especially if you plan on gracing any more questionable streets with your presence."

I straighten my shoulders, sliding the right one out from under his hand, and look him full in the face. His eyes are dark, his features fine, almost femininely delicate, save his strong jawline. "With all due respect, sir, I'm not about to trade one strange man for another, and I have no interest in showing you where I live."

His smile broadens. "Then I insist you let me buy you supper, and we will part as friends with no knowledge of the other's residence."

I open my mouth to inform him I've no time for supper, but before I can, he takes off his hat and I find myself entranced by the impossible gold of his hair. I have never seen such hair in my life. It's like the sunshine of my childhood is concentrated there.

A door opens beside us, and his hand once again presses against my back. My feet trip forward of their own accord—*traitor feet, what's happening?*—and suddenly we're sitting in a warmly lit booth in a restaurant that smells of garlic and spice. My stomach and heart react at the same time: one with famished hunger and the other with renewed longing for home.

"I thought this would do nicely," he says, and his smile reminds me of the expression my mother's cat, Tubbins, would get when he'd done something particularly clever. "Why did you travel from Melei to attend school?"

"I never said I was a student. And how do you know where I'm from?"

"The beguiling way your mouth forms S and O gives away your island home."

I raise an eyebrow at his attempt to be clever. "It wasn't my dark skin and black hair?"

He laughs. "Well, those were rather large clues as well. As for the school, see—" He reaches across the table and takes my right hand in his. I try to pull it back, but his long fingers are insistent. "Look at your callus." He points to the raised bump on the top knuckle of my middle finger. "And see how it is stained black? If you were a secretary, no doubt they'd have you on one of those horrible new typewriters. You don't have the pinched look of someone who keeps ledgers, either. And, much like your skin, your school uniform is a bit of a giveaway."

I stifle a snort of laughter, not wanting to give him that point. Then, realizing he still has my hand in his, I pull it back and take a sip of tea. When did the tea get here? Have I been so distracted by his hair? I am not that shallow, surely. But I use the tea to buy myself a moment to look at him. "And what am I studying?"

He taps his chin thoughtfully. "In your final year of preparatory, yes? So you'd have to be in your focus. You have the soulful eyes of a writer and the heavy bag of a reader. Literature, certainly."

"History."

He narrows his eyes. "But that is not your first choice."

"Alas, apparently the feminine mind is not suited to the mathematical arts, all my test scores to the contrary. Now you, sir. Or is it 'lord'?"

"You may address me as anything you wish."

"Well then. You have all the grace and manners of nobility, not to mention clothes that cost more than our server's yearly wages. Your quick smile indicates an arrogance born and bred into you through generations of never having to answer to anyone, so I'm guessing lord, or perhaps earl, but lord suits your savior complex better. In your spare time, because being wealthy and privileged is a full-time occupation, you like mingling with those too far beneath you for notice. Chambermaids, waitresses," I glance meaningfully at where our serving girl is leaning against the counter gazing moons at him, "and even the occasional student. Unfortunately, sometimes you miscalculate your appeal and try to use your charms on girls who grew up on an island spotted with bastard children who were fathered by visiting Albens. I am therefore immune to being overwhelmed by your exceptional ancestry. You will, however, be able to console yourself with your vast lands and holdings and never again have to consider the student who paid for her own tea and then begged leave."

I dig out my purse and drop a few coins on the table, expecting him to sneer or curse, but instead I look up to find his first genuinely delighted smile. It makes him look younger and I realize he's probably not much older than me. Eighteen, perhaps.

"Oh, please stay and eat, won't you?" he asks. "I haven't had someone be so honest with me in ages, and I cannot tell you how refreshing it is."

Something in the open happiness of his face, the almost childlike hope there, whisks away my resolve to be cold.

"Very well." I sit back and consider my strange companion. "Though you haven't told me whether or not I'm right, my lord."

"I've no doubt you're right with startling frequency, and while I'd very much like to be yours, I am not a lord. Sandwiches to start?"

The meal is the best I've had since I left Melei. Halfway through, I'm struck with sudden fear for the cost of such a meal, but in one of those odd, sliding moments where I seem to be entranced by the light playing on his hair, the plates are gone and the bill is paid.

"Thank you," I stutter, unsure what else to say. I am out of sorts; I know we've spoken of many things, but I cannot grasp the particulars of any of it.

"Thank *you*, my dear Jessamin. Are you quite sure I can't walk you back to the dormitories?"

I stop midway to standing. "I told you my name?"

His sly smile is back, all innocence gone. "I plucked it from the air around your lips. And for the privilege of knowing it, I'll tell you that mine is Finn."

"Well then, Finn, I wish you the best of luck in your future endeavors, whatever they may be. I do not live in the dormitories, nor do I care to tell you any other details." I scamper from the restaurant. He follows, slower, and I turn to see him over my shoulder, watching me. When I round a corner toward the hotel, I check again to see if he is following, unsure if the thought makes me feel safer or scared.

A large black bird caws over my head, nearly startling me out of my boots. Frowning at it, I unlock the servants' entrance to the Grande Sylvie. Checking over my shoulder one last time, I notice a movement and jump backward.

I shake my head at my nerves. Only my shadow cast by the dim gas lamp.

But for the oddest moment it looked as though I had two.

Two

"AND WHO CAN TELL ME THE TOP IMPROVEMENTS made during colonization?"

The professor teaching our Advanced Alben History course has every degree available, and is teaching for one year here as a special guest of the school. His owlish eyes peer out between round spectacles. Wisps of hair make a last desperate attempt to cover his shiny bald pate, and he is thin everywhere except a small paunch pushing out the buttons of his vest.

And yet, beneath the gradual wearing-down of age, it's obvious he was once handsome. No matter how hard I look, I can see nothing of myself in him. And he has never, not once, so much as looked me in the eyes to try and find himself.

Oh, Mama, why?

A mousy girl shoots her hand into the air. "Improved infrastructure. Eradication of pagan superstitions and beliefs. Education. Increased safety with Alben police forces and state protection. Introduction of advanced medical discipline."

"Very good."

She beams, either besotted or trying to get a better grade. Please let it be the latter. "Anyone who follows your column on the theoretical benefits of Alben policies on Iverian continental countries would be able to say the same. The colonization case studies are perfect examples."

I cannot stop myself and raise my hand.

Professor Miller does not call on me.

I talk anyway. "What about the steep rise in infant mortality for the period of twenty years after colonization? Taking Melei as an example, death rates among infants went from one in ten to one in five and have only recently begun to taper off."

Professor Miller clears his throat, and the sound does not cover a blond girl on the end of my row sighing, "Island rat."

"Why is she even here?" the mousy girl whispers over her shoulder.

"My father has complained to the superintendent about the decline in quality of students." The blond girl does not look at me as she says it. None of them ever do.

Professor Miller, having finally cleared his throat but not his ears, which remain deaf to my comments, lists the chapters we are to study for our next class and then leaves without dismissing us.

I feel utterly dismissed nonetheless.

Leaving in a cocoon of silence amidst the chattering of my classmates, I find a bench outside and begin writing my calculations with fierce strokes. I'm not in a mathematics course, and barely have time to balance my actual studies with work at the hotel, but I don't care. I will learn *everything* I can. I wish I were like the other students and that studying was my only task.

Fortunately for them, none of them are poor.

I have never been poor before. I had everything I needed on Melei, with a private tutor to teach me the hard consonants and neglected vowels of this language. Mama wouldn't even let me speak Melenese at home. She sent me to classes on the manners and social customs of Albion. My friends got to learn traditional dances from their grandmothers while I was forced to memorize the stiff measures of this country's music, the stilted, passionless steps to their waltzes.

Sighing, I pull out a paper and, balancing it on top of the library's mathematics book, compose another letter to Mama, as always writing lies and telling the truth in my head.

Dear Mama,

    I hope this letter finds you well. It contains all my love and affection. (It also contains all my questions about how you could ever have loved a man like Professor Miller.)

    You asked about where I live. I cannot believe I haven't mentioned it, but I suppose I'm so used to it now I don't think of it. The dorms are small and plain, but as a student I don't need much more. (I cannot afford the dorms. I do not live in them.) The food is dreadful, all heavy meat and sauce. I miss fruit! (I am always hungry; a supper with a strange man was the fullest my stomach has been since I got here.)

As I have mentioned in every letter, my professors are all interesting and I take copious notes during lectures. (If you do not bring up my father, I am certainly not going to offer you information on that louse of a man.) The course work is challenging but I am excelling. (I have to be perfect so they can find no excuse to dock my grades.)

I have delivered Aunt Nani's package to Jacabo. He was so happy to receive it, and I take tea with him once a week. It is a great comfort to speak Melenese with someone. (I live in the hotel where Jacabo works. He saved me when I realized I could not afford room and board at the school. I work long, hard hours in the evenings to earn a tiny hole of a servant's room and whatever scraps of food are left over.)

Please give everyone my love and tell them how much I am learning to bring back to the island as a teacher. (I will not fail, and I will use everything I learn here to make Melei better.)

Your affectionate daughter,
Jessamin

A large black bird lands on the bench beside me, brazenly close. "Hello there," I say as it considers me with flat, yellow eyes. "Where I am from, you're known as an *acawl* for that awful noise you make."

It cocks its head reproachfully.

"No disrespect, Sir Bird. You cannot help your harsh voice any more than these Albens can help their love of ugly words and sounds."

A boy walks by, not bothering to hide his snicker at the quaint island girl talking to the local wildlife. Sir Bird caws sharply at him. I approve.

"Anyone who shares my distaste for the men of this country can also share my lunch." I break off the stale heel of my bread, crumble it in my palm, and then toss it onto the bench next to my friend. If birds had eyebrows, I'd swear it was raising them at me. "Spirits bless you, you arrogant little thing. I suppose I wouldn't eat it if I didn't have to, either. Good day, Sir Bird."

Unaware it has been excused, Sir Bird continues to sit and stare until I have to report for my next lecture. Even the birds here are strange.

Two days in a row of the sun breaking through clouds, and while it isn't anywhere near what a rational person would deem warm, it feels as though the whole city has sighed in relief.

Everyone is shedding their outermost layers of clothing to sit outside and soak in the light they can.

I elect to stroll through Haigh Park, a lonely jewel of green adjacent to my school. Humming to myself, I wander a twisting path and play with the lines in the park, tracing imaginary triangles between points and calculating their areas based on estimated lengths.

"Why, Jessamin, are you following me?"

I look up, shocked, to see Finn sitting on a slatted bench ahead of me, his arm draped over the scrolling ironwork along the back. The sun catches in his hair, hat discarded next to him, and I've never seen anything quite so lovely as those shades of gold.

I blink rapidly, feeling like I'm coming up for air from the swimming hole behind the village. *Speak, Jessamin.* "I could ask the same of you, sir."

"Ah, but I was here first, which makes you the follower and me the followee."

"Following requires intent, and I can assure you that I have none where you are concerned. Good day."

I hurry past, my boots kicking up gravel, and pull my most recent letter from Mama out of my bag for something to do. A few seconds later, he appears at my side, matching my determined stride. I read with a scowl, hoping to communicate how busy I am.

"Bad news?"

"No."

"You seem unhappy with the contents of the letter. What does it say?"

I glance over and my resolve to be distant drifts away. I really am a shallow thing if a handsome face affects me so. "It's from my mother. She informs me of the minute goings-on of a man she had hoped I would marry."

"Aren't you a bit young for matrimony?"

"On Melei, I was an old maid. It's safer to be married."

His eyebrows draw closer together. "*Safer* is an interesting word for marriage. But you did not want to marry this suitor."

I wave a hand, but he is not Melenese and will not understand that it's an unspoken gesture for "it doesn't matter." "Henry was a friend I tutored. I do not wish to wed him or any other Alben on the island she had her eye on. That's why I left."

"So." His face is solemn, but an amused tone undercuts his voice. "You left your home to avoid being married to an Alben man and came to a country entirely filled with them."

I'm torn between offense and amusement. Amusement wins, and I laugh at myself. "It made sense at the time."

"I'm certain it did."

We walk in silence, and I go back to the letter, waiting for him to bid me good day. He doesn't. "I've never been to this park before." He swings his cane at the tip of a bush. "It's rather filled with children, isn't it?"

As if on cue, a small, round thing runs in front of us, legs flying to keep from falling forward with momentum.

"Charlie! Oy, Charlie, you get back here before I tan your hide!" A harassed nurse runs past us, skirts held in her hands.

"Do you dislike children?" I ask, entertained at the little one's cleverness in dodging capture attempts.

"I don't dislike them, nor do I like them. I've never understood why one must love children simply because they are children. I don't love people because they are people; in fact, I rarely like any people at all. If a child is somehow deserving of admiration, I certainly won't deny it, but why hand it out like candy on Queen's Day?"

I laugh, surprising him.

"Do you think me terribly cruel, then?"

"Actually, I agree. It is another great fault of mine my mother endeavored to correct. Children in general I've never cared for, though individual children I love very much."

"I knew you had taste. Though your lack of hat is rather shocking."

"Oh, fie on this country and its inordinate affection for hats. I would sooner love every child alive than I would wear a hat. My head is perfectly covered by my hair."

"But the sun! We Albens have a terrible fear of letting it touch more of our bodies than absolutely necessary."

"Which would explain the dour and listless spirit that pervades this country. Perhaps if you gave the sun a bit more attention, it would be flattered and come out more often."

"Perhaps." He smiles, cane tucked behind his back as he leads with his angular shoulders and long strides. Everything about him is graceful, from the cut of his suit to the curve of his brow. "Jessamin, I should very much like to call on you."

I stop in my tracks. He turns immediately with his sly grin, as though he'd anticipated my reaction.

"I—I'm sorry, I—"

"But," he says with a drawn-out sigh, "I'm afraid I cannot, simply because I do like you, ever so much. I should not have stolen this moment as it is. And so I'll wish you safe wanderings, an utter absence of distasteful suitors, and many more days of sunshine for your hatless head." He takes my hand in his and bends at the waist. A spark flames through me as his lips brush against my skin. I barely stifle a gasp.

"If things were simpler," he says. And this time in his smile I am shocked to see the same ache I feel for Melei.

With that, he turns and leaves. I watch, bewildered as he walks away, his shadow stretching longer than any others around him, like it wants to stay.

I press my fingers to my chest. What nonsense is my heart pattering out? I barely know him, and I'm almost certain I don't care for him in the slightest.

What an odd, beautiful man. I will never understand the customs of this insane country. Frowning, I find the nearest bench to rest on and another bird, as big and black as Sir Bird, lands next to me and caws.

"I don't have any food for you." I feel strangely melancholic in spite of the sunshine. The last two conversations with Finn are the most personal I've had with anyone since I left home. "That's that, I suppose. Just you and me, Sir Bird."

The bird answers with another loud caw, then a clacking attack of wings as it flies in my face. I scream and throw my arms up, trying to protect myself as it scrabbles for a hold on my shoulders. Standing, I twist and turn, stumbling down the path, but the possessed bird continues its attack until I feel a sharp burning sensation in my bun. It flies away, a clump of my hair and the blue ribbon that held it back dangling from its claws.

There's a strange note of regret in its fading caws. Feeling the back of my head with probing fingers, I find a tender spot where the hair was ripped out.

I do *not* accept that blighted bird's apology. I collapse onto another bench, warm tears tracing down my face, less from the pain than from the shock of it all. I hate this wretched country.

Three

"WHAT'S GNAWING YOUR SOUL?" JACABO ASKS IN the soft, musical language of our home. Here everyone calls him Jacky Boy, but he's rather less a boy than a man—a large man at that, with his head shaved bald and a pronounced limp. When I looked him up to deliver his parcel, he knew without asking just what the city was doing to me, and immediately offered work and lodging.

He's the type of man I am proud to know.

I wave a hand in the air. He chuckles at the familiarity of the gesture. I wish I could bare my soul to him in Melenese with the same ease, but the sad fact is, thanks to my mother's determination, I am more fluent in Alben. I don't even think in Melenese, and most of my dreams are narrated in the harsher tones of this country's language.

It makes a soul lonely when even your tongue has no home.

Last night's dreams required no language, though. I dreamt of beady yellow eyes watching me from the darkness. The memory of claws and feathers and beaks has me on edge. Today I begged a hat from Ma'ati, a maid here sweet on Jacky Boy, and wore it to my classes. Partly to protect my hair, but mostly so I could resist the temptation to watch the sky.

"Thinner on the carrots." Jacky Boy nods at my work, and wordlessly I follow his instructions. I helped with the cooking some as a child, but we had a woman from the village who bore the brunt of the meal-making. This, however, is nothing like what we supped on. All creams, heavy sauces, and meat, with vegetables nothing but an afterthought.

I work mainly with chopping. Jacky Boy likes consistency in his kitchen, and I am very good at creating even, calculated amounts. Then he adds the artful touches that turn a tenpenny cut of meat into a queen's head dollar. The ways of the rich. They will pay ten times as much for a meal because it is served on a beautiful plate, just as they will pay ten times as much for a bed and a roof if well-decorated.

Though I do envy them the goose-feather down.

I'll bet Finn sleeps on goose-feather down. I'll bet his sheets are the finest and softest materials, and that—

"Jessa." Jacky Boy nudges me with his elbow. "That's enough

carrots to garnish a full cow."

I jump guiltily, as though Jacky Boy knows I was thinking of a boy's bed. "Oh, sorry!"

"Delivery," says an oddly familiar voice, and I look up to see a tall, young man, his sharp, almond eyes instantly recognizable though it takes me a few moments to connect them with the younger version I remember.

"Kelen?" I gasp.

His face breaks into a smile as he looks me up and down. His brown skin isn't as tan as it was on the island, and his hair is cut closer to his head in the Avebury style, but there's no mistaking him.

I drop my knife and run, throwing my arms around him. "Kelen! I thought I'd never see you again. I asked Mama if you were in Avebury, but she said your mother didn't know."

Kelen laughs, squeezing me so that my feet leave the floor. *Kelen, Kelen!* "That's very odd," he says, his Alben accent nearly as good as mine. "Since my mother writes me once a week."

I huff and shake my head as he sets me down. No doubt Mama didn't want me running off to Albion and giving my heart to a Melenese boy. But this boy already *had* my heart for a few summer months when we were fifteen. Seeing him makes me think of cool, hidden pools, fruit-sweetened stolen kisses, and the glorious freedom it felt like we'd have forever.

We didn't, of course. Kelen feels utterly out of place in this kitchen, in a way that is both joyous and painful.

"This is my cousin, Jacabo."

"Hello," Kelen says, nodding. He picks up a large, brown parcel from where he dropped it on the floor and hands it to Jacky Boy.

I want to drink him up, reveling in the familiar comfort of a shared childhood. That dizzy summer aside, we grew up running wild together, Kelen, me, Nuna, all of the village children. It feels like more than a lifetime ago, and I want to live in those memories, if only for a few stolen minutes. "Are you staying nearby? What are you doing? How have you been?"

A shadow passes over his face and I remember too late exactly why he came here. Not all the half-Alben children were as fortunate as me. His mother had turned to prostitution after Kelen's father left. Some soldiers hurt her, and Kelen beat them near to death. We never saw him again after that. It was the end of my childhood in many ways, and the end of our easy romance.

I take his hands in mine. "I'm so very, very glad to see you are well."

He nods. "Likewise. Though I'll admit I never expected to see Miss High and Mighty working in a kitchen."

"Oh, I'm not—" I pause, about to deny that this is why I'm here, but realize Jacky Boy is standing right next to me. I won't demean what he does. "I'm also a student."

"That sounds more like you. I live near the docks—no, you shouldn't come visit," he adds, seeing me open my mouth. "It's not very safe. I know where you are now. I won't be a stranger."

My whole face is a smile as I pull him close for another hug.

The physical contact is a balm to my soul. No one touches each other here, not like on Melei, where no conversation passed without touching each other. "I'm so happy, it feels like home."

Kelen laughs darkly. "You and I remember home very differently then."

I pull away and he nods again at Jacky Boy. "I'll be seeing you, then," he says, giving me his smile that always felt like a secret as he walks out of the kitchen.

I hum quietly to myself as I finish plating the food. The world feels much smaller tonight, and I like it. Kelen will be part of my life. I can hardly wait to sit and talk with him of the people we know and the island we love.

Finished, I show the plate to Jacky Boy for approval before taking it up.

I'm the only kitchen maid allowed to deliver things with the day staff gone. The entire night staff is Melenese, but apparently I'm the only one the managers find acceptable to present to their distinguished guests. It does not endear me to those receiving the meals.

I carefully lift the covered platter, Jacky Boy makes sure my white cap is in place, and then I navigate around the tables and out of the steamy heat of the kitchen. "Go straight to bed when you're done now," he calls after me, and I nod with gratitude.

Though the hotel is small and operating at half capacity, of course the guest ordering food at nearly midnight would be on the third floor. I blame the electric lights newly installed. If you can make night burn as bright as day, how does the body know when to sleep? My arms are trembling by the time I've climbed the narrow stairs hidden in back of the building.

Sleep, sweet sleep, calls to me. I'm exhausted but happy after seeing Kelen again. I balance the tray on my hip and knock three times. So close to sleep.

"Yes, what?" an annoyed voice calls.

"Meal service." If he doesn't open the door soon, my arms are liable to drop off, and then I'll be no good as either a kitchen worker or a student.

"I ordered no—" The door swings open, and I find myself face-to-face with an equally shocked Finn. He's in a dressing robe, deep wine red and open at the neck. It's obvious from his sharp, pale collarbones that he has nothing on beneath.

"What are you doing here?" I shout.

He grabs the tray and yanks it forward, pulling me with it into his room. Before I can back out, he spins me around and shoves me farther inside, the tray smashing against my ribs, then slams and locks the door behind himself.

"Open it right now!" I keep the food between us like it will somehow protect me. "How dare you follow me here! The entire kitchen staff knows where I am, and they'll come looking for me." He doesn't know Jacky Boy told me I could go straight to bed.

"Lie." His eyes are narrowed and his body is tense. He picks up his cane from where it rests against the wall. I knock the cover off my tray and grab the steak knife, dropping the rest— food and all—onto the thick, green carpet.

I force my voice to come out calmly. "I will kill you before I allow you to touch me."

A ghost of a smile pulls at his lips. "Truth. Now." He puts a hand into a deep pocket in his robe. "Who are you working for?"

"What are you on about? I work for this hotel, as you well know since you followed me here and trapped me in your room!"

"I never ordered food."

"Humblest apologies, sir, it must have been the other maniac in room 312! Is he here? Because I'll cut him if he comes near me, too!"

"More than one way to trace the path of a liar." He pulls his hand out of his pocket. The crystal chandelier overhead gives dim light, and I cannot see what he has in his fist. He brings it to his mouth, blowing out. White powder, fine as chalk dust, billows and surrounds my head. I breathe it in and cough. It tastes like the harsh soap my mother used to wash the cleaning rags.

"Let me by, or I swear I'll slit your throat." My panic is rising. There is no safe way out of this situation. Either I fight my way free and am jailed for attacking a nobleman or . . . he does whatever he has planned.

I'll take prison.

But how could I have been so wrong about him? I liked him. He never felt threatening.

"What do you know about my parents?" His voice pierces through me, and it's as though I can feel it, tugging outward on the tender spot at the hollow of my neck.

"Nothing! Other than that they raised a madman."

"Whom do you work for?"

"I work for my cousin Jacky Boy in the kitchen, you daft wretch."

"I thought you were a student."

"I *am* a student! How do you think I survive in this spirit-blasted city?"

"How did you get into the boarding school then, a simple girl coming from the colonies?"

"My father is a professor there, and I threatened to tell his wife about me if he didn't secure my admission after I passed all the tests." I gasp, bringing my free hand to my mouth. I've told no one this; not even Mama knows how I really earned my place here.

"And you practice no arts, Hallin or Cromberg?"

"I don't understand what that question even means." I am horrified and trembling, unsure what has come over me. "Please let me leave." I cannot believe what I've admitted to. My head feels slick and slippery, like a path has formed between my brain and my tongue. I want nothing else sliding free.

He taps his fingers together as though he's trying to divine more than my words have told him. "Why are you here?"

"Because you ordered food and I work in the kitchen!"

"Someone is playing us for fools," he mutters. His hand snakes out and before I can raise the knife, he pulls something from my bun. Between his fingers is a single black feather.

How was that in my hair? I've washed it since the bird attack.

Finn holds it over a candle on the small table next to the door, and instead of lighting on fire, it evaporates in a puff of pale smoke. He looks back at me and sighs, a finger placed thoughtfully over his lips. "I'm sorry. I mean you no harm. You obviously have no part in this. My apologies for a less-than-graceful strategy. But I wonder . . ."

Abruptly standing straight, he brushes past me and leaves the scents of candle smoke and spicy cloves in his wake. The door! I dart forward but the doorknob burns my hand. I yank it back, hissing.

"Not yet, Jessamin. I need you to do something for me."

I let out every curse I know in my own tongue, most of which revolve around the shriveling death of his manhood. I rip off my white cap and wrap it around the doorknob as a buffer, but it's still too hot. Blowing on my burned fingers, I turn around to find Finn standing much too close. His dark eyes are locked on to mine and behind them is a frantic light—madness, anger, lust, I cannot distinguish. I am frozen between wanting to lean closer and wanting to lean away.

"I still have the knife." My voice trembles.

"No, you don't."

I look down. My hands, both burned and unharmed, are empty.

"It will be fine." He takes a deep breath, and I frown, wondering which of us he is trying to reassure. "It will be fine," he repeats. "Pull a card from this deck, and you may go."

I look down to see that, where his hands had been as empty as mine, he now holds a deck of cards. The backs are painted a uniform midnight blue with golden stars, and though they're not worn, they seem old.

He cannot be serious.

"A card trick? You lured me up here and locked me in your chambers to perform a card trick?"

The smile he gives me lacks both warmth and humor. "Please," he says through gritted teeth. "A single card. I must be sure."

I fold my arms and lean back against the door to put more space between us. He's so close, too close, and I am painfully aware of how little clothing he's wearing. If anyone were to walk in on us, my reputation would be ruined.

I will not humor him. "I refuse."

"Just one card and you are free to go, everything that has been said between us this night forgotten." He raises an eyebrow in challenge, and I scowl. He now holds my dearest secret—the truth about my father that not even Jacky Boy knows. I couldn't bear it if the school knew I blackmailed my way in. Though I am at the top of my classes, they would never again take me seriously. They hardly do so now.

"Just one card"—he knows he has me—"and you walk out the door and never see me again."

I square my shoulders. "Is that a promise?"

"Take a card."

Gritting my teeth, I pluck a single card from the deck. I don't break eye contact. "Your card," I snap.

I hold it up, and he staggers back as though I've dealt him a physical blow. The rest of the cards fall from his hands and whisper down to the carpet.

"Wretched fates," he whispers. "I am sorrier than I can tell you."

A cold something prickles down my spine, and I look at the card. In my hand—though I am certain—*certain*—I took one card, are two.

"Please leave." His voice is strangled, and his eyes are wide with fear.

I drop the cards without looking at them and flee. It's only after I'm safely in my room that I realize his door had unlocked itself.

Four

AS I LEAVE THE LIBRARY, I'M NOT LOOKING WHERE
I walk and nearly bump into a man.

"Oh, I'm so—" I stop, the apology trapped on my tongue.
Professor Miller looks back at me, eyes opened as round as his
glasses. My first instinct is to run, to flee, to do anything to get
away from the awkwardness of this moment.

But then something mean and stubborn inside of me rears
its ugly head and instead I stand there, not breaking eye contact, my back and shoulders straight with defiance. I dare him
to speak to me.

He ducks his head and hurries away, misjudging the space
and smashing his shoulder into one of the bookshelves.

"I hope that hurt," I whisper, not sure whether I won or lost.

Sighing, I push out of the building. The day is heavy with clouds, even the green of the grass and shrubs losing their sharper edge of color, and I rub at my sleeves wishing I had brought a shawl.

Finding an open bench is no issue. I crack open a book written by the very man I just passed. Usually the chapters are tedious, but today something catches my eye. This section focuses on the royal families of the Iverian continent, Albion's across-the-channel neighbor and constantly rotating source of enemies and allies.

Hallin. I'd never heard the term before Finn and his crazy questions (and my shameful answers, the honesty of which I still cannot account for). But Hallin is the name of the family from which all the Iverian continental countries draw their royals.

Skimming with a new urgency, I find the other name: *Cromberg.* The royal family from which all Alben gentry descends.

I try to connect it, but it leaves me even more confused than that entire encounter did. Why would Finn ask me which royal line I practiced? How does one *practice* a royal line? And why would anyone think I had associations with either?

Perhaps Finn is in some sort of trouble. Perhaps he's a spy, or a traitor, or . . . a prince in disguise. Yes. Because that makes as much sense as anything. I laugh quietly, imagining all of our encounters with this filter. The poor prince in hiding. The exotic, too-good-for-her-circumstances woman who breaks through his barriers. I ought to be making my money by writing the penny romances sold to bored house-keepers.

A caw makes me slam the book shut with a startled excla-mation. "You!" I glare at the large black bird on the bench next to me. It's foolish to think it's the same foul creature, but I can-not help it. This bird is missing a claw from its left foot. I take note, if only to prove to myself that I am not seeing the same bird everywhere I go.

It reminds me of the feather Finn found in my hair. But the feather is gone, and so is Finn—checked out of the hotel. Hope-fully forever, and good riddance. I shouldn't spare him any more thoughts.

The image of his collarbones beneath the open robe rises unbidden in my mind, and I curse at myself in Melenese. Penny romance indeed.

The bird caws again and I shoo at it with my hands. "I am very cross with you. Please leave at once." It ignores my attempts at banishment, so I turn my head to face directly forward, nose in the air. Part of me wants to run inside, but I refuse to be cowed by a bird. This is *my* bench today.

It lets out another caw, this time softer. I hadn't realized birds had the capacity for volume control. Out of the corner of my eye, I see it bob up and down like it wants my attention—silly thought, birds are not cats, it is not trying to communicate—and then, with another caw, it flies away.

More relieved than I care to admit, I look at the empty spot where it had been, only to find a long, green satin ribbon.

This city has a veritable plague of large black birds. I cannot understand how I never noticed until now. I see them everywhere I go. But none get close enough for me to determine whether or not they are my ribbon-fascinated stalker.

Which is why being awoken by one of the brutes tapping on my tiny window sets my heart racing and my teeth on edge. I flop back down onto my cot, hand cool against my fevered brow. There was a dream, with . . .

Finn. I can still feel the curve of his collarbone where I traced it with my finger. He was apologizing, and I was in his arms, the angles of his sharp shoulders wrapped toward me.

Another tap against my windowpane. I jump out of bed and scream, pushing the window out on its hinge and dislodging the bird in a flurry of black feathers. "And don't come back!" I shout.

I lean my head out, closing my eyes against the soft mist drizzle the sky has been weeping for a fortnight. If it would only rain, that would accomplish a cleansing of the city, but this drizzle simply coats everything in a layer of slick damp over the usual grime and dirt.

Poor bird. I spend nearly all my time indoors and still I'm going mad with the weather. It was probably trying to find an alcove to get dry. I grab a tin of biscuits from my nightstand and set them out along the ledge as a peace offering.

To my surprise, the bird comes back immediately, claws

grabbing onto the narrow stone ledge just outside my reach. A missing claw. Maybe the odd creature has imprinted on me? Though it is far from a new hatchling. It turns its head outward toward the rain, but one yellow eye remains fixed on me reproachfully. "Yes, fine. I apologize. Get dry and stay warm with a snack."

Shaking my head, I close the window and sit back on my cot. The school is on holiday, which means as much studying, only done in this tomb instead of the library. I have become intimately acquainted with every inch of my tiny room. At one point I charted the precise rate at which the plaster splits, and extended the formula to predict when the next crack will appear and how many finger-lengths it will span.

I *am* going mad.

I wish Kelen had told me where he lived. I could use an outing, some excuse to leave the hotel. And I'd dearly love to talk about Melei and our childhoods there.

I hate that I have to wait for him to visit in order to see him. I don't like being locked in my own thoughts. He'd be such a nice distraction.

There is a soft knock at my door, and I call, "Come in!" with a great deal of relief and urgency.

Ma'ati enters, closing the door behind her with a whisper of sound. She is the perfect maid—even when you are in the same room together it's difficult to notice her. Her face is sweet and plain and round, her hair always pinned beneath a white cap. We cannot tell whether her Alben or my Melenese is worse, and our conversations always vary between the two in a confusing jumble of not-quite-right words before we settle on Melenese.

"How are you?" she asks, her eyes taking in books strewn on every surface.

I wave my hand. "I wish this rain could wash away the gray, but it seems to be adding even more."

"I miss color." Her eyes drift to my window. "And fruit ripe off the tree."

"And the warm brown skin of men who work an honest day."

"Oh, I still see some of that." She blushes and her hand goes to her mouth as though she can pluck the words out of the air and put them back beneath her tongue.

I smile. "When will you and Jacky Boy marry?" She's younger than I am, only sixteen, but there is something in the way she carries herself, telling a sad history that made her far older. It makes my soul light to think that she has found someone as strong and gentle as my cousin.

"You cannot speak of it! I haven't—we haven't—I would never do anything improper." The word *improper* is in Alben, of course. It has much more meaning here.

"Ma'ati, sweet, I know that! But it's obvious you two are meant to be together."

Her dark eyes twinkle with light. "Spirits willing, next spring. We think the managers will let us stay on rather than lose two good workers."

"Oh, Ma'ati!" I draw her in for a hug and wonder if, had they not left the island, Ma'ati and Jacky Boy would have ever found each other. Perhaps this dreary country is good for something after all.

"Oh, but that is not the reason I am here!" Ma'ati pulls back, her eyes alight with even more excitement. "You've had a package. It came just now. They brought it to me by mistake. Come on!" She takes my hand in hers and we run past the other servant quarters' doors and into her room.

I see now why she elected to leave it rather than move it herself—it's nearly as tall as I am and half again as wide.

"I have no idea what this is." The box is made of wood so thin it's nearly translucent, and a red ribbon encircles it, with a cream envelope tucked into the bow. I pull it out—the paper is heavy and thick in my hands. *Jessamin Olea* is written in elegant strokes.

"Open it, open it! I have three rooms to finish before midmorning and I cannot handle the suspense!"

Smiling nervously, I break the seal—an unmarked circle of black wax—and slide out two cards. The first is an invitation to a gala ball celebrating the opening of a new royal conservatory; the date is tomorrow night. I pass it to Ma'ati, shrugging my shoulders. The second is handwritten in the same elegant script from the envelope.

> *Please attend as my guest. I must see you again, if only to apologize and explain myself. I cannot banish you from my thoughts and no longer want to. Until then, F.*

I realize only when Ma'ati holds out her hand for the second note that I am covering my mouth, barely breathing. I had not thought to hear from him ever again.

A rebellious anger stirs in my breast and I set my mouth in a grim smile. I will not attend. He can wait all night. I'll not do him the honor of playing to his whims, nor will I ever again give him opportunity to unsettle me like he did that night in his room.

"Open the package!" Ma'ati demands, still eyeing the note I have not yet passed to her. I tuck it into my dressing robe instead, and undo the ribbon. It takes both of us to pry the lid free, but when we do neither of us can find words for what we see.

Five

I WEAR THE SINGLE MOST BEAUTIFUL DRESS I
have ever seen in my life. Set against the brilliant scarlet material, crystals are sewn down the neckline and across the bodice
in a dizzying pattern. The skirts hang with a gauzy lightness
that feels like a dream on my legs. It's sleeveless, in the fashionable cut of the season, with a sash over my shoulders.

"You'll look like a fire-petal, dancing in that," Ma'ati whispers, referencing the flowers that bloom in the high heat of
summer all over Melei, turning the hillsides into a violent riot
of red.

Spirits take that rotten Finn. I didn't have the strength in
me to say no to this dress. And the shoes, delicate black heels, fit

perfectly with the gartered stockings. As though these details were not enough to win me over, a silver hair comb with the same red crystal accents as my dress was included and is now tucked into my twisted bun.

I am worried bordering on terrified of this evening—so much so that were it not for Ma'ati's excitement over dressing me I might have called the whole thing off. She even talked Jacky Boy out of needing me in the kitchens tonight.

"Wait!" Ma'ati runs out of my room and comes back with a small bronze jar in her hand. "Please don't tell, but one of the guests left this lip rouge in her room, and she never asked for it back." She dips her finger in and pulls it out, tracing my lips as carefully as an artist.

"Oh," she says, her voice like a sigh. "You look like the queen."

"The queen is eighty years old."

Ma'ati swats my shoulder. "You know what I mean. Like a queen ought to look."

"How do you know how to do this? The corsets and the hair and the stockings. I'd have been lost without you." My regular dresses are sturdy and plain—buying the student uniform cost all my savings, so that's all I wear. And my hair is a mystery even to myself, but Ma'ati's deft fingers twisted and pulled it into something of a miracle.

"I used to be a lady's maid."

"How did she ever let you go?" A lady's maid would have been a much higher position than head maid of even a fine hotel.

Ma'ati smiles with one side of her mouth, but there is no happiness there. "The lady's gentleman became too fond of me."

"I'm so sorry."

"Nothing to me now. I came here and found Jacky Boy, and he's better than all the fine manors in the country. Now then, a mirror."

I pull on the shiny, black, elbow-length gloves, admiring how such a simple thing can transform plain scholar's hands into mysterious things of beauty.

"Jessamin, there's—" Jacky Boy stops midsentence, staring at me from the open doorway. I am instantly aflame with embarrassment.

"Yes?"

"Your friend. Kelen? He's downstairs in the kitchen with a delivery. Wanted to see you."

I take a step toward the door and then pause. I look ridiculous. How will I explain any of this to Kelen? *Oh, yes, a strange and infuriating person I barely know sent me the dress so I can go to a grand gala! Isn't it nice?* Kelen has even more reason to hate Albens than I do. I couldn't bear the derision I know I'd see on his face.

Why did he have to show up now? Any other time I would have been thrilled to see him. Now I feel like a traitor. Maybe I am a traitor. I ought to take off all this nonsense and go see him.

But tonight, for once, I don't feel like remembering the island we can't have. I want to have a night *here*, now, rather than wallowing in what I left behind.

"Will you—will you tell him I'm not here?"

Jacky Boy nods. I expect him to look disappointed in me, but he seems almost relieved at the deception. He leaves and I follow Ma'ati out into the hall. We nearly bump into Simon, the tiny and perpetually terrified bellhop.

"Miss Jessamin! Outside, for you, there's—" He takes a deep, steadying breath. "There's a *motor*. Outside. For *you*."

"No," Ma'ati whispers, her eyes wide with wonder.

"But I—he said nothing about—I was going to hail a cabbie." It's no difficult task to find a horse carriage circling the city for hire, though tonight would have been my first ride. "Is there a man in the car?" My chest should not be so tight at the thought of seeing Finn again. I blame the corset.

"No, no one but the driver, who said he was to pick you up at eight o'clock on the dot. And the motor—oh, it's a wicked sharp-looking thing, no mistake, and the way it rumbles like a miniature train! Can I stand long enough to see you drive away? Please?"

I laugh, unsure how to feel. A motor! "I insist on you seeing me off. You, too, Ma'ati. You must both do it to reassure me I haven't gone mad."

We hurry down the servant stairs, past two maids, who give me looks of wonder mixed with scorn, then go out the side exit around to the front of the hotel. I'm afraid we'll run into Kelen and my lie will be revealed, but to my relief he's nowhere to be seen.

Simon spoke the truth: there is a motor in front of the hotel. I beam at Ma'ati. I have no idea what to expect from this night, but if it starts out like this it cannot be all bad. "Wish me luck."

"How can I wish you any more than you already have!"

I walk with as much grace as I can manage, hoping to mask

the fact that I want nothing more than to jump up and down and run my gloved fingers down the length of the motor.

"Milady." A man in a black suit and bowler hat bows and opens a door for me.

"Thank you." I climb in, careful of my stockings, and sit on the leather seat. Turning to the pane of glass closing off the tiny cabin, I wave at Ma'ati and Simon, and then, feeling foolish for all my borrowed finery, I stick my tongue out at both of them.

A bird hops up onto the runner. I laugh, noticing the missing claw. It's *my* bird. "Well," I say as it fixes a beady yellow eye on me, "you came to see me off, too?"

The motor starts and my bird flaps away, its noisy calls drowned out by the engine. I settle back to watch the city pass by. Something about viewing it through glass makes everything shine more—the lights reflected and glimmering in the droplets of water clinging to the panes.

I feel a sickening mix of fear and excitement. Any time I think I know what I want from this evening it all slips away from me. Do I want Finn to court me? Am I agreeing to such by accepting his gifts and attending? Should I have returned them immediately? But I cannot deny the thrill that runs through me when I anticipate seeing him again.

It's aggravating. And I will be certain to demand answers from him about his behavior. I reassure myself that this is the biggest reason I am going.

And through it all is an undercurrent of guilt. I worry that leaving Kelen behind while dressed in Alben finery is symbolic.

He would certainly see it that way. Several times I open my mouth to ask the driver to take me back, but it's too late to see Kelen anyway.

Before long—far too soon, in fact—the motor pulls to a stop in front of a building lit up like high noon on the warmest summer day. Light spills from the entire glass-encased structure, a palatial testament to engineering and science. I hadn't understood what the conservatory was, but the glimpse of shrouded green I can see from here has me even more excited than I was before.

It's a greenhouse! A tropical island in the midst of the great gray city.

My door opens and the driver stands to the side. I realize with a knife twist of embarrassment that I have no concept of whether or not I am to pay him. I have only a few coins on me, just enough tucked into the satin purse around my wrist for a cabbie. No doubt this was a far more expensive ride.

"I—"

"Everything is taken care of, milady."

I nod, grateful that he anticipated my question. "That was the most I have ever enjoyed the streets of this city. In fact, I shall never again love them so much as I did this night."

He finally looks up, the brim of his hat high enough to let him meet my eyes. "I'll not be escorting you home, I'm afraid. But it's all been arranged." He sounds regretful and I smile, putting my hand on his arm. He seems surprised—both at the eye contact and at the touch. I know what it is to be ignored while providing service, and I refuse to do it to others.

"Well, nothing can compare to your exceptional motoring skills. Thank you."

He nods, lips tight in a smile, and I release his arm. Pulling out the invitation, I walk down a path lit with hundreds of crystal-encased candles and try not to look like a wide-eyed girl incredibly out of her depth.

I am failing miserably, and I can't find it in me to care.

At the doors, twelve feet tall with a blue-green patina of old copper, two liveried servants stand, their backs as straight as the spine of a book. One holds out a white-gloved hand and I place my invitation there. Without so much as looking at it, he bows and opens the door to me.

I'm hit by a rush of air. These doors are a portal to another world, one of green, growing things and warm, living air in the midst of this cold city. I have not been truly warm since I moved here. Blessed heat! Beaming, I step through and am greeted on one side by a woman in scarlet.

She is beautiful, I think with a pang of jealousy, before realizing that I am greeting my reflection. But it is a vision of myself I have never before seen. The dress makes me look more a woman than a girl, and I suddenly feel far too revealed. Not only my skin—though there is more of that on display than normal— but *myself*.

I am a girl playing at womanhood, bright lips and brighter dress. With the heady scent of plants so close to those I grew up with, I feel young, painfully young, and remember a time my mother walked in on me, wrapped up in her finest dress. She had laughed.

I dearly hope no one laughs at me tonight.

I hear the door opening behind me and hurry forward so as not to be caught holding court with my own reflection. The gravel path is lined with palms carefully coaxed to arch overhead, the space between filled with the fuzzy, soft fronds of smaller ferns. And then, just when I begin to wonder if the path ever ends, it opens into a massive room filled with riotous flowers and oddly shaped trees, the humidity-fogged glass ceilings at least twenty feet tall. There are islands of plants everywhere.

And people.

So many people.

Any hope I'd harbored of quietly finding Finn vanishes. There must be three hundred people in the room, and to my horror I am the only woman dressed in a shade other than charcoal gray, silver, or black. They congregate like austere and glittering chunks of volcanoes long since passed.

I look like the flame erupting from a living volcano, and my face is burning to match.

I walk into the room with my head held high as though I attend galas in wildly inappropriate colors every day. As if it weren't enough to be alone in such a brilliant dress, I am also the only woman with a shade of skin darker than ivory. I would have been remarkable no matter what I wore.

I scan the crowd, walking with as measured a pace as I can manage, though I'm feeling more and more frantic. I crave Finn's face, desperate for someone familiar, even someone as confusing as him. Shocked and appraising glances follow me, and I try to pay them no mind.

Weak, stringed music drifts on the air, barely able to fill so large a space. Some couples dance, their movements formal and perfectly scripted.

After traversing nearly the length of the room, I'm close to despair. *Why wasn't he by the front, waiting for me? Why isn't he looking for me?* Surely he's not indifferent, not after the lengths he went to get me here.

I let out a sigh of relief. There, in a brightly lit corner, Finn stands surrounded by three women who glitter like obsidian peacocks. My heart picks up, and I raise a hand.

"Finn!" I call. His suit sets off his dark eyes and fine shoulders, and how his hair catches the light! He looks up from his conversation and his eyes widen. Instead of greeting me, he lifts a gloved hand to his heart and his chest retracts inward as though in pain. Then he looks back at the woman who is speaking, dismissing me without a word.

Six

I STAND GAPING AT HIM, HIS REFUSAL TO acknowledge my existence like a sharp stone in my throat.

I know this pain, this raw ache—it's what always precedes crying. I glance to either side, desperate for an exit. I'll run out, flee, pretend tonight never happened, and then . . .

I clench my jaw and narrow my eyes. I am no wilting Alben, I am a fierce and strong Melenese woman. And I am not the victim of any cruel jokes. Spirits below, I will make certain he knows I am not to be toyed with.

I march directly over and take the small space left between two of his admirers. He tries to avoid my gaze, suddenly intent on whatever the tallest peacock has to say.

"Good evening, Finn." I smile brightly. "What a marvelous building this is."

He finally looks at me, dragging his eyes as though it takes physical effort. "I'm sorry, have we met?"

I will not be embarrassed. I will *not*. I grasp hold of the anger flaring ever higher in my chest as a lifeline. "I believe we have."

"You're mistaken," says the shortest peacock, her brown hair adorned with a massively jeweled headband. "This is Lord Ackerly of North Aston."

I raise my eyebrows, not looking away from Finn. "A lord? How nice for you."

"Yes, quite. Good evening." He turns back to the tallest peacock, but the last peacock, in a clinging slip of charcoal gray, cannot resist.

"How pretty you are," she says with a cloying smile. "You must feel so at home here in this horrid, muggy heat with all of these wild plants. You look like one yourself!"

The worst part is, she's right. I did feel at home when I walked in, but I know how far I am from it now. Lifting my chin, I return her smile with a pointed one of my own. "Why thank you, I *do* feel comfortable here, just as you must feel perfectly suited to this city of cold, gray rocks."

Her eyes grow bigger than I'd have imagined possible. I look triumphantly at Finn, who is trying his hardest not to see me. Fine then. "So nice to meet you all. I think I should prefer a dance. Lord Ackerly, ladies." I bob my head at them and turn on my heel.

A shadow looms behind mine and I turn, expecting Finn to

have followed me, a sharp word already on the tip of my tongue. I frown, confused. He hasn't moved, but in some trick of the light from so many electric torches, his shadow stretches farther than the women's, mingling with my own. He looks down as though he notices it, too, and his face is as white as a ghost.

Ghost-faced spirit cursers. It's a nasty phrase in Melenese, filled with hissing noises. Mama spanked me the one time I used it in front of her. That's what Kelen always called them. Kelen, whom I should be laughing with right now instead of pretending at finery I despise.

Ghost-faced spirit cursers. I hold the words on my tongue, relishing their feel as I march into the crowd, determined to stay the entire evening so that Finn sees me dancing and enjoying myself and knows he hasn't won. Whatever his game is with the strangeness in the hotel, then the dress and the invitation, I have not gotten this far to be beaten by simple humiliation.

Sweeping my filmy shawl over one shoulder, I smile as though I am the queen Ma'ati said I looked like. And, to my surprise, it works.

First one man, then another, then another, asks me to dance. I am twirled and curtsied around the length and width of the room. Mama would be so proud to see the lessons I threw fits about attending paying off so well. I laugh and make charming remarks. Why *yes*, I do love tropical flowers, why *no*, not everyone from Melei is as fair of skin as I am and in fact I envy them their darker shade, why *yes*, I am here to further my studies.

My partners are all charmed by my "exotic beauty." I do not

feel exotic. I feel strange and small and false, but I smile and smile and smile.

This building is a wonder. Not even the cold night can get through the glass, fogged with steam. Everything glows in a bright haze of progress, and I think I understand why Albion assumes it does the rest of the world a favor by installing itself and its standards wherever it lands. If they can bring the hot, green glory of Melei here, why can they not bring the rigid structure and social "progress" of Albion there?

One man, in his late teens with ginger hair and clever eyes, asks me to dance several times. I can tell he is pleased with his own deviance, happy to be the focal point of the room when I am on his arm. I don't like being used that way, but he is pleasant and a good conversationalist.

"And how do you find the school?" he asks.

"Well, seeing as it's always in the same location, it's never very difficult to find."

He laughs, delighted, and I can't help but really smile. "Are all women from your island this charming?"

"Far more so, sir. That's why they sent me here. I was a blight on the whole village."

"I cannot imagine you being a blight on anything."

Another man, this one older but indistinguishable from the last three with his well-trimmed mustache and slick-combed hair, taps my shoulder to cut in. I would rather turn them both down—I am out of breath and near dizzy from the heat and the spinning.

"If I may?" the older gentleman asks. My ginger-haired

suitor looks disappointed and oddly worried. But he nods.

The new man smiles at me and I have the briefest impression of sharp teeth and sharper eyes, though when I shake my head to clear it his teeth are perfectly normal and there's nothing remarkable about his face.

"I'm afraid I have to steal her away now," a soft voice says next to me. I turn to find a woman I've never met, young and fair with reddish curls, her dress shimmering silver. "My brother, Ernest, has been monopolizing her. He can be quite selfish that way. If you'll excuse us, gentlemen, I've promised to show her the outer rooms and at this rate the sun will rise before she makes it off the dance floor."

My foiled new dance partner bows to us, and my savior takes my gloved hand and puts it through her arm. Ernest gives his sister a glare softened with a smile.

She leads me away from the press of bodies in the center of the room. I try not to scan for Finn. I do not need to see him; I know he's seen me. Everyone has seen me.

"Now then," the girl says, "I've been watching you for some time and, seeing as how this gala is the first I've planned, I'd feel simply awful if someone were to pass out from overexertion. They'd never let me be in charge again. My brother, bless him, would dance you into the floor."

I laugh, my throat raw. "I cannot thank you enough. Nor can my feet in these wretched heels."

"I admire your courage, coming to the gala knowing how you would stand out." She must feel me stiffen, because she hurries on. "I don't mean to offend. Unlike many of my lovely associates." She smiles at two women who hold fans over their faces and lean in to whisper as we pass. "I mean, I cannot imagine what it must be like to enter a room and know beyond a doubt that everyone will notice you. The very thought sets me to the edge of panic. But here you come to a new land and allow no one to tell you that you cannot stand out. Well done."

"And if I admit tonight is among the worst of my life?"

"Is my brother really that terrible a dancer?" She laughs as I stammer to correct her, and shakes her head. "I know he's awful. But I will proudly inform you that no one here would ever have guessed you were unhappy, so you have played your part to perfection." Her face is narrow, the features too pinched to be traditionally pretty, but her eyes are clever and a beautiful pale color. I can certainly see the resemblance between her and Ernest.

"That is a relief. Now I would like to find somewhere quiet and hidden to sit and be unnoticed by anyone."

"I can do that, as well. I'm Eleanor. I should have mentioned that sooner. My uncle is the Earl of South Deacon. He granted me the favor of being the planner for this event."

I squeeze her arm. "It's incredible. Granted, I haven't much to compare it to, but I cannot imagine a finer celebration."

"I knew I was right to rescue you. Now, take a drink." She turns me toward a long, white-covered table manned by a row of servants and covered with glasses of sparkling amber liquid. "Then wander until you find one of the quiet side rooms unattended by men looking to dance with the talk of the evening. Here is my card—" She slips me a tiny rectangle of thick paper.

"I want you to visit me next week after your feet have recovered from this evening. I will take you to dinner to thank you for giving people something to gossip about. They'll speak of tonight's tropical flower of a girl for weeks and remember what a resounding success I am."

I put my hand against my forehead, closing my eyes. "Was I that terrible?"

"No! You were that wonderful. Now go and hide." She waves me away with a smile that lights up her face and I return it, surprisingly gratified to have made a friend. It is a small balm to the humiliation of tonight.

Drink in hand, I read the address on her card, then take the first trail that appears to lead away from the vast main space of the conservatory. Through one room dominated by lilies and another so saturated with the scent of roses I can scarcely breathe, I find one that, to my delight, is filled with fire-petals in full bloom.

I sink onto a bench in the corner, wondering how unforgivable a gaffe removing my shoes would be. I cannot make any stranger of an impression than I already have, so I slip them off and stretch my toes. I sip at my drink, wrinkling my nose at the bubbles. They tickle my raw throat, and I drink more.

If Eleanor is correct, whomever Finn dines or speaks with over the next few weeks will bring me up in conversation. He may have meant to mock me, or meant for others to, but regardless of their assessment I will be inescapable. I hope he is utterly plagued by my memory.

The fuzzy, white electric lights in the room go out, leaving only the light from the adjoining room spilling into this one. I stand, stocking feet on gravel, and slide back into my shoes. "Pardon me, is this room closed now?"

Someone stands, silhouetted against the entrance, his shadow stretching all the way to my feet. I frown and set down my glass.

"Jessamin." Finn quickly closes the distance between us and stands directly in front of me. His silly cane is, as always, clasped in one hand.

"So you've remembered my name."

He grabs my arm, fingers squeezing as I try to pull away. "What are you doing here?"

"Perhaps I am unfamiliar with the strange customs of the gentry. Did you not *mean* for me to come when you sent the dress, the motor, and the invitation that begged my presence?"

He lets go of my arm and puts a hand over his face, his shoulders stooped as though bearing a great weight. It is so dim I can see only the barest expression on his face, but he looks defeated. "I sent none of those things."

"What?" My heart pounds. That was not the answer I was expecting.

"It wasn't me. We've been set up, and I can only pray that I played my part well enough for no damage to be done."

"I don't understand. Are you saying that the dress, the letter—they weren't from you?"

"Of course not. I would never do that."

I let out a sharp breath, wishing this didn't cut through me with icy pain. I have no reason to stay, no further levels of shame and embarrassment to drop to. My night is complete.

I sweep out past him, ignoring the urgency with which he calls my name.

Back in the great room, I accept another card pressed into my palm with a smile as mechanized as the motor I rode here in. I stay on the outskirts, searching for a door other than the ones I came through, and am mostly ignored save a few curious souls.

I cannot puzzle this out.

If Finn did not send me the letter, invitation, dress, and motor, who did? It is a cruel joke, elegant and expensive in execution. Surely I have no enemies of this caliber. I just want to go home. My driver said another way to the hotel had been arranged, and the thought gives me pause.

Either it is part of the joke and there is no ride home, or some form of transportation will be waiting for me, possibly with answers as to how this whole nightmare of an evening happened.

I want to face neither of those options. It was Finn or it wasn't, and the only person who can answer my questions is the same one I never want to see again.

I finally spy a side door and slip out. The night hits me with jealous greed, eager to steal away the memory of humid warmth, and for once I am glad of the shock of it.

"Fie on this whole country and everyone in it," I declare, setting off across the grounds perpendicular to where the main road crosses in the front. If I can get back to the heart of the city, I'll find a cabbie eventually.

"Fie on stupid men who see dark skin as an exotic temptation.

Fie on these accursed shoes." I kick them off into the grass, knowing I will regret it when I hit the street but simply not caring. "And fie on whoever sent them."

A loud caw sounds behind me and I spin, nearly falling off balance. "Fie on birds, too!" A big, black one bobs up and down in the grass behind me, its eyes glowing reflectively in the dark night.

I rub my arms and walk a bit faster. "Fie on creepy glowing eyes, especially."

Another caw, echoed from the other side behind me. Then another, and another, and finally I look over my shoulder to see dozens of pairs of glowing yellow eyes, all fixed on me.

As one, they lift into the air with a great rush of wings and I scream, throwing my arms over my head. I run forward, away from the birds, but they surround me, flying with a cacophony of wings and horrid, croaking cries. I see a break in their formation and run through it, trying to make it back to the conservatory. My feet pound against the grass, the demon birds right behind me, flying up to block me at every turn with sharp beaks and razor claws.

They are blacker than the night, a tunnel around me, herding me and giving me only one way to escape: into the darkness of the trees surrounding the lawn. As I give up on the beacon of light from the conservatory, the ground slips and slides beneath me, reality shifting. I turn to look over my shoulder one last time, running as fast as ever I have, when I slam into something.

Something with a set of teeth and eyes equally sharp.

Seven

I AM HOME, IN MY BED, MY NIGHTCLOTHES
tangled around me so that I cannot move. My mother talks
to me in the low, sibilant sounds of our language, though her
voice is deep, too deep. Her words don't comfort—their tone
is chiding, accusatory, but my memory fails me and I cannot
understand what she is saying as her fingers brush my forehead.

Her fingers turn into the touch of feathers and I scream,
fighting upward out of the blackness. I'm in the conservatory,
spinning, spinning, passed from partner to partner down an
infinite line. I look up, begging to stop, to see that it's Finn who
holds me, his hands tight around my waist. Then he passes me
to the next man—Finn again, always Finn, and none of them

will look me in the eyes, none of them will answer my pleas to be released.

I try to break through but I can't, and I'm twirled and danced farther and farther down the line of bodies, an endless path.

Just when I can bear no more, Finn pulls me close and finally meets my eyes. "I am so sorry," he says. And then he spins me into the sharp man, whose arms wrap around me once more, turning into great black wings.

I am smothered in feathers and pulled into darkness so complete I cannot even scream.

Eight

I GROAN, MY HEAD ACHING WITH SHARP PULSES.
For a moment I am utterly disoriented—I was home—but no,
I'm in Avebury, and . . .

I sit up, the soft shuffling of feathered wings sending panic
through my whole body. I am *not* home, nor am I at the hotel.
I'm in a study of some sort. Dark and masculine furniture with
bulky rigid lines takes up more space than required. The room
is paneled in wood, the single window shuttered and letting
in only the merest mention of light. A fire burns in a stone
fireplace covered with an ornamental iron gate, and the room
smells overpoweringly of resin. Books line the walls, but there is
something off-putting about their unmarked black spines.

Perched on the back of an imposing leather armchair, a single black bird with wicked eyes glares at me. I avoid its stare, hoping that if I ignore it, it will cease to exist.

Nothing is familiar, no clues as to where I am or whose couch I was sleeping on. I'm still in my red dress, my feet bare of shoes, stockings torn but in place.

I'm missing something. I scan my surroundings again. And then I realize: the room has no door.

I stand. I'm wrong. I have to be. I'm feverish or suffering the ill effects of something strange in the drinks from the gala. Keeping the demon bird in my peripheral vision, I pace the walls, pushing on bookcases, searching for seams, but there is nothing, no egress. The window shutter will not move; I cannot even budge the slats to see outside.

"Tea?"

I scream, spinning around to find a man sitting in the now birdless leather armchair, perfectly at ease, as though he did not just appear in a doorless room. My heart races with fear.

"How did you get in here?" I ask.

He smiles, lips thin under a stylishly clipped mustache. He is older, handsome in the way of Albens. Carefully styled black-and-gray hair sets off his pale skin, so white it is nearly blue in this light. There is nothing remarkable about him, though I know I've seen him before. "I should think myself perfectly capable of entering my own study."

"But there are no doors!"

"Oh?" He raises his eyebrows as he stirs a cup of tea—where did the tray come from? That coffee table was empty before, I know it was. And then I see over his shoulder, plain as day, a door.

I stumble forward and collapse on the couch. "My apologies, sir. There is something wrong with me. There was a bird, and no door, and—" I pull off a glove and put my hand to my forehead, but it feels cool to the touch. "Where am I? How did I get here?"

"I found you outside the conservatory. Fearing you had too much to drink and that others might take advantage, I had my man carry you to the carriage and brought you here." He smiles knowingly and I try not to bristle—one glass of fizzy champagne would never render me unconscious.

"I thank you for your gracious actions, sir, but I cannot account for the circumstances." I shake my head, remembering the birds, and the man, and the dreams. "I suspect I was drugged."

"Doubtless." But his smile indicates he doubts it very much. There is something wrong with his face, with the way it moves—almost mechanical, the lines of his eyes not matching the expressions, his lips not quite keeping pace with the words he speaks. "Sugar?"

He holds out a delicate teacup and I take it, staring down at the milky brown liquid as though it has answers for me. I set it on the table without drinking any, and then stand. "I should be going. My friends will be worried." I'm unnerved and have no desire to remain in a room alone with a man I do not know.

"Sit down," he says.

I sit.

"Drink your tea," he says.

I reach for the cup and bring it to my lips, but smash them shut before I can take a sip. My arms trembling, I set the tea back down on the table. "I am leaving," I say, and now I am certain I am still trapped in a dream, one of those horrible nightmares where I tell my body to run but it does not listen to me. I force myself to stand, every movement slow and labored, like the very air around me has solidified.

The man laughs, and the film around his face parts for a split second. I see the sharp teeth and sharper eyes of my nightmares.

"You," I whisper. *Wake up, wake up, oh please, Jessamin, wake up.*

"Stubborn. Any good Alben girl would have downed the whole pot of tea at the slightest suggestion. I've spent a remarkable amount of force on you." He cocks his head, the movement like a bird, and his blue eyes flash to black.

My legs shake. I am telling them, screaming at them to move toward the door, fighting the overwhelming urge to drink that accursed tea.

"You may as well be comfortable and sit. You'll wear yourself out, and we've barely begun."

I strain for a moment longer until I realize the door behind him has disappeared once more. I slump down to the couch, sitting on my hands to keep them away from the tea.

"I should very much like to wake up now," I say to no one in particular, because I am done dealing with this nightmare.

"It is a puzzle," the nightmare man says, and I avoid looking at him by staring at the bookshelves and trying to determine why they unnerve me so. "I can't understand why he would notice you. You're utterly without potential for a man like him."

I count the spines: twenty-five across. I count the same row again: thirty-three. Again: twenty-seven. And yet I can detect no movement, no change.

"How did you catch Lord Ackerly's affections?"

He succeeds in yanking back my attention. "Is he going to show up, too? This dream keeps getting worse." I've reached for the teacup again. Furious with myself, I swipe it off the table to the floor. There. No more tea to tempt my wayward hands.

"It is puzzling. I shouldn't think a girl like you would be more than a trifle to him. Poor Lord Ackerly, my great challenge. He's been untouchable all this time, only to trip and drop the key to his undoing."

My head aches where the silver comb is digging into my scalp, and I reach back to pull it out. Several hairs come away with it. I pull them free from the comb's prongs. *Wake up, wake up.*

"Give them here," he says, holding out his hand, and I've placed the hairs there before I can stop myself. "Let's add them to the collection, shall we?" He opens a polished ebony box and places the hairs gently next to my blue ribbon and the strands already there.

"That's mine."

"I am pleased to see my taste is impeccable. The dress was the final test for Ackerly." He reaches out and fingers the gauzy material of my skirts, and my stomach turns.

I think perhaps this is real, and I wish, oh, how I wish it were a nightmare.

He continues. "I couldn't know whether you were important enough to work, whether our coldhearted friend had fallen far enough to care. It seemed improbable. But shadows never lie, and the way you looked last night sealed his fate. For that I thank you." He bends and takes my ungloved hand in his, bringing it to his lips. His mouth on my skin feels so cold it burns, or so hot it freezes. I cannot tell the difference.

"Please." I hate the way the word tastes in my mouth directed at him. "I want no part in any issue between you and Finn—Lord Ackerly—whoever he is. He is nothing to me and I assure you I am less than nothing to him."

"Oh, little rabbit." He sits back in his chair across from me, and I find I can breathe easier again. "You have no idea what he's pulled you into, do you?"

"No, and I should like very much to leave now."

"Not just yet, I'm afraid. You missed your chance to avoid all this last night. I gave you the option, you know." He picks up the sugar dish and carefully pours a small pile of the crystals into his palm. As they touch his skin, they turn from white to gleaming black. He traces a circle with them, and then cuts the circle evenly down the middle. The room brightens to an almost painful degree of brilliance. The light is coming from my right side, throwing our shadows into sharp relief along the wall.

"Please join us, Lord Ackerly." The man throws the crystals at my shadow, and there is a hiss like water hitting fire. My shadow splits in two.

I put my hand to my mouth, but my second shadow does not follow the movement. *It's not my shadow*. The shoulders are angled, the body smooth, the head free of long hair. I look to my right, but no one is there.

I close my eyes, try to force reality back into place. I must be drugged. "What have you given me?"

"You didn't prepare her at all, did you, Lord Ackerly? This will be a hard initiation. As a kindness, I'll use a method she'll understand, something she will not be able to dismiss as a trick of her mind." Cold glee undercuts his voice. "Please remember that you brought this on her. You thought you could have her. You can't. And now that I know you're observing us, it's time to set the terms. You will give me access to the Hallin book, and you will give it to me immediately."

My eyes open again, and I can no longer hide my terror. "Please, please. I have nothing. There's nothing for me to give you."

"Not you. Him." He waves cheerily at my second shadow, then pulls out a hammer, the head heavy and battered, the handle worn and plain. It's out of place in this elegant room, a blunt instrument with nothing but utility built into its design. He swings it experimentally through the air, nods, and then places it next to the floral china of the tea set.

"Dear little rabbit, if you'd place your hand on the table."

I look at him in horror. "I will not."

The other shadow looms even larger on the wall. The nightmare man smiles. "You will."

My hand snakes forward of its own accord, and I grab it with my free hand, the one still gloved. I am pulled off the couch to the rug beneath, wrestling with my own possessed limb.

"That's a good girl. Keep fighting me." The nightmare man takes more sugar. He traces something on his palm that I cannot see, and then sprinkles the bloodred crystals onto my head.

I release my hand, and it pulls itself forward to the center of the table, lying flat with fingers evenly spread. I'm on my knees, unable to move, eye level with the hammer. He picks it up, and his smile does not fade a fraction as he says, "I *am* sorry about this."

Nine

THE SOBS RACK MY BODY. MY HEAD HANGS NEARLY to the carpet, everything anchored by my hand stuck to the table.

"Three out of five. We're nearly finished now, that's a good little rabbit." The pain crescendos in a blinding white burst of agony and I scream, scream, and scream until it breaks up into more sobs. He always gives me enough time between fingers to go back to crying.

"By all means you should blame yourself for this, Lord Ackerly. It could have been avoided. Making me chase your magic for so long, well, of course I need a way to release the frustration."

I open my eyes. My second shadow is so large it takes up nearly the entire wall now, and it vibrates with menace.

"You'll say, must you have smashed *all* her precious fingers? Perhaps one would have been clear enough, but I want to leave no question in your mind that you are doing the right thing. The only thing. And if you do not lay yourself at my mercy within the hour, I will begin doing things that no amount of time will mend."

The world explodes in agony again, and I haven't even the energy to scream this time. There is blood in my mouth, and my vision blurs with spots. I'm going to faint. I want to faint. *Please, please, blessed spirits, let me faint.*

Suddenly, my hand is released. I slump to the floor, curled in a ball around my ruined fingers. I cannot bear to look at them. If I do not lose consciousness soon I will be sick. The pain radiates out from my hand, claws in my stomach, bursts in my head.

The nightmare man is still talking, carrying on his one-sided conversation. I tune in and out, trying to find blackness, but pulled back from the brink of unconsciousness time and again by his voice.

". . . all settled then, I assume. I expect you shortly. This next bit will hurt, but we cannot have you here without a handicap, now can we?"

I brace for whatever is coming, but, to my surprise, nothing happens. Then I hear a shrill scream, like air escaping a boiling kettle, as the nightmare man cheerfully flings venomously green sugar crystals at the extra shadow. Each eats a hole where it strikes, and though the shadow darts around, the nightmare man continues to hit it.

I move onto my knees, biting my lip at the rolling pain—there is the source of the blood—and use my good hand to push against the table and get to my feet. The sugar bowl sits unguarded on the table. I snatch it and throw the contents into the fire, which pops and sparks in brilliant miniature fireworks.

The nightmare man turns around, twisted smile falling into puzzled frown, and I swing the sugar bowl up, knocking it into the hand cupping his shadow-burning crystals. They fly free, landing on the unprotected skin of his face with sizzling hisses.

He screams and shoves me to the ground. The impact jars my destroyed hand and it is too much. I lean over and vomit onto the rug.

A stream of words I do not understand but instinctively recognize as foul and evil stream from his mouth, but then, to my surprise and disappointment, he laughs.

I wipe the corners of my lips and sit up against the edge of the couch, barely able to see him through the red haze of pain.

His face has angry holes eaten into it, opening onto dark patches. He takes out a pristine handkerchief and wipes one side and then the other. But rather than wiping the burns off, it's as though he has wiped his old face back on. No evidence of my momentary victory remains.

He sniffs genteelly, tucking the handkerchief back into his suit pocket. "I like you. You have all the spirit and passion they've been careful to breed out of Alben women. To thank you for finally giving Lord Ackerly a weakness I could exploit, I will keep you for my own."

My head lolls back on the couch, and I close my eyes, letting out a sharp breath in place of a laugh. "I would sooner die."

"Never worry about that. You'll want me. You'll be perfectly at home. And only I can keep you safe from the coming war." A finger touches my cheek, and I shudder. I concentrate on the pain in my hand since it is preferable to the sensation of his skin on mine. "You shouldn't have gone to the gala, Jessa. Men like Lord Ackerly will bring you nothing but suffering. I'm so disappointed in you. Still, you've learned your lesson, and we will move on as soon as this is settled. Now if you'll excuse me, I've a guest to prepare for."

The door closes, and I open my eyes to find the room once again without an exit. I angle my neck so I can see the wall. Though the light has dimmed, I can still see my two shadows. They're slumped in defeat, but tiny dots of light have eaten through the extra shadow's silhouette.

Could it really be Finn's shadow, as the nightmare man seemed to believe?

This is not the same world I woke up in yesterday. I know none of the rules, and I have none of the power. All the things I've learned, all the ways I've tried to make a place for myself where I am not at the mercy of others, none of it matters in this new, bizarre reality.

A harsh caw draws up my head. Three of the horrid black birds are staring at me from the armchair. One of them hops forward, darting close and pecking my leg with its bone-hard beak, then flapping back with a chorus of croaking laughter.

Another moves to do the same, and I cringe, shielding my

ruined hand and ducking my face into my shoulder.

There is a clatter of wings and a chorus of angry caws, but nothing touches me. I raise my head to see one of the birds—missing a single claw—bobbing in front of me, flapping its wings and viciously attacking the other two when they get too close. It draws blood and rips a pinion out of the wing of one of my would-be assailants. They flap away, cawing reproachfully, and disappear into the bookshelf.

I wipe my eyes and look at the remaining bird. "Well," I say, "spirits' mercies. I am sorry I didn't leave better food for you outside my window."

The bird turns so one yellow eye is fixed on mine.

I sniffle, swallowing back another wave of nausea. "I should have known you weren't evil. You're far handsomer than those other wretched birds."

It ducks its head and tucks some stray feathers back into place along its wing. "Are you a boy?" I ask, and it bobs its head. "Sir Bird it is, officially. Now, Sir Bird, is there a door to this room?"

He hesitates, and then weaves his head back and forth in what I assume is an approximation of shaking it no.

I squeeze my eyes shut against a welling of tears. "I'm afraid that if I do not escape right now, I shall never leave this place." I don't know what the nightmare man has in store for me, but any kindness he thinks of is one I want no part of. My hand pains me to distraction, though, and I haven't any hope of fighting my way free.

There's a frantic scratching, and I open my eyes to see Sir

Bird hopping the length of the table, twisting and twitching as though fighting some internal war. Finally, he shakes himself from beak to tail, caws, and flies to the iron grate over the fire.

I close my eyes again. Perhaps if I can sleep I can wake up somewhere safe, my hand intact, this nightmare over.

Sir Bird caws again, louder than ever, and I look at him, irritated. "What is it?"

He pecks at the iron grate, hops down behind it, and then flaps directly into the fire.

"No!" I gasp, standing and rushing forward. But Sir Bird hops back out of the fire, tapping impatiently on the grate with his beak. I gasp my surprise, and he hops through the fire and back once more.

"I—through there? But the fire!"

As if to prove a point, Sir Bird hops directly into the center of it and stares at me, his eyes reflecting the flames that do not touch him.

Well. It makes as much sense as anything else that has happened since last night. Grasping the heavy iron grate with my good hand, I drag it away. It makes a horrid screech against the floor, and Sir Bird caws a warning a moment too late. Books explode off the shelves, turning into birds in midair, the room a whirling mass of cries.

I duck my head, screaming, but Sir Bird flies out past me and into the melee, scratching and pecking and, in a process my eyes cannot comprehend, swallowing other birds. They converge on him, attacking, and though he fights more fiercely than any, he will be overwhelmed. There is an iron poker next to the fireplace and I grab it, flinging it wildly and batting the demon birds into the walls. They turn back into books on impact, falling to the floor with dusty thuds.

Sir Bird goes down in a tangled mass of feathers. I can only tell which one he is because so many other birds are trying to kill him. I grab his foot and yank him free of the pile, cradling him to my chest and diving into the fire.

I pull the grate shut behind us, not a moment too soon. Black bodies slam against it, beaks straining through the gaps in the pattern. I tug it tight, leaving no space at the top like the one Sir Bird used to get in.

I do not know how badly Sir Bird is hurt, but my fingers are slick with his blood. I tuck him into the crook of my elbow where I hold my ruined hand against my chest. The pain is so all-consuming that it's a relief to focus on something else: figuring out what I am supposed to do now that I am crouched in a roaring fire.

Sir Bird croaks and jabs his head toward the back of the fireplace. It's solid bricks, stained with years of soot.

I look up—the chimney narrows into two pipes. There's no way I will fit in either of them. Not even Sir Bird could, were he able to fly. I suppose he meant for me to hide here, but it won't take the nightmare man long to find me. If his bird knew I could sit in the fire unharmed, surely he will know as well. I take a deep, smoke-free breath, and collapse to rest against the bricks until I am discovered.

Thus it is I am greatly shocked to fall straight through the wall into a small, dark passage.

Ten

SIR BIRD CROAKS REPROACHFULLY, AND I VOW
to never again question his directions. Half laughing, half sob-
bing, I crawl using my knees and my one good arm. Every bump
and jolt sends a scream of pain through my hand. The ground is
cold stone slick with layers of grime and—judging by the overwhelming smell—bird droppings.

After what feels like an eternity, I see tiny cracks of light
ahead and crawl faster, desperate to take a full breath and to
be out of this cramped, dark place. I push my shoulder against
rough wooden slats and a trapdoor flips down on spring
hinges. Taking Sir Bird in my good hand, I gently lift him
through and then wriggle my way out of the opening, grateful,

for once, for my corset.

I'm free. I'm free! I stand, every muscle quivering, and again tuck Sir Bird against my chest, trusting him not to touch my hand. I finally force myself to look at it. My fingers are a blue-and-purple mess, knuckles bent at wrong angles. Three are split open and bleeding, and I see slivers of white I can only assume are bone. Even after I get them properly set, they will never be the same.

My stomach threatens to give out on me again, but I refuse. Finish escaping now. There will be plenty of time to mourn my writing hand later. I follow the small space between the gray bricks of a house and the hedge, and arrive at an opening large enough to squeeze out of. Valuing speed over caution, I shove myself through, hair catching on twigs and dress ripping as I burst into the cloud-dimmed light of an Aveburian afternoon.

I turn to my right and am unsurprised to see Finn, standing on the step of a fine townhouse, cane poised in the air midway to knocking on the door. It was his shadow, after all. His angular shoulders droop, and even his hair appears dimmer than usual. But his dark eyes are fixed on mine, and his mouth is frozen open in the pleasing round shape of an O.

"For spirits' sake, do *not* knock on that door." And then I collapse onto the ground.

"Jessamin!" He kneels beside me, hands hovering as though he isn't sure what to do with them. "You must want me to explain everything."

"No." I watch in horror as a massive plume of smoke shoots out of the chimney and transforms into a cloud of black birds so thick it obscures the sun. "I want to run away from here as fast as possible."

He follows my eyes and curses, then slides his hands beneath my legs and back.

"What are you doing?"

"Picking you up so we can run!"

"Don't be daft, my hand is broken, not my feet!"

"Right, that was stupid. Stupid." He helps me up by my elbow. "This way!"

We run across the lane and down the street. We're surrounded by solid row homes, finer than any I've ever been in, with attached walls and no alleys or side streets to offer us escape. The cloud of birds circles overhead, a swirling mass of terror.

There are a few people out, but judging from their dress they are all servants. They glue their eyes on the ground and hurry in the opposite direction of us. Is this so normal an occasion for them that it does not merit so much as a shout of fear?

I do not realize I am cursing in Melenese until Finn—one hand on my elbow and the other waving his cane in mad circles overhead—gasps, "What *are* you saying?"

"I am saying that my hand hurts so much I want to die and will you kindly shut up and let me focus on running?"

"If you will kindly shut up and let me focus on a spell to save our lives!"

He glares at me but then stops dead, nearly jerking me from my feet. "One of the familiars is with you!" He raises his cane, eyes blazing with murder toward Sir Bird.

"Don't you dare!" I hunch my shoulders around Sir Bird, angling him away from Finn.

"We haven't time for this!"

"So keep running!" I shrug away from him and continue my mad flight.

He catches up to me quickly, falling into pace though I do not doubt he could outrun me in my current state. "That bird belongs to him."

"This bird saved my life."

"I am saving your life!"

"You were ready to give in! I saved my own life. You are simply keeping me company on this leg of my escape." Sir Bird caws brokenly in support of my statements.

One of the birds dives at us and smashes against an unseen barrier, exploding in a poof of feathers that turns into ash. "And how," Finn says, huffing with anger or exertion, his cane still tracing patterns into the air, "do you intend to evade the flock of familiars even now conveying our every move?"

"I can't do *all* the work! Surely if you are so important as to merit the smashing of my every finger, you can figure this out."

"Stop!" he says. I fear he is going to leave me, but he nods. "Here, this should work." He traces a rectangle onto the blank space of a head-high wall, then knocks the tip of his cane on it three times in rapid succession. The wall melts away and, instead of a view into the small front lot of the house, it opens into blackness.

He ducks to go through, then looks back and sees my hesitation. "Trust me?"

"Of course I don't." I grit my teeth and swish sideways past him, but I miscalculate the width of the door and brush my ruined hand against the brick. I cry out, the pain intensified to a blinding wave.

This time when his arms come around me, lifting and cradling, I do not object. He hurries down a flight of stairs in the pitch black. The wall seals behind us, cutting off the harsh screams of the birds. At the bottom, Finn taps his cane against the wall and a line of sconces burst into flame, illuminating a stone tunnel with periodic holes in the ceiling. It drips with the slick collection of water from the cobbled stones of the street above us. Finn's fine shoes *splosh* through the accumulated slush and stone-strained filth.

"Not far now," he says.

"I can walk." I do not want to, of course, but most of the dizziness has passed and the pain has dulled to merely overwhelming.

"Don't be ridiculous. I need you close for this next part anyhow. And will you please get rid of the bird."

I cradle Sir Bird closer to my chest. "You will have to get rid of me first." Sir Bird squawks loudly.

"Accursed stubborn creature."

"He is not accursed!"

"I was speaking of you."

He stops and I brace myself to be dropped, but he shifts me with the gentlest of movements to free his cane for wider access. I turn to see a circle, inscribed with patterns, burned into the wall. Beneath us, a wider circle glows faintly under the streaming water Finn stands in.

"Running water helps," he says as if that is any explanation at all. "But I cannot have any part of you outside of the circle. If you would stand on my feet and"—he pauses and looks down as though unwilling to meet my gaze—"wrap your arms around me in as tight an embrace you can manage without pain, that should be enough."

"Must we?"

I do not know why this sounds more intimate than being carried in his arms, but my cheeks burn. He nods and removes his arm from beneath the bend of my knees, easing me down until my toes meet the water and the tops of his shoes. Keeping Sir Bird between us and angling my hand so that it touches nothing, I wrap my free arm around Finn, trying not to note the smooth muscles of his back beneath his long, black overcoat.

"If you could—that is, would you mind terribly—tucking your head in as well?"

I close my eyes and lean in. My head fits right at the hollow of his neck, and the image of his collarbone springs unbidden into my mind. My breath must catch because he murmurs about having hurt me again. I shake my head, pressing it closer into his neck. "It's fine," I whisper, not trusting my voice.

"This won't be painful, but you will be disoriented. Try not to let go when it's finished. I fear you would fall."

I nod into his neck, his pulse beneath my cheek.

He whispers a series of foreign words, and we are swept away, twirling and tumbling in a rush of water that is neither cold nor wet. It takes me several seconds to realize I am still upright, clinging to Finn, and even longer to process that we are not in any river, nor are we in the sewer system, but rather in a bright room where every square foot is covered in books—crammed on shelves, piled on tables and chairs and couches, strewn haphazardly in teetering stacks on the floor.

"You're trembling," Finn's voice is a low song beside my ear, and I know I should let him go, but the commands refuse to transfer from my brain to my arm.

"Here is the back of the couch. Use it to steady yourself. I'm going to clear a spot for you to lie down." He's careful and gentle, as though addressing a spooked animal.

I nod and pull my head away from his neck, keeping my eyes down. I cannot look him in the face, not so soon. I shift to lean against the couch, and he slowly releases me. I sway but manage to stay upright, and he darts out of view. The sound of books being flung to the floor punctuates an otherwise silent room.

"How are you?" I whisper to Sir Bird.

He is breathing, I can feel it, but I have no knowledge of normal bird breathing, much less magical bird breathing, to determine whether it is too fast or too slow. It is easier, though, to focus on the bird rather than let my mind dwell on my own pain.

"Here," Finn says. His arm is around my shoulders again, and he guides me around the couch to where I can sit. I don't want to lie down. It feels too vulnerable, too personal, and brings to mind the other strange couch I woke up on today.

The coffee table.

The hammer.

"Are you going to be sick?" He sounds alarmed.

I lie down and squeeze my eyes shut. I feel fingers reaching to take Sir Bird and flex my arm instinctively.

"I promise not to harm your beastly little friend. But I need your hand. Will you trust me?"

This time I nod, and his hands are soft as he lifts Sir Bird away. "I have my eye on you," he says in a low, menacing tone, and I am relieved to hear Sir Bird caw ill-naturedly in return.

Something warm and comfortingly heavy is placed over my waist and legs. I am shivering, shaking all over. Now that I no longer need to run, my body is shutting down.

"Your hand." Finn's voice is cold. I've done something to anger him, and I open my eyes, confused. He's kneeling next to me, fingers outstretched, just barely above my injuries. They shake until he draws them into a fist. "I will kill him."

"Wait your turn," I try to say, but my voice breaks and I seal my lips shut.

"Will you let me fix them?"

"Are you a doctor?"

"I would not let a doctor within twenty feet of your fingers. I can make them right again."

"Will it hurt?" I hate that tears pool in my eyes, but I cannot help it.

He nods. "It will. Terribly. But only for a moment."

"Couldn't you knock me over the head with something first?"

He smiles, but it doesn't touch his eyes. "Then I would have to fix your head, too, and I'm much better with fingers."

I take a deep breath and hold out my hand. I cannot move it past my wrist.

He surveys the damage. Then he reaches into his vest pocket and pulls out a black satin, wrist-length glove. "I already made it," he says. "As soon as he started . . . well, I wanted to be ready when I got into the house. I didn't count on you meeting me at the porch."

He sets the glove down next to me and then looks into my eyes. "It may be best not to watch."

"You cannot compete with any of the horrors today has already delivered. I'd prefer to see."

This time the sad smile makes it to his eyes. He reaches out like he would tuck a loose strand of hair behind my ear, but stops short and turns back to his work. "Very well. Take a deep breath. On the count of three—"

I draw in the deepest breath I can, holding it, watching and waiting for him to start twisting and popping my fingers back into place. He picks up the glove, then says, "One . . . two . . ."

Without warning, he pulls the glove over my hand. I scream and kick out, catching him on the chin with my knee, but as soon as the pain registers it is gone, replaced by a strange, crawling, cold sensation, prickling beneath my skin.

I stop midscream and look in wonder at the glove, perfectly fit like a second skin, each finger straight and placed as though they had never known a hammer. I brace myself, then wiggle my hand to find that there is no pain at all, and each finger bends where a finger ought to.

"Now." Finn rubs his chin where I struck him. "Are you ready for an explanation?"

Eleven

I NOD, DISTRACTED, STILL FLEXING MY FINGERS with wonder. I broke a toe once, when I was six or seven, and even after my friends popped it back into place, it ached for months. Wanting to look at my fingers to see if the discoloration and splits in the skin have mended as well, I move to tug off the glove.

"No! Don't do that!" Finn grabs my gloved hand and holds it protectively in both of his. "You cannot remove it."

"Ever?"

"No, no, not that long. But it must stay in place until everything has settled. Can you feel it? The sort of itching crawl beneath your skin?"

I nod. It's like pins and needles, the way my foot feels when I've been reading with it tucked under me for too long. But colder. "What is it?"

"Magic." But the word sounds tired and ordinary coming out of his mouth. I know I should be shocked, disbelieving, but after everything I have seen and been through, it's a relief. I'm not losing my mind.

I shake my hand as though I can dislodge the sensation there. "I am not sure I like it, but it's better than the pain. You've felt it before?"

His eyes focused on nothing, one corner of his lips pulls up. "Every waking hour throughout my entire body."

"Well, a glove and a strange sensation is more than a fair trade. Thank you."

"I am—you must know how sorry I am for all of this."

"Yes, though what 'all of this' is I cannot begin to fathom." Needing some fidget to break eye contact—his dark eyes are piercing, and I begin to feel those strange pins and needles across my whole body under their gaze—I pull off my regular glove, wrinkling my nose at the filth caked there. It is then that I'm finally aware enough to take into account the relative state of my clothes and person.

The dress is snagged and torn. The skirts around my knees are black with grime, and I want nothing more than to be shot of it and the associations with the man who sent it to me.

"This is an explanation best made in clean, dry clothes, worn over full stomachs," Finn says, anticipating my discomfort. "Though I have no women's clothing here, I'm afraid."

"I should wonder greatly if you did." I smile, attempting levity, and then realize I know next to nothing about him. He could be married. He certainly wouldn't be the first married Alben man to pursue a Melenese mistress.

"How old are you?" I blurt out.

"I am the oldest nineteen-year-old alive," he says, smiling sadly. "This way." He waits for me to stand, watching to see how steady I am. I'm pleased to be able to walk more or less confidently. He leads me out a door—which does not disappear, I have kept half an eye on it the whole time—and into an electric lantern–lit hall. I look down both ends, but it stretches beyond what I can see, blurring far sooner than it should. I cannot make out how many doors there are, and they seem too close together to lead to any rooms other than closets.

Finn opens one onto a washroom. It's generously sized, bigger than my room at the hotel, and far larger than the doors in the hallway would account for. But inside, the walls are free from extra doors, a pale blue color with waist-high wainscoting.

This house makes me dizzy.

I decide to willfully ignore the problem of the doors and inspect the washroom, instead. There's a claw-foot bath, and a pillar washbasin against the wall, complete with in-room faucet. Running water! A large, gilt mirror hangs above a dressing table and a plush chair. Against the far wall is a window, through which I can see branches of a tree and the late afternoon sky.

"Towels, here." He opens an armoire. "And a clean night-shirt with a dressing robe. I am sorry I cannot offer better, and that it's not pressed."

"It's fine, thank you." Something nags at me, however, and though it should be the least of my worries, I cannot help but ask. "What will you tell the servants?"

"I keep secrets in this house. I have found that one can either keep secrets or keep servants. The two are incompatible. I'll leave you to it, and prepare a luncheon in the library." He closes the door quietly behind himself, and I turn the lock.

As I struggle to undo the lacings of my corset, I look out the window, needing distractions. Odd. The windows in the library were streaming warm golden light, but this window overlooks a tree-lined park, the day drizzling and gray as it was when we fled the nightmare man's house. I suppose I should no longer expect anything in the world to make sense, but I find this annoying in the extreme. Other memories demand to be felt, tugging at the edge of my mind and emotions, but I cling to the annoyance so I can delay addressing what the nightmare man did to me.

Finally managing to rip free of the corset, I slide out of the whole mess and toss it in a bin along with my ruined stockings.

The prospect of soaking—actually soaking!—in a bath sings a siren song and in a few minutes I am up to my chin in hot water. I have no concept of the time. The fact that I no longer feel hungry means I have gone beyond the point of complaint from my stomach. My fingers tremble as I undo my bun and let my hair fall onto my shoulders.

I stay until the water cools, then towel dry. I kept my gloved hand out of the water. I will have to ask Finn how to wash it. The nightshirt I choose from the many options is light and thin, and feels marvelous against my skin. I wrap a black dressing gown around it, and though I am now more covered than I was in the dress, I feel exposed.

I try on a pair of slippers, but they are far too large, so I leave the washroom and pad silently down the plush rug in the hall. One door is cracked open, so I push it but stop short of entering the library.

Finn is wearing a fresh suit. He sits on the couch facing me, but with his head bowed and cradled in his hands. He looks so despairing, so raw with pain or worry, I know I have intruded on a private moment. My first impulse is to go to him, to put my arm around his shoulders and comfort him. But this is not done here. Nobles are proper and distant, and no doubt that is the best comfort I can offer him. I back silently through the door, pulling it closed behind me and then wait a few minutes before knocking.

"Yes, come in," Finn calls, and I reenter the library to find him standing, straight and assured as ever, with falsely bright eyes.

We wear faces as disguises. I hold back a shudder, remembering the nightmare man's true face revealed in snatches behind the one he wears for the world. I suspect I was seeing straight to his soul.

"I've some sandwiches, and there's tea—"

"No tea!"

Finn startles at my exclamation, and I stutter to explain. "It's—you see, there was tea—I could smell it so strongly while he was—" I twist my hands, running my fingers over the glove.

"Of course. We need brandy." He grabs the silver service set and whisks it away. I sit, jumbled with nerves, on the edge of the couch. He is going to explain everything. I am not sure how, but he will. I long for the security of the world I lived in yesterday, but it is lost to me forever.

He returns with two cut crystal glasses filled with amber liquid, and sets one on the table in front of me. I eat half a carefully cut sandwich and find it is all I can manage. Sipping at the warm brandy, I wait for him to start.

"I'm sorry. I didn't see the tea," he says.

I frown. "How could you have? And how did you know what . . ." I cannot say aloud what the nightmare man did, because then I have to acknowledge it happened. "How did you know to prepare the glove?"

"You saw my shadow, correct?"

I nod.

"It is a . . . peculiar sort of connection and separation. I could choose to see through it, which is much like looking into a dim room from outside in the brilliant sunshine, or hear through it, which is much like listening with cotton in your ears. Since I needed to prepare the glove, I was forced to listen instead." He stares into his cup of brandy and then takes a gulp. I remember my screams. Clearly, he does, as well.

"Why *was* your shadow there? Is it like his birds, a sort of errand runner?" I look for Sir Bird and instead find a massive black volume atop one of the piles of books. I hope he's resting.

"The bird!" Finn stands, whirling and frantically searching the room. "Curse that bird, he'll—"

"Here!" I grab the book, waving it at Finn. "Unless this is one of yours."

Finn's eyes narrow, and he reaches out to take it. I hug it to my chest, matching his glare.

"Curious." He sits again, still staring at the book. I place it on my lap. The cover is pure black, with a faint hint of iridescence, much like Sir Bird's wings. But it is far heavier than Sir Bird, and much larger than any of the bird-books that were on the shelves. I wonder if it has anything to do with his having swallowed so many of the other creatures.

"Your shadow?" I am impatient for actual answers now that we have begun. Denial and avoidance will get me nowhere. I want to learn as much as I can about this . . . *magic* . . . that is now a painful and confusing part of my life.

"Oh, yes, well. That's a complicated bit to explain." He tugs at his collar as though it is bothering him. "I should rather tell you about Lord Downpike."

I shudder, twitching my neck to relieve the prickling of discomfort there. "Is that his name? It sounds familiar."

"It should. He is the minister of defense."

Twelve

I GASP, STUNNED. "THAT MADMAN IS THE MINISTER of defense?" In the hierarchy of Alben rule, the minister of defense was just below the prime minister.

"Unfortunately, yes."

"This country just gets worse and worse."

Finn laughs sadly. "It does have some good parts. But he is not one of them."

"Well, go on, before I decide I've gone mad after all."

He nods. "Doubtless you have surmised that, for lack of a better word, magic exists in the world."

"I had noticed," I say dryly.

"Subtlety is not a strong point of Downpike's."

"Nor is sanity."

"No, nor sanity. The distribution of power is not always what it should be, and men like Downpike are born with more than their fair share."

"Is that what it is? An issue of the nobility? You secretly use magic because it gives you privilege?"

"You misunderstand. I could show you, step-by-step, the precise method to, say, turn this brandy to ice. But even after learning the symbols and words and following all of the directions to the letter, you would be missing the final . . . how do I put it . . ."

"Variable?"

"Yes! Exactly. There is a variable that you lack. Nearly everyone lacks it except those of noble bloodlines."

"So there *is* a reason you're born into privilege and take what you have not earned!" I glower at him.

"You of all people should know what it is to be relegated to one side of the great power struggle due to factors about yourself you cannot control. It is not my fault I was born with these abilities. Please do not hold me accountable for my birth, as I assure you I would never do you the same dishonor."

I lean back and fold my arms across my chest. "Very well. Your noble birth is the variable needed to make magic. Wonderful! How lovely to have it in the hands of a madman who also controls so much of the country."

"I am sorry." His voice has lost its sting. "I did my best to keep you from crossing paths with this world. And I shall do my best to protect you now that you have been so violently initiated."

"Why *did* Lord Downpike choose me? I have nothing to do with any of this."

Finn stands and goes to the window, his back to me. "You know of the tenuous peace between Albion and the Iverian continental countries. Our history is long and fraught with conflict, though the last few decades we've found balance. There are some who wish to tip that balance back in favor of Albion. Lord Downpike wants something he thinks I have, and will do anything to secure it. For the last two years, I've managed to subvert his efforts, never giving him ground or opportunity to manipulate me. Then I met you." His voice is bitter.

"What am I to you?" I am angry, growing angrier, that I have somehow become a pawn in a game I did not even know was being played. "Why would he think you would care?"

Finn reaches into his waistcoat pocket and pulls out a familiar deck of blue-backed cards.

I scoff. "You cannot tell me this has anything to do with silly, superstitious cards."

"If it is silly, you won't mind drawing again. One card."

We match glares, neither of us backing down. Finally, just to move on to actual answers, I reach out and snatch a card from the middle of the deck.

He doesn't look at the card, keeping his eyes locked on me. He simply whispers, "Fate and lovers."

I roll my eyes and hold up the card.

The cards.

Again, where I am certain I took only one, I hold two. I turn them so I can see what they are, and my breath catches. The first card shows two bodies twined around each other, blending until I cannot tell where one begins and the other ends. A red ribbon encircling them twists out LOVERS.

But it is the second card that hits me like a blow. Two roads converge in a tangled wood tunneling into darkness. The branches of the trees spell out FATE.

"I know this path," I whisper.

"You do?"

"I've dreamt it. But it wasn't trees, it was bodies, and we danced down the line. . . ." I look up to find Finn's stony glare has melted into something like hope, and I stop myself. "Let me see the deck."

"What?"

I hold out my hand. "You knew which cards I'd get before you saw them. Let me see the deck."

He hands it over and I thumb through it, my triumphant *aha!* ready to be unleashed when I proved that all of the cards were FATE or LOVERS dying on my lips as I see dozens of cards, all distinct.

I drop the cards on the floor, feeling dirty for having touched them. "It means nothing. This isn't magic, it's superstition of the basest kind. And you've told me nothing to explain why Lord Downpike would target me."

"I tried," Finn says, staring at the mess of cards. "I tried so very hard. After our first meeting, I thought I could put you out of my head. And then when I saw you in the park, I aimed to test myself, to prove that you meant nothing. I found myself checking into your hotel afterward. Not to see you—I didn't

want to see you, I couldn't—but simply to be near enough to—"
He shrugs helplessly. "It was obviously indulgent and selfish. I
should have known I was being watched. When you drew the
cards . . . well, I resolved to never speak to you again and that
would end things. I did not count on the reach of Downpike's
spies, though, and he presented an impossible task at the gala.
How could I see you and not—"

My heart beats rapidly as I wait for him to look up, to finish
the sentence. I'm disappointed. He stops, gathering the cards
and tucking them away. "Well. He played the game better than
I. But he underestimated you."

Blast that unfinished sentence. But something else is off. He
is not telling me enough. Then I notice that, though the light
streams in all around Finn, *he has no shadow*. I run to the window
next to him, then turn and look at the ground. My shadow is
there, silhouette of long hair and robed body, but there is something fuzzy, something not quite the same about it. I raise one
arm as fast as I can, and there! The hint of another shadow
behind it.

"I still have your shadow!" I gasp. "Take it back!"

"Would that I could."

"No, I don't want it, you must—" I stop, my heart racing as
I remember what he said earlier. "You . . . you can see and hear
through your shadow." Minutes ago I was naked in his bathroom, with his shadow there the whole time! "How dare you!" I
slap him, and he has the audacity to look surprised.

"No, it doesn't work like that! I don't see and hear through
it all the time. It takes a great deal of concentration and power,

and I'm entirely tapped out at the moment. I promise I would never intrude on your privacy."

My face is burning, and I cannot find it in me to believe him. "Take it back. Immediately."

He raises both hands in the air, exasperated. "I can't! These things don't work like that. You don't understand."

"Then tell me how they work! Why did you attach it to me in the first place?" Had he suspected Lord Downpike would do something? If so, why hadn't he protected me?

Finn looks to the side, taking a deep breath and folding his hands in front of himself. I can actually *see* him regaining control of his temper. "I would prefer not to discuss it at the moment. In due time we will figure out . . . a solution."

I want to strangle him. The cool, smooth planes of his face, the sharp contours of his jaw, the perfectly combed golden hairs atop his head. It infuriates me how he can be so put together and calm when my whole world has shifted.

I lift a hand. He cringes expecting another slap, but does not move, as if he knows he deserves it. Instead, I push my fingers through his hair, making it stand at wild angles, horribly mussed.

"There." I mimic his imperious, disengaged face. "Now." I sit back down and take a sip of my brandy. "You have more to tell me, but first I would like to send a letter to my friends at the hotel telling them I am safe and will be home soon. They're probably sick with worry."

"I'll send notice that you're safe, but I am afraid you can't go back."

"Pardon?"

He moves away from the window and stands, examining a bookshelf as though it contains something more interesting than a rainbow of cracked and worn spines. "I think it best if you go to my home in the country. You'll be safe there until this is sorted. The grounds are well kept, and you'd love the greenhouse. I can hire a few servants for you."

"And how long am I to stay?"

"As long as it takes for me to neutralize Downpike as a threat to you and others. If you are where he cannot reach you, then that problem is solved."

I set my glass carefully onto the table, my voice measured. "I am a problem to be solved."

"Yes. I mean, no. But I could not live with myself if you came to any more harm from my enemies. It's the best solution for everyone."

"You mean it is the most convenient solution for yourself! What about me? I have school, and a job!"

He shakes his head dismissively, and I hate him for it. He has dismissed my entire life with that one gesture, whether intentional or not. "You cannot go back to the hotel, he knows where you live. But you needn't worry about money. I will take care of everything. And you can tell me which books you want, and I'll have them sent there. I can't imagine you learn more from your professors than you do on your own."

"It's all settled, then."

He nods, clearly relieved. "Yes. This will work out nicely."

"And how shall I dress? Will you pick out my clothing for

me? Perhaps you'd prefer I give up scholarly pursuits entirely. I could take up painting! Would you also advise me on how to style my hair so that, if you decide to visit, it is most pleasing to your tastes?"

He frowns. "It's not my place to—"

"To tell me *anything* about how to live my life and protect myself. You tell me that you do not ask for the power you were born with, and yet you wield it like the Great Gentle Sword of Mother Albion, coming in to tell the simple primitives how they should be living their lives! You couch your motivations under the banner of protecting me, when it comes down to the fact that you think you are better than I am and more equipped to rule my life."

His eyebrows raise. "That is not fair."

"No, it's not fair. None of this is fair. But I will decide what to do with the lack of fairness in my circumstances."

"There is more at stake here than your well-being. You don't understand the elements at play, the lives that hang in the balance. Downpike isn't only after you. He has his sights set on inciting conflict, perhaps even war, and I alone stand in opposition!"

"If I don't understand, it's because you think me unworthy of the knowledge and that is where you fail." I stand. "Now, if you will show me the front door, I'll be on my way."

He leans against the bookshelf, arms crossed, face set. "And where, pray tell, will you go? He will have you in an instant if you return to the hotel. Is that what you want?"

I try not to blanche at the idea of being back in Lord

Downpike's horrible room. "I have other options. You needn't concern yourself."

"I can't help it!" For a moment, his coolness cracks and he looks beside himself with anguish. Then his smile slides back into place. "I am afraid I cannot show you to the door." He taps his cane against the floor, perhaps thinking I do not notice the motion. "They are all locked at the moment."

We both stare, eyes hard, neither breaking down or backing off. Then I sigh, putting on the meek face I gave to Mama when she needed to be right. "Very well. I'm not agreeing to anything, but I'm in no condition to argue right now."

He lifts his cane, pleased. Clearly he does not know me if he thinks I am *ever* in a condition where arguing is not possible.

"I'm feeling faint. I'd like to wash my face with some cool water."

"Of course!" He walks ahead of me, and I take Sir Bird's book and tuck it into the robe, crossing my arms in front of its hidden bulk.

"Thank you," I say, entering the washroom. "Is there a bed you could prepare for me? I would be grateful."

He nods, all polite concern now that he is getting what he wants, and closes the door behind himself. I roll my eyes at how easily he accepts me as meek and courteous. I play an Alben woman well when I want to. I cross to the window overlooking a park in the city, push it open, and climb out.

Thirteen

THE GRAY-HATTED WOMAN UNDER THE BATTERED umbrella cannot seem to understand what I am asking.

I repeat myself. "The park, madam. What is it called? What area are we in?"

She looks nervously from side to side, as though unsure whether to call for a constable to deal with me. I am a sight, in my man's dressing robe, bare feet, single glove, and undone hair, but one cannot be expected to be fashionable under such circumstances.

I wait as calmly as I can manage. Finn will check on me soon, and I'd prefer to be far removed. But if she calls for a constable, I'll have to run. No telling where they would take me if I answered their questions honestly. *Yes, sir, I am hiding from two mad magicians, one of whom tortured me, and the other of whom wishes to set me up in a beautiful estate with servants and anything I require.*

"The park?" I repeat.

"Greenhaven. Greenhaven Park. In the southern neighborhood of Kingston. Can I . . . do you need . . . would you like my umbrella?" She holds it out. The handle is worn but sturdy.

For some reason this small gesture from a woman I don't know, whom I assumed was judging me, puts me on the verge of tears. "Thank you. You are so kind." I take the umbrella, because I do not have it in me to pass up such a simple generosity.

She pats my hand and smiles. "You're young yet. These troubles are never as serious as we make them out to be."

I sniffle, nodding and holding back a laugh. "I'm certain you are right."

"Well, then." She seems to stand a bit straighter—in spite of the drizzle now hitting her hat—and walks away.

Kingston. It's on the opposite end of the city from where I live, but something feels familiar. I laugh. I *do* have other places I can go. A few minutes later, I stand on the front steps of a beautiful dark stone town house in a stylish Kingston neighborhood, my umbrella dripping a halo of water around me. The butler, a stout man with polished glasses and hair brutally combed into submission, blocks the door with a perplexed frown.

"And you know Miss Eleanor how?"

"She gave me her card and told me to call on her."

"Do you . . . have the card with you?"

"I am afraid my purse was stolen. Along with my shoes."

I can tell he thinks me mad—with good reason. He would sooner set me out with the rubbish bins than allow me into the parlor of Eleanor's fine town house, but if my story is true, he might earn the ire of his mistress by being rude and dismissing me.

I have a feeling I will be standing on this porch for a long time.

A man's voice comes from behind me. "What in the queen's name is going on here, Mr. Carlisle?"

I turn to find Ernest trying to figure out who exactly I am. When he finally connects me to his dance partner at the gala, the realization is written in humorous clarity across his face. He immediately looks to either side as though caught doing something wrong.

"I . . . erm . . . what are you doing here?"

I silently thank the spirits when Eleanor, dressed in a tailored burgundy day gown with an art piece of a hat, climbs out of the black carriage and joins her brother. She frowns, clearly stumped, until recognition lights up her face. Instead of guilty, she looks delighted. "Jessamin? Is that you?"

I give her a wry smile, hoping I didn't misjudge her friendliness last night. "I have had a series of misfortunes since we met and wondered if I might trouble you with some questions."

She laughs, hands her umbrella to Mr. Carlisle, and then wraps her hand through my elbow. "Oh, I knew I was right to make you my friend. Finally, someone interesting in this whole sleeping town. Let's get you off the porch before you're attached to Ernest in some vicious gossip he is no doubt already fearing will ruin his political aspirations."

"I—of course not, I—" he stammers, his face as red as his hair.

Eleanor ignores him. "Mr. Carlisle, we will be in the parlor. Have Mrs. Jenkins bring dry clothes for my friend, and we'll take some tea—" She notices my expression change, and narrows her eyes. "No tea then. We'll have some chocolate. You do like chocolate?"

Relieved, I squeeze her hand with my own. "Nothing could sound better at the moment."

After my umbrella is taken, my clothes are changed, and the chocolate is delivered, we settle near a cozy fireplace in Eleanor's parlor. It is decorated in stripes and cream colors, far less ornate than I would have expected.

Ernest walks in to join us, but Eleanor cuts him a look and shakes her head. "I think this is a ladies' talk." Again his skin tone matches his hair and he bows out. She leans in, her eyes gleaming. "I must warn you. I am the biggest gossip in all of Avebury."

I take a sip of the thick, bittersweet drink. "Well, at least you're honest about it. And if you are a gossip, then I hope you know something of the people I'm avoiding."

"Oh, dear," she says, but her smile grows bigger.

"Do you know anything about Lord Downpike? The minister of defense?"

Her smile vanishes, replaced with genuine concern. "What has he done? Are you all right? I'm so sorry, I tried to protect you last night. That's why I pulled you away when he tried to cut in on the dance floor. It had nothing to do with Ernest. You were probably the highlight of my brother's entire year. But Lord Downpike had been watching you so closely and I simply couldn't stand idle. I would not wish that man on my worst enemy. Dark rumors. Besides, Uncle and he don't get on at all. They had a dreadful falling-out a couple of years ago."

I find I am stroking the smooth surface of my glove. "Yes, he . . . well, let's just say I find your enmity with him greatly comforting."

"What did he do?"

I debate lying, but if she's nobility, she should know about the magic. And if she doesn't, she is not much use to me in avoiding this mess. "He spied on me with his familiars, kidnapped me, trapped me in a room without a door, and then proceeded to smash each of the fingers on this hand with a hammer."

She leans back as though I have struck a blow, and then pulls out a snuffbox. Pinching some between her fingers, she whispers and, to my surprise, blows it straight into my face.

I sneeze.

She clicks the snuffbox shut emphatically. "Well, I'm confused. Whatever would he want with you? You're lovely, but you haven't a drop of magical blood in you. He never concerns himself with commoners. Oh, sorry. Here." She holds out an embroidered handkerchief, and I take it to dab my nose, glaring at her.

"I could have *told* you I have nothing to do with the secret magical societies apparently flourishing in Albion."

"Uncle will want to hear about this. Oh, he will be simply livid when he finds that Lord Downpike has revealed himself to you! It's not done, you see."

"*You've* just done it. I had no idea whether you were capable of magic."

She waves a hand dismissively. "I am barely fit to fill a teacup with the amount of power I have. No one cares about me."

"So it's true then, that all the gentry can do these things?"

"More or less. Some of us barely bother, we can do so little. We're all required to learn the basics, is all. But some, like Uncle and Downpike, could move mountains. I think Uncle *has*, now that I am on the topic. Ernest studies as hard as he can, hoping to join their ranks among the powerful someday. However, I aspire only to join the ranks of the well-dressed and fashionably late."

I frown, stirring my chocolate. "But if I recall my lessons correctly, wasn't there a period in Alben history where accused witches were hunted and burned at the stake? How did you all become gentry, then?" I had thought the accusations of witchcraft and magic were entirely false, but apparently not.

"Oh, that. It was a nasty business. You know how men can . . . sow seeds where seeds ought not be sown? Well, we had just come through the Lily War, and the royal line was finally settled. The king thought magical power ought to be consolidated to loyal families, and that the security of the crown depended on keeping power with the wealthy and educated. So, those who had been born outside of the approved family lines . . ."

"Were exterminated." I set down my cup, no longer thirsty. "That is horrible."

"Worse things have been done in the name of crown and country. But yes. I think we can both agree it was." She frowns and then shakes her head as though shaking away bad associations and thoughts. "Back to you! This is very exciting. We haven't had a real shake-up in the hierarchy since Lord Ackerly showed up two years ago, all dashing and aloof and powerful. Ever since then it's been the most dreary sort of political posturing without any action. I loathe politics. But if Downpike is misbehaving, things are bound to get interesting! Whatever did you do to catch his eye?"

The door to the parlor opens. We look up to see Finn, cane in hand and none too pleased. Mr. Carlisle is next to him. "Lord Ackerly here to see you, milady. He said it was urgent." Carlisle bows and backs away, closing the door.

"Lord Ackerly!" Eleanor stands, dropping a slight curtsy. "To what do we owe the pleasure?"

"Spying again, were you?" I glare at him.

Eleanor follows my scowl to where it meets Finn's, and then back, as though watching a game of tennis. The silence is a heavy thing, as electric as the overhead chandelier. She frowns, clearly puzzled, then looks down at the floor at my feet and bursts out with a sharp laugh. "Oh, dear spirits below, this is the best thing that I have ever been privy to. Lord Ackerly shadowed a commoner from the colonies!"

"That's enough," Finn snaps.

She leans in to me conspiratorially. "You must tell me your

secret. There isn't a girl out in society who hasn't tried to catch his eye, and here you are with the greatest prize of them all."

He is not amused. "You will kindly bite your tongue, Eleanor."

"Or you will bite it for me?"

He taps his cane once on the tiles, and Eleanor sits as though her legs have been knocked out from beneath her.

"I may well at that," he says.

She smiles, delight undampened. "This explains Lord Downpike's interest in Jessamin. You know, he's been trying to get you on his side for so long. It would be such a coup for his anti-Iverian cause. Everyone's been too afraid of you to really support him. I am beside myself with nerves! This changes everything. Lord Ackerly is no longer untouchable in the infernal machinations and subtleties of political blackmail and extortion. How *will* it all play out?"

"Without your aid," Finn says, tone dismissive. "Now." He sits near me on the couch, takes off his hat, and leans in, carrying with him a whiff of clove and something richer, darker, something that reminds me of heady velvet nights of a year ago, when I would sneak out of my house at night and run like a wild thing through the trees with my friends. I am pulled to his eyes. They seem to be larger than before, depthless, with flecks of gold dancing in them, and I have never seen anything so beautiful.

My hand is in his before I realize it. "We'll be going then," he says, and I nod. Of course I will go with him. He's pretty, so very, very pretty, and I would be a fool to say no to anything he asks of me.

I blink. *No,* I think. And then I manage to say it out loud. "No."

He sits back with an angry huff, now exhausted with dark circles under his eyes. It's as though a fog has been lifted from my brain. *Magic! He tried to use magic on me!* And I realize it is not the first time. "If you ever try that again," I say, taking a sip of chocolate to wet my suddenly parched throat, "I will beat you silly with your own cane."

"This is the best day of my life," Eleanor says.

I cannot agree with her.

Fourteen

"I'LL SEND FOR UNCLE. HE MUST HEAR ABOUT THIS."
Eleanor paces, her hands flying at such a rate as she talks I am
nearly dizzy watching them.

"You will do no such thing," Finn says, all ice to Eleanor's
flame.

"But he'll want to hear the details of what Lord Downpike
did. He can help you! Alliances, how I adore alliances. And
weddings. Which are really the same thing."

"I don't need help."

"Is that so?" She leans toward him and bats her eyelashes.
"Because that charm spell you were working was so strong I
was ready to pack my trunk and elope with you, and yet your

intended target threw it off. It seems to me that Lord Downpike is not the only issue here."

"It is none of your concern, Eleanor. All I need from you is a promise that you will keep this information to yourself."

"Lord Ackerly, if you asked me to deliver you the moon on a platter, I should think my odds of success slightly higher."

"I can make it worth your while, of course. Or, if you prefer, I can simply *make* you."

"Now we're dealing in threats! I feel so important. I wish you had done this last week. Aunt Agatha was in town, and I thought I would die from boredom."

The creak of the door gives me away. They both look up, surprised to remember that I am still in the room, and perhaps more surprised to find me leaving.

"Where do you think you're going?" Finn says at the same time Eleanor says, "Oh, please don't leave!"

"I do not care to be talked around. Call it a defect of my common breeding."

Eleanor rushes to my side, taking my hands in hers. "No, no, I'm sorry. Of course. Please, sit. You've clearly been through so much. I insist you stay here with me."

"You can't keep her safe," Finn says.

"I can! Well, no. I probably can't. But Ernest is here. And Uncle! Yes, Jessamin and I will go to stay at Uncle's. Lord Downpike wouldn't dare cross him, and Uncle is ever so powerful."

Finn slams his cane against the table. "I will not have her under the earl's thumb, nor have her leveraged against me. Not by Downpike, and not by your family. She should be somewhere away from all of this. It's nothing to do with her."

"You made it to do with her, though, didn't you?" Eleanor looks pointedly at the ground where my shadow pools at my feet. "Can I see it? Wiggle around or something. I've never actually seen someone shadowed before! It's so romantic!"

"It is nothing of the sort! It's . . ." I glance at Finn, who is avoiding my eyes. "He was just spying, and . . ." *Romantic? Preposterous.* But suddenly I am desperate to understand. "What does it mean? He wouldn't explain it to me."

"Open your mouth, Eleanor, and I will cut out your tongue and use it as fertilizer for my personal herb garden."

"But she should know!" Eleanor whines, pulling me back to the couch across from Finn. "It's adorable."

From the look on Finn's face, it's clear that no one has ever used "adorable" in conjunction with him before. And that he is not overly fond of it.

"If you don't explain it to me right now, I will never speak to either of you again. Which means no more gossip for you." I point at Eleanor and then at Finn. "And no more . . ." My sharp words fall to pieces at the look he pierces me with. Perhaps he *would* mind it if I never spoke to him again.

This room is very hot.

"Will you leave us for a moment, Eleanor?" Finn asks.

"I would not miss this for—"

"Leave."

Eleanor's legs walk her out of the room. She cranes her neck around to yell, "She'll tell me later, you know! We're the best of friends now!" The door slams behind her. "I would have told it better than you!" she yells, her voice muffled.

Finn clasps his hands behind his back and begins pacing. "Most of what you call magic is carefully controlled. Like chemistry. I assume you have studied chemistry."

"Yes," I snap.

"When the right elements are combined—whether they are plants or minerals or symbols or simply words—by someone of noble blood, they produce a reaction. It's more science than anything, and the best practitioners are the ones who have studied the most, and who have access to the most information. It's a delicate process. In the more complex instances, a single misplaced word or line could change the entire thing."

"Yes, fine."

"But there are some . . . aspects . . . that we still do not understand and that are beyond our control. Much like the potential being in blood. Some generations are skipped entirely, some people are born with far greater capabilities for no apparent reason. Many believe that a good deal of what we access exists outside of us, all the time. We can find evidence of it, in things like . . ." He pauses. "Well, in things like the cards. No reading is ever the same, and the interpretations vary. It lacks the precision of the more learned methods, but there is something elemental about it, something that we cannot control or change."

I don't hold back an unladylike snort. "Pretty pictures on a card tell the future."

"I know how it sounds. I was resistant to it as well, but my mother—" His voice catches, and he clears his throat. "She was gifted with the cards and taught me what she could. I have had the evidences I need."

"Will your mother tell me my fortune as well?"

Something shifts in Finn's eyes at my snide tone, and he looks farther away. "She's dead. My father, too."

Badly done, Jessamin. I cringe. "I'm sorry. But you have still said nothing of shadows."

His jaw twitches, whether with annoyance or amusement I do not know him well enough to say. "Your professors must be constantly exhausted."

I smile. "I do try."

His tone shifts from a pedantic, scholarly drone to a rushed tumble of words, as though by saying them faster, I will understand them less. "Shadows go in front of you, leading into your future, and trail behind you, leaving a part of you in the past. They are clearest when we are in the light, and disappear when we lose ourselves in darkness. When a shadow elects to jump to another person, it is an indication that they are your present and your future, that in light you will find them, in darkness you will lose them. It is highly unusual and very important and, might I add, extremely dangerous for the owner of the shadow.

"I have always been able to use mine as an extension of myself, in a form like Lord Downpike's familiars, but much more stable because it's actually a part of me. Thus separated, both myself and my shadow are vulnerable to attack. The fact that I have lost it represents Lord Downpike's greatest opportunity to manipulate and blackmail me, and surely you understand now why it is best for you to be secreted away."

I frown, trying to process the rush of information. "You

mean . . . it would be safer for you if I went away."

"For both of us, naturally. We are connected."

I throw my hands in the air, beyond exasperated. "We've already discussed this! Take it back! I don't want it!"

"I cannot! I would not even if I could!"

"Why not, you daft boy? I never asked you to grace me with your precious shadow or to give up your future and past and whatever other nonsense that accompanies it!"

"If you had asked, I wouldn't have given it to you! I couldn't have! It is precisely because you are so maddening that I had no other—"

Eleanor's voice sounds unnaturally loud from the entryway. We both freeze. "To what do I owe the pleasure of this surprise visit, *Lord Downpike?*"

Fifteen

A PIT OF TERROR OPENS IN MY STOMACH. "ELEANOR betrayed us," I whisper. I cannot face Lord Downpike again, not now, not with the memory of my pain so fresh.

"She's warning us," Finn hisses, grabbing my hand and pulling me toward a large armoire tucked into the corner. He opens it and we climb in. He has to stoop, and only by tucking myself into him, my back against his chest, can we both be hidden with the door shut.

My breath is fast and ragged. The walls are closing in on us. The flimsy wood that conceals us is not enough, not enough to block Lord Downpike's piercing black eyes. He will see through and then—

"Shh," Finn breathes, his lips next to my ear. He puts both arms around me and pulls me in closer. "I will kill him before he touches you again."

I close my eyes and mentally recite the quadratic equation in an effort to slow my heart. Maybe they will leave without ever coming in this room.

The door to the parlor opens. "In here is quite adequate," Lord Downpike says.

Finn tightens his arms around my waist and they are all that keep me on my feet. No. I can accept hiding, but certainly not cowering. I'm better than this. I squeeze Finn's hand to let him know that I am in control of myself. He does not loosen his grasp.

"Tea?" Eleanor's voice is as cheerful as ever.

"I see you have already had visitors."

"Oh, is the chocolate still here? My cousin was by this morning. I should think the maid would have cleared it by now. No matter, here is Mr. Carlisle with the tea. Mr. Carlisle, would you please remove the cups left out from this morning? We cannot have Lord Downpike thinking I keep an untidy house."

There are a few sounds, the clinking of spoons, and I picture the small bowl of sugar. At least it is Eleanor's and not Lord Downpike's.

"I will admit the suspense of why you are here is sending me near to fits! I cannot imagine the girls at the club will believe me when I tell them that I hosted the minister of defense himself!" She titters, and I am suddenly afraid for her.

"This is not a social call. It is about a girl. You met her last night at the gala."

"Oh, the gala! I met so many wonderful people. Did you enjoy it? It was my first large event, but I do so hope to have made an impression. Were you to want aid in the future with parties or balls or—"

"Jessamin. You would recall her. Red dress, dark skin."

"From the colonies! Yes, of course. She was quite the coquette, wasn't she? I think Ernest is half in love with her. And she's such a nice reminder of the work we are doing, spreading solid Alben values to savage nations."

"She stole something from me."

"No! How horrible! She seemed trustworthy to me, but one never can tell these days."

Lord Downpike continues on, failing to acknowledge anything Eleanor is actually saying. "It is of personal value only. I need it back."

Sir Bird! I left him in book form, tucked beneath the couch after I changed. Lord Downpike is probably sitting directly above him right now. I hold my breath, praying that the bird is either unaware of his master's presence or faithful enough to me not to give us all away.

"Have you contacted the royal arms?" Eleanor asks.

"I prefer to deal with it myself. You will let me know if she contacts you."

"Certainly! Anything I can do to be of service."

"Hold out your hand."

"Whatever for? Oh, did I spill some sugar—" Her voice cuts out with a sharp squeak of pain. I flinch, raise a hand to the door. I can't let him hurt her.

Finn's lips brush my ear. "Not yet," he whispers near soundlessly.

"A reminder," Lord Downpike says. "Sides must be chosen. I do hope you stand firmly with the might of Mother Albion."

There is a stumbling noise, and then the sound of the parlor door opening. Eleanor's voice is strained with the effort of suppressing tears. "Yes, thank you, do come again. I—Ernest! And Uncle?"

A voice who must be the elusive earl says, "What is it, Eleanor? Ernest said to come immediately, that you told him it was urgent."

Her laugh sounds like a bird with broken wings; it borders on hysterical. "Did I? Urgent? You know how prone to exaggeration I am. I merely wanted to visit with you. You needn't have hurried. Silly Ernest, you shouldn't have nagged him so."

Finn lets out a sharp breath, and I realize that Eleanor must have sent her brother for the earl while we were discussing shadows.

"Is that Lord Downpike?"

"Well met, Lord Rupert."

"I feel like the prettiest maid at the ball, all of these men visiting. Tea?"

"What did you do to your hand?" Lord Rupert asks. When he speaks again his voice is a low rumble of a threat. "Lord Downpike, if you had any part in this . . ."

Eleanor speaks first. "Oh, that! I burned it this morning trying to make myself toast! Aren't I the silliest creature alive? That is what I get for trying to give Cook a morning off."

"You did no such thing," Ernest says, not as sure-sounding as the Earl, but obviously upset.

The Earl's voice contains all the force of generations of power. "I will *not* allow you to bully my own blood. You cannot threaten us in our homes."

Lord Downpike sounds bored. "Then where shall I threaten you?"

Eleanor coughs. "Tea! We need more tea! I'll see to that, yes?"

"Lord Rupert, you may stand behind me or stand to the side, but I warn you not to get in my way."

After several tense seconds, Lord Rupert says, "Why did you let that man in here?"

Finn loosens his grasp on my waist, and I allow myself to breathe more fully. Lord Downpike must be gone.

"How does one say no to Lord Downpike?" Eleanor answers. "Please, I would very much like to know."

"It's a good thing I had already fetched Uncle," Ernest says. "But where did Jessamin go? He wasn't here about her, was he?"

Eleanor giggles. "Spirits below, what would a man like Lord Downpike want with a colony rat? She left right after you. Lord Downpike just wanted to . . . recruit me for his anti-Continent cause. Apparently, word of my excellent connections has gotten around." I have to hand it to Eleanor—she can spin lies faster than anyone I know.

"Stay out of this," Lord Rupert says. "You haven't the power or the intelligence to deal with a man like him."

"Of course," she answers, and I want to shake both of them. "He asked me to let him know of any interesting news I hear. Should I? What are you going to do about him?"

There is a long silence, and then Lord Rupert sounds more tired than angry. "If Lord Ackerly cannot hold out defending the Hallin lines, I fear there is nothing to be done. And sometimes I wonder if perhaps Downpike isn't right, after all. If we are not moving forward, we will perish. For all our history and might, we're not a large country. The resources Iveria offers . . . Well, there's a good girl. Keep a low profile. Alert me at once if Downpike comes around again, but I cannot see him taking any further interest in you."

"Spirits' blessings," she says, and then their voices trail away, Ernest bringing up some new motion in Parliament.

In the silence they leave in their wake, I become very aware of Finn's body against mine. I have the overwhelming impulse to lean back, let myself rest against him, and tuck my head again into the hollow of his neck. I imagine the release of letting go, letting myself be held by him simply because I want to, not because we are hiding or fleeing.

"Stop it!" I hiss.

"Stop what?"

"Stop doing that magic where you make me think I want to do things that I don't actually want to do!"

"I did no such thing!" He pauses. "What did you want to do?"

The armoire door opens, and I nearly scream until I realize it's only Eleanor. She looks tired and frayed around the edges, all her happy energy gone. "I think," she says, "that I am not quite so excited to be in on secrets as I was a few minutes ago."

Finn and I step out. He puts an arm around Eleanor's slight shoulders and steers her to the couch. "Let me see your burn."

I hurry to a side table where a decanter is filled with rich, dark wine and pour a glass. "Here," I say, handing it to her. She drinks it in one long draft. Finn holds her hand in his, palm up, gently rolling the silver top of his cane back and forth along the angry red slash there. With each pass the line gets lighter and the tightness around Eleanor's eyes loosens.

"Thank you," I say, kneeling on the floor next to her legs and resting my head against them. She puts her hand on my hair, and I wonder which of us is providing more comfort to the other. "You kept me safe."

"It was nothing. If I had a frock for every time I had to hide someone in that armoire, I would need another house just to hold them all."

"They're wrong, you know. About you. Your uncle and Lord Downpike. You are smart and brave and terribly important."

She laughs. "Oh, I know that, silly. But it's easier not to let them realize it, because then they'd stop ignoring me, and they'd realize how much mischief I really get up to. Now, Lord Ackerly, I will have to ask you to stop stroking my hand, or my own shadow might replace your missing one."

He clears his throat awkwardly, and I laugh. I shift from the floor to the couch and pull Eleanor into a hug. She sighs with her head against my shoulder. "You cannot stay here. It's not safe, though I would love to keep you."

Finn stands, shoulders straight and confident. "It's settled then. Eleanor, if you feel threatened, you are welcome to join Jessamin at my country estate."

I shake my head. "That will be difficult, as I am not going to your country estate."

"But—you heard—if even Eleanor's uncle won't come to your defense, how can you hope to hide from Lord Downpike?"

A pair of bright yellow eyes blinks at me from beneath the couch, and I smile with relief that Sir Bird is alive and well and on my side. It gives me an idea. I hold out my arm, and Sir Bird hops out, flapping a few times to land there.

I stroke his feathers and smile. "I think I will not have to hide at all."

Sixteen

Dear Sir,

   I am writing to inform you of the whereabouts of a certain book which frequently doubles as a bird. I understand you are concerned about it, and no wonder! Such a large volume containing so much knowledge. In fact, I believe it is actually several volumes in one, due to the rather impressive appetite of said bird in devouring many of its comrades.

   Perhaps you will recall that I left your home without a word of good-bye, and for this you must pardon my poor manners. I find myself averse to

being trapped in doorless rooms, to say nothing
of being methodically tortured. It is a character
defect owing to my savage ancestry.

To atone, I have entrusted the book into the
care of your friend Lord Ackerly. He assures me
that he will keep the volume perfectly safe, so long
as I myself remain unmolested and left entirely
to my own devices. To this end, he has worked
a magical connection that will destroy the book
should I meet harm at your lordship's hands, or
anyone working on behalf of your lordship, as
your lordship's time is precious and sometimes
these things must be delegated.

Looking forward to never meeting again,
Jessamin Olea

I sign a flourish under my name, and then shake out my hand. "The pins and needles are worse."

"Because you are remembering what happened, and the magic has to work harder to combat the memory of pain." Finn is reading the letter over my shoulder with a scowl.

"How is it that you have such dark eyebrows and yet your hair is golden?"

"Oh, that," Eleanor says, tucked up into the corner of the love seat with a shawl draped over her legs. She's still recovering from her own encounter with Lord Downpike. "Hadn't you guessed? You already discovered he uses a very potent charm spell. It's woven into his hair. Some would consider constantly charming everyone a bit of an excess, but Lord Ackerly needs all the help he can get."

"Such vanity." I tsk, trying to hold back a smile. No wonder his hair was both so enchanting and so aggravating.

"This will never work." Finn shakes his head.

"Of course it will. You said that the most powerful practitioners are the ones who study. Would he risk losing so much knowledge?" I stroke Sir Bird's head where he sits next to me, picking apart a biscuit.

"But I can't just magic up a connection between the two of you. Even if I have a spell that can accomplish it, it would take me several days of research to find and prepare it."

"Yes, but he doesn't know that! As far as Lord Downpike is concerned, a wealth of his magical lore is intricately tied to my own well-being. I'll give you Sir Bird to complete the ruse." Sir Bird caws in protest. "Hush. It's for the best. And if Finn does not take perfect care of you, we will plot his destruction together."

"I think she's done it," Eleanor says. "She's cleverer even than you."

Finn's scowl deepens. "This will do nothing but delay him. He will not stop until he extends his power past Albion and into the entire Iverian continent. His end goals are far larger than a few lost books of magical knowledge."

"That is your problem, not mine." I take the letter and blot it dry, then crease it shut.

"Please." Finn's voice has lost the arrogance it normally carries. Instead, it conveys a note of . . . desperation? "You may be cavalier with your own safety, but I can't forget the sound of your screams. They will haunt me to my dying day. I couldn't live with it if something else were to happen to you."

His hand is flat on the table, and I want to lay my own on top of his. Eleanor sighs dreamily, and I am snapped back to reality. "I'm sorry. But if I agree to run and hide I would only be giving him control of my life."

"You'd be safe from him!"

"No, I'd be as much a captive to my fear of him as I was when I was locked in that room. I refuse to be ruled, whether by those with bad intentions or those with good." I grab a small candle with deep red wax and dribble it onto the letter's fold to seal it shut.

Finn slides it away from my hand and then lowers his knuckle to press a large, gold ring into the wax seal. It leaves a symbol of two trees, the branches intertwining with each other. It must be his family crest.

"It's done, then." He scowls. "He won't doubt my part in it, false though it is."

"I'll have Carlisle send it out immediately." Eleanor stands and takes the letter, leaving us alone.

My head lolls against the couch. I have never been so tired in my life. Finn paces the floor, hands clasped behind his back.

"Will you at least agree to stay in my town house? It's very near your school."

I let myself imagine how soft his beds must be, how luxurious the sheets. And a washroom all to myself.

No. I will not become Mama, dependent on a man who thinks himself better than her and grateful for the privilege of his condescension. "Thank you, no. I'm comfortable at the hotel."

"I've seen servants' quarters, Jessamin. You cannot be comfortable there."

"A great many people live in servants' quarters, and they have yet to die from acute claustrophobia. I'm fine. Stop pacing, you make my nerves stand on end."

He sits on the love seat across from me, and I close my eyes, mentally calculating how long it will take for the letter to get to Lord Downpike. Perhaps Eleanor will let me sleep here for the night, until we can be certain of the letter's receipt and my safety in going home.

"This does not resolve the issue of my shadow," Finn says softly.

I wave my hand. "I have the utmost faith in your ability to figure out how to fix that problem."

He doesn't respond and I open my eyes to find a look of hurt on his face. "Problem," he whispers. Then his feline smile slides back into place. "Well, I have a great deal of work ahead of me."

I don't like the way he says it, the promise behind his words. And yet an odd sort of thrill courses through my body and I find myself hoping . . . for what?

Nothing. I am overtired, that is all. Getting back to my routine of attending classes and working in the hotel will be a comfort. I've simply been around Finn's elevated charm for too long.

He stands and bows at the waist. "If you'll be so kind as to excuse me, I have letters to write."

"Yes, of course. And thank you again for all your help." I

raise my gloved hand.

"Thanks are not necessary, as it was my own fault that you needed help. I would never dare presume to help you otherwise. I'd fear your wrath something terrible were I to try. Though..." He looks at me thoughtfully. "A wrathful Jessamin is a wondrous thing to behold."

Before I can finish blushing, he's held out his arm to Sir Bird. "Come along."

Sir Bird caws ill-temperedly. "Go on." I hand him an extra biscuit. "I promise to visit."

Finn's face lights up. "Suddenly, I am intensely fond of this bird. We shall be great friends, you and I." Sir Bird squawks and then, in his place, there's the great black book. Finn tucks it under his arm. "This suits me, as well. Until tomorrow." He's through the door before I can tell him that we certainly won't be seeing each other that soon.

Fie on the tired melancholy that descends on the room as soon as Finn is gone from it.

Bright—relatively so, by Alben standards—and early the next morning, I leave Eleanor's, refreshed after a solid night's sleep. Ernest escorts me, despite my protestations, and I know he suspects more than Eleanor told him about my surprise "reappearance" at their home. I'm wearing another borrowed dress of hers, jeweled green and finer than anything I own, but one she insisted she never wears.

I changed in the dark, and can't help but look over my shoulder at my shadow constantly. Though Finn claimed watching and listening through his shadow is difficult, I feel as though he is hovering at my side. It is not a comfortable sensation.

We weave through the push of a crowd that seems to part easier for me in this dress and on Ernest's arm than they normally do. "My sister likes you," Ernest says as we walk the many blocks back to the hotel. He offered the carriage, but I thought if I were walking, he'd let me go alone.

"I like her, too. She's rather remarkable, isn't she?"

Ernest smiles. "She would have us all dismiss her as a flirt and a gossip, but I suspect she is a more formidable force than even our uncle. I think she will be a great advantage to me in politics."

Perhaps Ernest is not so gullible and trusting as his open, honest face would indicate.

"What of your parents?" I ask. "You both seem young to be on your own."

"Mother died when we were children. Father passed last year."

"I'm so sorry."

Ernest smiles, but it's distant. An Alben smile is rarely an expression of joy. More often it is a way to deflect true emotion. "We are quite well taken care of. I come into my full inheritance next year, at which point I'll purchase a seat in the Higher House, following in our uncle's footsteps."

"And Eleanor?"

"She has a suitable dowry upon her eighteenth birthday. I think we'll find her a good match."

"Doubtless." Actually, I doubt very much that any man her

brother or uncle deems worthy will, in fact, deserve her. And the way Ernest says "we'll find her a good match" crawls under my skin and leaves my soul feeling itchy on Eleanor's behalf. Shouldn't she be able to choose someone that makes her heart sing?

It would appear Eleanor's birth does not free her from the same binding restrictions and marital expectations my own did.

"Perhaps, with all her connections, Eleanor ought to go into politics, too."

Ernest actually laughs at this, throwing his head back, his throat bobbing. "I would fear very much for Albion if she did." He pauses outside the Grande Sylvie, straightening his tie. "I wanted to say . . . that is, I hope you understand that . . . well, Eleanor may like things to be interesting, but a future in politics is not well-served by scandal, real or imagined. I would very much hate to see any talk involving my sister."

His words are carefully weighted, and I can feel them tugging on my shoulders, willing me to shrink back. I don't know whether he is asking me to stop being her friend because I, myself, am unacceptable, or because he suspects my connection to Lord Downpike's threats. I hope it's the latter.

I stand taller, pasting a smile any Alben would be proud of onto my face. "She is lucky to have you as a brother."

He relaxes his shoulders in relief. "It was nice to see you again, Jessamin. I almost wish, if things were different—well, but they aren't." His look is wistful as he pats my hand on his arm. I draw it back and wave good-bye.

I slip in through the servants' door, anticipating a reunion with Ma'ati and Jacky Boy. But first, to change into normal clothes.

I sneak into my room and am undoing the buttons on my blouse when I hear soft snores behind me. Screaming, I turn to find a strange girl in my cot.

"What are you doing in here?" I demand, hurrying to the narrow wardrobe and flinging it open. I recognize nothing in it. "And what have you done with my things?"

The girl sits up, hair a messy black halo around her head, clutching the blanket to her chest. "I'm sorry, milady, I only started last night, and I was told I needn't wake until eight, please don't fire me."

"Jessamin?"

I whirl around to find Ma'ati standing in the doorway. "You replaced me already? I've only been gone two nights!"

"I don't understand." She takes my hand and pulls me out of my room. "The letter said you wouldn't be returning to work."

"What letter?"

"Here, I'll show you."

I follow her to her room where she pulls out a cream envelope with Finn's double-tree seal. The seal is the only thing that keeps me from suspecting Lord Downpike meddling again. Violence brimming in my thoughts, I rip out the letter and scan the contents.

... no longer requires employment ... studies will take up the bulk of her time ... thanks you for the kindness and generosity ...

will be staying in room 312, which I have paid out in full to the end of the year.

"Spirits take that meddlesome dolt, I will wring his neck."

"We moved your things up to the room, Jessamin, books and everything. We didn't know what to make of it, but the instructions were quite clear and, well, it's such a fancy room!" A door slams next to us and I meet a glaring pair of eyes as one of the chambermaids swishes away. Clearly not everyone is as pleased with my fortune as Ma'ati.

I rub my forehead. "And you've already replaced me?"

"I'm sorry, but the girl came with the letter and her references were all good. And Jacky Boy has been needing someone who can give more hours."

"Well, you've done no wrong, of course. I have to get to class. We can sort it out when I return."

Ma'ati smiles and hands me the key to room 312. "Oh, your friend was by last night to see you. Kelen?"

I grimace. He's going to think I'm avoiding him. I do want to see him, really, but he feels rather low on my list of priorities right now. "Did he leave an address?"

"No. He wanted to wait in your room, but Jacky Boy wouldn't let him. He's very protective of you."

I laugh. "Kelen isn't good enough for him?"

She shrugs. I want to ask more, but I'm already running late. I kiss Ma'ati's cheek and head to my room. No. Not my room. *Finn's* room. I refuse to take the guest stairs, and instead make my way up the narrow hidden flight. Someone bumps me roughly from behind.

"Oh, beg pardon, milady. Only shouldn't you ought to be using the stairs for proper folks?" The chambermaid glares at me.

I don't have time to set her straight. I hurry up, angry at her and at myself and especially at Finn. "This isn't funny," I hiss in the general direction of my shadow as I walk into the room. "You have no right."

My books are carefully stacked on the generous desk, but I try to ignore the opulence of the room. The sky-blue silk duvet and matching drapes. The mounds of feather pillows. The window seat perfect for reading. The dressing table. The private bathroom.

I fail at ignoring it. But I will not accept it. I grab my books and barely have time to change into my school uniform. My satin gloves—Eleanor found a near-match—look ridiculously out of place.

"And now you've made me late." I throw one of the pillows at my shadow and stomp out of the hotel.

I arrive out of breath and cross as a hornet to pick up a book from my carrel in the library. When I see the back of someone sitting in my spot, it is too much. "Sir, if you tell me this is no longer my carrel, I cannot be held accountable for my reaction."

Finn turns—the black book known as Sir Bird open in his hands—and smiles.

Seventeen

"I WONDER WHETHER THE ACADEMICS AT THIS institution are as rigid as they ought to be." Finn looks pointedly at the slate I left on my desk. Someone has drawn a crude rendition of a woman's body—mine, probably—along with mathematical equations for the size of her rather impressive bosom.

Go back to your island, rat is scrawled at the bottom.

"Yes," I say, dryly. "Their calculations are entirely wrong. It reflects poorly on the school." I drop my satchel at my feet. The sight of Finn in his dark blue three-piece suit sitting in my study carrel is too much. "What are you doing here? And what did you do at the hotel? You had no right!"

"I'm sorry about that. But I intend on taking up more of your time than you can afford to lose, and thought it only fair you have fewer responsibilities."

"That's not your decision! And—wait, what is that on my slate?" I lean over his shoulder, squinting. Next to the line about going back to my island is an odd symbol that I don't recognize. It seems to have been etched there. I reach out a finger to run over it, but Finn blocks my arm.

"I wouldn't touch that if I were you."

Hugh, a lanky boy with a perpetual sniffle, stands up from his carrel three down from mine. "Can I borrow a pen and ink-well? Mine won't seem to work." A boy next to him hands one over. "No, this one won't work either."

"It was working fine for me, give it here. See?"

"But it won't write for me! Neither will this pen." Hugh growls in frustration and then sits back down out of sight. "Spirits below, what is happening? Not even my chalk will show up on slate. Here, let me have a go at yours."

There's low, confused murmuring. Again the other boy says, "It works fine for me."

"Why won't any of my instruments mark?" Hugh walks by, smashing a piece of chalk against a small slate. It leaves no mark.

Finn stands, moving out of the way for me to sit in my carrel. "Hmm. Puzzling."

"It wouldn't have anything to do with you, now, would it?" I ask.

He shrugs, long, slender shoulders lazily rising. "I *may* have put a curse on whoever wrote that horrid thing. Just a small one.

Though I suppose a month without being able to write something down will be inconvenient for a student."

The laugh that bursts out of my mouth earns me the ire of everyone around us. I put my gloved fingers to my mouth, trying to push some of the mirth back in. "I am still very cross with you."

"Making you cross with me is a full-time occupation." He wanders to a leather chair near a series of shelves holding old newspapers and sits down. I follow him, shoving the needed book into my satchel.

"I have class."

He waves a hand, mimicking my Melenese gesture perfectly. "Quit bothering me. I'm reading. This is a library, after all."

"We're not done discussing what you did at the hotel."

"I should hope not." His lips curl into a smile, but his eyes remain fixed on the pages of the book.

Infuriating boy!

When I return to my carrel that afternoon, Finn is still in the same chair. This time he's thumbing through a newspaper.

"You can't stay in the library all day!" I hiss, sitting next to him.

"This is a school. Studying is encouraged."

"What exactly are you studying?"

He folds the paper and gives me his cat grin. "History students."

My face burns, and I need something to do with my hands. And my feet. My whole body, really. I stand and gather my things, then stalk outside toward home until I realize I haven't any work to hurry back to. "Curse you," I mutter at my shadow. "You may be content with doing nothing, but some of us need to be busy."

"Who *are* you talking to?" Finn asks, and I turn to find him walking several steps behind me, swinging his cane in time to his pace. Sir Bird is on his shoulder but hops to mine.

I abruptly change directions and head instead for Eleanor's house.

"Eleanor's is rather a long walk. Shall I call for my carriage?"

I whirl around and Finn nearly crashes into me. "Shouldn't you be doing something productive with your time instead of following me around? I thought you were figuring out how to get your shadow back!"

"I'm hungry. Are you hungry?" He reaches up to take off his hat.

I stand on the tips of my toes and slam it back down. "Leave that on!" I realize a second too late that this position puts us face-to-face. I haven't been this close to him other than in immediate peril situations.

This feels far more perilous.

His smile spreads. "I'll leave my hat on if you'll have supper with me and allow me to walk you home."

I scowl and let go of his hat, backing away to a respectable speaking distance. "I'm safe. You have no further obligations."

"Is that so?" He nods toward the roof of the school. My stomach flips to discover it is lined with large black birds.

They are watching me.

Sir Bird shifts closer to my neck, a low, comforting sound

in his throat. I stroke his feathered head but cannot look away from the silent sentries.

I swallow hard and clench my gloved hand. "Supper then."

"Marvelous idea! Should we eat in the hotel dining room?"

"Oh, no! I couldn't. I'd be mortified."

He frowns. "Why?"

I shake my head. It would be utterly humiliating to sit while being served by the same people I work—worked—with.

"We'll order up to your sitting room, then."

"Is that appropriate? I mean, for us to be there together, alone."

He puts a hand over his heart, expression shocked. "Why, Jessamin, you'd try to take advantage of me?"

I scowl and kick his cane out so that he misses a step. He laughs.

"Fine. We'll order up."

Thankfully, it's Ma'ati who delivers our meal. She beams at me, curtsying and keeping her eyes low. Finn thanks her profusely and tells her that the cook is exemplary. On her way out, she winks and I want to strangle her.

I stab sullenly at my food. All the times I helped prepare and serve it has made it far less palatable than I thought it would be.

Finn clears his throat but I interrupt him before he can speak. "And another thing," I say, jabbing my fork through the air. "This ability is utterly wasted on the gentry. As far as I've seen, all you do with magic is make it dull and uninteresting, or utterly horrendous. It would be better off in the hands of more creative users."

He has the audacity to laugh. "I'm sorry magic is such a disappointment."

"It's very disheartening." I try my hardest not to smile. "I'd do more exciting things if I had it."

He leans back, toying with his silverware. "Such as?"

"I don't know. I'd make this accursed country warm, for one. Blast away some of this dreadful gray that seeps into my bones and makes me cold all the time."

"You think us far more powerful than we actually are."

"See? Disappointing."

"It's true, it's not very exciting. I mainly studied healing magic. The mending of bones, the repair of the body. Not very glamorous."

I flex my fingers. "That's how you worked up the glove so quickly. But you said 'studied.' Why did you stop? Too middle class for a nobleman to be playing at doctor?"

His smile effectively shuts him off from me, tight as a mask. "I found my interests shifted significantly when I had to come to Avebury."

We spend the rest of the meal in silence. But when he stands to leave, his mask drops off into mischievousness. "I have a gift for you."

"No more gifts!"

"You'll want this one." He hurries to a side table and lights a lamp there. Muttering to himself like I do when working out a particularly complex equation, he blocks my view with his body. After a minute, he turns around, a perfect sphere of glowing brightness hovering above his palm. It looks like a miniature sun.

"There! I can't fix the whole country, and it will only last a few days, but I present you with the sun, on behalf of my dreadfully boring magic."

He bows low, holding out his hand. I reach out tentatively, afraid of being burned, but the globe merely hovers above my hand where I slide it on top of Finn's. It's golden and deliciously warm and instantly makes me happier and more at ease than I've been in weeks.

I laugh, delighted, and by the look on Finn's face you'd think I was the one who had given *him* an absurd and wonderful gift.

Eighteen

TWO DAYS LATER, I SIT IN ELEANOR'S PARLOR drinking the sourest lemonade in the history of liquids. The birds have not followed me here. Neither has Finn, for once.

"Sorry," Eleanor says. "I am afraid Mrs. Jenkins is at a loss for what to serve to someone who dislikes tea. She's not good at improvisation."

"It's very fresh." My voice squeezes out from my tortured throat.

"I am glad you stopped by, though! I have so much news."

"I had to figure out somewhere Finn—" When I use his first name, Eleanor's eyebrows raise slyly, and I realize I've given her more gossip. "*Lord Ackerly* wouldn't come. He's been like a shadow." I pause, "Well. I mean less literally, of course. He waits outside the hotel when I leave in the morning, no matter which part I try to sneak out of. He haunts the library, insists on walking me through the park, joins me for every meal."

Eleanor stirs her third heaping spoonful of sugar into her tea, a dreamy smile on her face. "That's wonderful."

"No, it's not! He's hovering." Not that he's not good company, it's just that I have no say in the matter. I glare at my shadow, though I know he can only be either listening or watching. He assures me he does neither.

"You should hear what Arabella Crawford had to say when she heard that he'd shadowed you. You'll remember her from the gala—encased in her shiny, black dress like a sausage?"

A note of panic sounds in my ears. "How did she hear?"

"I told her, of course."

"But Finn threatened you! Oh, no. I'll forbid him from cursing you, but I can't say how much he'll listen." After Hugh missed two important exams, I asked Finn to remove the curse early. He felt I was entirely too forgiving, but when I heard Hugh crying softly in his carrel I couldn't help but relent.

Eleanor laughs. "Silly girl. Self-preservation is a skill of mine. I would never cross Lord Ackerly. At least not in a way he's likely to discover. No, he told me to tell."

"He *what?*"

"The morning after that horrid business with Lord Downpike, your *Finn* came for a visit and asked if I would please tell everyone I could possibly think of that he had shadowed you. I was to spread it like the gossip of the season, which was no great task, because it is."

"But—I thought he—well, the night of the gala, he only spoke to me in secret. And the past two days we have gone nowhere where your crowd would see us. I assumed he was . . ."

"Ashamed?"

Blushing, I nod.

"If he is, he has an odd way of showing it. There isn't a cousin-of-a-cousin-of-a-noble that has not heard about it now."

I don't know what to do with this information. The way he has been acting, and now to so openly claim me . . . but why spread the word among people whom I don't know? Why not talk to me about it? Perhaps it is a step on the way to regaining his shadow.

That's what I want, of course. To be rid of my involvement in the entire matter. Whatever political tension there is here, whatever designs Albion has on the Iverian continent, it's nothing to do with me.

My eyes flick to my shadow, and I realize I cannot remember exactly how it looked before the edges were blurred.

Eleanor continues chatting about the various stunned and devastated reactions among eligible girls who had long been pining after untouchable Lord Ackerly, obviously taking great pleasure in their dismay.

"Oh, that reminds me, I've been clearing out my wardrobe and I came across another dress I thought you might like. I'll have it sent to your room at the Grande Sylvie."

I nod dumbly. "Thank you. You've been so kind."

She laughs, a private smile on her face. "Yes, I am *very* kind."

That evening after she has lent me her carriage for the ride back to the hotel, I find a letter from Mama. I also find Sir Bird with a note from Finn. Apparently, Sir Bird has been rebelling against book form, and taken to chasing Finn around his library, pecking at his hands. Finn thought some time apart would be good for both of them, so long as I do not take Sir Bird out without him.

I laugh, picturing Sir Bird terrorizing stately Finn. "Good boy," I murmur, emptying my pockets of brass buttons and coins I've been collecting, and Sir Bird caws contentedly as he begins sorting them.

I sit on the brushed-velvet chaise longue. The room is wonderful, I will admit that, but I feel false staying in it and insist on taking care of my own linens and cleaning. The bright side is giving Ma'ati extra free time, but a large part of this is an effort to avoid the ire of the chambermaids, who whisper poisonous things.

"You've put me in an impossible situation," I say to my shadow. "I had a hard enough time fitting in with my peers before. Now I am neither here nor there with any class. It is very inconsiderate of you." I pause. "While I am thinking of it, your tie yesterday was ghastly. You shouldn't wear brown. I much prefer the blue one. And stay out of my room."

I turn to the letter, which is written in Alben. I sigh, wondering whether Mama speaks it at home without me there anymore. As usual, I supply my own interpretations of what she says.

Dearest Jessamin,

I have not had a letter from you in a month. (You are a terrible daughter.) *I blame the slowness of the boats and hate the distance between us.* (How could you leave me?)

Your cousin Jacabo responded to my inquiries after your well-being with only the vaguest of terms. (I threatened Jacky Boy if he did not update me on your life.) *I take this to mean you have seen him regularly and have also forbidden him from updating me on your life in the big city.* (Why are you spending your time with him when he is clearly not running in the right circles?)

How are your studies? Have you met anyone interesting? (Why have you not given me news of your father?)

I suspect you do not write because you have found someone. (Please, please tell me you have found someone.) *I know it.* (I beg the spirits for it each night.) *A mother can feel these things.* (I will drag you back to the island and force you into marriage if you do not take care of it yourself.) *Please tell me whether he is of a good family and when I can expect happy tidings to share with my friends.* (Do not do anything I cannot crow about to the neighbors.) *I knew you would not be on your own for long.* (Give me grandchildren. Soon.) *Dear Henry has asked after you, though, so if you are lonely you know you have many options here.* (I pestered Henry until he finally asked after you and took it as a sign he still wishes to marry you.)

Write me soon or I will perish for want of daughterly affection. (You are a terrible daughter.)

All my love, (All my love,)

Mama

I compose in my head:

> *Dear Mama,*
>
> *Am being stalked by not one but two men of exceptionally high birth. One is a madman who tortured me and promised to make me love him forever. The other is a madman who gave me his shadow and lives to make my life difficult. No doubt you would be pleased, but I intend to deny you grandchildren for the foreseeable future. Henry is a dear, but I suspect the only reason his parents were willing to consider me for his bride was that he does not, in fact, like women at all. In place of comforting news about my marriageability and future grandchildren, please know I have adopted a bird. You would like him.*
>
> *Much love,*
>
> *Hopeless Jessamin*

A knock at my door distracts me from fictional letter writing. I open it to find Simon holding a garment bag and a letter. He bows, and I knock his cap off his head. "Don't start that nonsense with me. Come in and have a biscuit, or I'll box your ears."

Grinning, he picks up his cap, bouncing on his toes and nervous to be in the room. I realize I cannot explain why I have a large black bird in my room, but Sir Bird has elected to be a book again. Simon sets the bag on the edge of my bed.

"Is that man around?" I ask. "The one who's been following me?"

"Lord Ackerly? Yes. He said you'd have a book for me to deliver to him? The letter is from him, too. He tips something handsome, Miss Jessamin. Everyone likes him."

"Hmm. I'm sure. Did you let him into my room earlier?"

"No, Miss Jessamin. This is the first he's been here all day."

I glance at Sir Bird, but as neither book nor bird can he tell me how Finn sneaked into my room. Annoyed, I hand Simon the book and open the letter. It's an invitation to a symphony to be held tomorrow evening. In the bag, I find a stunning gown of pale gold with a tag attached that reads:

> *Aren't my castoffs simply amazing and tailored to your exact frame? See you at the symphony. Love, Eleanor.*

Nineteen

"AND YOU ARE CERTAIN IT'S LORD ACKERLY WAITING downstairs for me? No strange birds hopping about?"

Ma'ati sounds confused as she finishes buttoning the back of my dress. "Why should you worry about birds?"

I shake my head, trying to calm myself. I have had three separate written confirmations from Eleanor and Finn that yes, the invitation came from him, and no, there is nothing sinister at play. Aside from false gifts, that is. I run my fingers down the front of the dress. Eleanor's castoff, indeed.

The dress is silk, pale gold with delicate beadwork on the empire-waist bodice. Sheer sleeves are open at the wrists. Finn—through Eleanor—was kind enough to include a perfectly matched black glove for my uninjured hand. I shake my right hand absentmindedly, trying to work out some of the pins and needles.

I notice it less lately, but the sensation is always there. I cannot imagine what it must be like to feel this way all the time, over your entire body. It makes me a bit more compassionate toward Finn. I would go mad in his place.

Then again, I'm fairly certain he already is.

"I wish we had something sparkly to put on your wrist or around your neck," Ma'ati says, considering the final product. This time we did not bundle my hair into a bun, but pulled it away from my face and neck with a twist and let it trail down my back.

"Never you mind. Thank you for your help." I stand and kiss her cheek. "You know, this dress would flatter you even more than me."

Ma'ati waves her hand. "When would I wear a thing like that?"

"Jacky Boy would like it very much on a certain special occasion. It'll keep until then."

Ma'ati's face blooms into the biggest smile I have ever seen on her. "Well, you know we were waiting to save up enough so we wouldn't have to live in the hotel. We were a ways off—years off—but then . . . oh, I shouldn't speak of it until it's certain."

"What? You must tell me now!"

"Lord Ackerly has offered Jacky Boy a position in his country estate! It's a good deal of responsibility. He would be in charge of the kitchens and head butler duties, and Lord Ackerly says he has never kept a staff so Jacky Boy would do well to bring someone with him. His words were 'perhaps a bride.' And then he gave Jacky Boy a good-faith payment and promised to arrange it all as soon as he is ready to staff his new home! We would have our own cottage on the property." She sits back onto the chaise longue, nearly overcome. "It's more than I ever hoped for. I was so scared when my aunt sent me here—I was afraid I'd be lost or killed or beaten daily. But I found Jacky Boy and now we've a real future and oh, Jessamin, I am so happy I might burst."

I cannot puzzle why Finn would be taking on servants now when he so recently told me he never kept them, but Ma'ati's joy is contagious. I wrap her into a hug. "You deserve every happiness in the world."

"Thank you. He's a good man, you know. Jacky Boy likes him, and Jacky Boy is the best judge of character."

I shrug noncommittally, but she doesn't let me go, pressing on. "He looks us in the eyes, Jessamin. All of us. You've worked here long enough to understand what that means. But, oh! Stop right now." She pulls back from our embrace, fussing over my dress. "We can't wrinkle you. Now go and enjoy your evening listening to terrible, boring Alben music."

I laugh and stand. "Yes, I can't say I am looking forward to that part. Perhaps I'll get in a good nap."

Ma'ati follows me into the hall, then grabs my elbow and turns me around. "Not the servants' stairs. Just this once, use the main ones. But give me half a minute to go ahead, so I can hide near the lobby and watch you walk down!"

She hitches her skirt and takes off at a run for the back

stairs. If it were anyone but her, I'd follow, refusing to make a spectacle. I cannot say no to Ma'ati.

Counting to sixty in my head, I walk slowly down the wood-paneled hallway toward the open flight of stairs that will take me to the lobby. I peek over the balcony to see if Ma'ati is ready. Standing in the center of the marble floor, looking straight up at me, is Finn.

His tailed tuxedo is trim and fitted, showcasing the slender lines of his body, and his golden hair catches the overhead electric chandelier. It's even a bit messy tonight, not so controlled as usual. He leans casually against his cane, and when he meets my eyes, a smile slowly spreads across his face.

Something inside of me breaks and re-forms into a new, unknown shape, and I do not know what has happened or why, only that I feel as though I am glowing from my toes to the tip of my head and I want to be beside Finn right now.

I take a deep breath to calm my racing heart, trying to tell myself that it's the effect of his silly charmed hair, but as I take the steps in measured pace, I realize this time it feels different. Before there was a sort of fuzzing, a misty separation from reality. But tonight everything is clearer, sharper, as though the sun has finally broken through the Alben clouds and lit the world in a new way.

As though Finn has created his wonderful miniature sun inside my heart.

I am down the stairs before I process having passed even one flight. I hear a soft, happy sigh and turn to see Ma'ati peeking from behind the dining room doors. I smile and wave at her. Then, hardly daring to look at him lest he somehow sees straight through to my wild, giddy panic, I turn to Finn.

"You look beautiful," he says, and that new something inside of me flares even higher. My eyes dart like a butterfly in a cage, alighting on everything but staying fixed on nothing. His jaw, his hair, his shoulders, his mouth.

"Yes," I answer, careful to keep my voice controlled, though I feel as if it should be two octaves higher. "How strange that Eleanor should purchase gowns so clearly the wrong size."

"The ways of women are a mystery to me." He holds out his elbow—in all the time we have walked with each other I have never taken it—and says, "Shall we?"

I slip my hand into place, and my voice trembles as I say, "Yes."

For some reason, it feels as though I am answering a far more important question.

Twenty

FINN TAKES MY HAND AS I CLIMB OUT OF THE carriage when we arrive at the Royal Hall. It's near the palace, across the river from the courthouse. All these are buildings I have walked by many times but never dreamt I would enter. Four soaring spires mark the corners of the Hall, the stone elegant and carved over arching stained-glass windows and massive scrolling iron doors. This is where the queen was wed, where her husband's funeral was held.

On Melei, the monarchy is officially ours, too, but we all grow up knowing the pale, unsmiling portraits in our schools are nothing like us—and care nothing for us. So, while I do not hold the monarchy in any regard, it is still more than a little intimidating to walk on such ceremonially important grounds.

When we pass guards in the queen's deep purple livery, Finn does not hand them the invitation as I expect him to. One of the guards holds out a golden platter, in the center of which a single sharp needle sticks up.

"Lord Finley Ackerly," he says in a deeper voice than I am used to. I had not known Finn was a nickname and feel both embarrassed and strangely privileged to know him as such. He then pricks his finger on the point. A spark ignites and the guard nods, withdrawing the platter.

I am cold with fear that he will expect me to do the same but Finn guides me forward without hesitation. "What was that?" I whisper.

"No one outside of the gentry is allowed at this concert. You'll understand why."

"Need I remind you I am not gentry?"

"But you are my very special guest, and no one enjoys telling me I cannot do things." He smiles confidently, and we walk through mingling clumps of people. I do not mind that I stand out so horribly this time, but I can feel many eyes on me.

Several people greet Finn as "Lord Ackerly," and he nods in acknowledgment but stops to talk to no one. He stays at my side, a hand at the small of my back, and leads me to our seats. We're on a private balcony overlooking a grand ballroom. People are drifting toward the seats set up on the floor. Two chairs beside us are open, and I wonder if anyone will fill them. The vantage point feels both privileged and exposed. I can see everyone, which means everyone can see me.

A small, raised stage in the center has a semicircle of chairs about a dozen in number, but no one is there yet. The walls of either side of the room are lined with guards—one group in the royal purple livery, the other in blue and gold.

Finn feels both too close and too far away, sitting with our arms nearly touching. I need something, anything, to cover my inner flutterings.

"What symphony will they be performing? Am I terrible if I admit I find Alben music dreadfully dull and somber?"

"I am terrible right along with you, then. But have no fear. It's an international group of musicians from the royal families of several continental countries."

"Ah. Thus the strangely liveried guards. I've always been partial to art and music from Gallen." The country immediately east across the channel from Albion, Gallen seems to suppress passion less.

"Spirits below," Finn says under his breath, shifting in his seat and angling himself toward me so half my view of the room is cut off. He smiles, but it is too bright, too forced. "I am so sorry. I had it on good authority that he wasn't coming tonight. Still, there is not a safer room for you in all of the city at the moment."

"Downpike?" I startle forward and there, in a balcony directly across from us, sits the nightmare man himself.

He raises a glass filled with bloodred wine in mock cheers and then takes a dignified sip, his eyes never leaving me.

My hand aches, spasming into a fist, and I want to flee, be anywhere but here with that man so close. I nearly ask Finn if we can leave, but the expression on Lord Downpike's face is too smug. It's not even a challenge. I'm not worth it in his estimation. Sitting straighter in my chair, I meet his horrid gaze from across the room and raise my right hand in a cheerful wave, being certain to wiggle all my fully functioning fingers. Then I fix my eyes firmly on the stage, resolving not to look that direction again.

"Well done," Finn murmurs.

Another couple joins us, the man maybe ten years our senior, handsome with reddish-brown hair. His wife is dripping in ostentatious jewelry, her face neither pretty nor plain, rather severe but offset by heavily curled blond hair. She gives me a slight nod and then settles in the farthest chair.

"Lord Ackerly," the man says, and I recognize his voice— Lord Rupert, Eleanor's uncle the earl. "I did not know we would have the honor of sharing a box this evening."

"The honor is mine. Might I introduce Miss Jessamin Olea?"

Lord Rupert takes my hand and inclines his head, but his eyes are shrewd, and he obviously knows who I am. "Charmed to make your acquaintance."

"Thank you, my lord. I am fortunate enough to count your niece, Eleanor, as a friend. She is a credit to your family name."

"Quite, yes." He sits next to his wife, whose chin is already bobbing into her pearls. Apparently, I am not the only one who thought to use the symphony as an excuse for a nap.

There is a strange sensation from my hand, and I look down to see the fingers of my right glove tugging free of their own accord. Finn clears his throat loudly, slamming his cane down against the floor, and immediately the tugging ceases, my glove no longer possessed.

"Now he is simply being petty," Finn says with a scowl, covering my hand with his own.

"It would appear Lord Downpike is intent on getting your attention," Lord Rupert says conversationally.

"I had noticed." Finn's tone is polite and unconcerned.

"Have you given any more thought to what he is proposing?"

"I cannot say that I have. What was wrong two years ago is still wrong today, and you will find my position unchanged."

"Yes, but the good of the country . . ."

"Is the good of the country, and I will always do my part to protect it. Why should we stretch further than needed? We have been independent and strong for decades now. The Continent holds nothing we cannot do for ourselves. I find myself perfectly satisfied with the amount of power we currently hold. Aggression would lead to war, which would benefit no one, least of all our own citizens. Oh, look! They're about to begin."

Finn still has not moved his hand from where it rests on mine. My stomach does not know how to feel about this development. Fortunately, I'm soon distracted as the lights dim and the music begins.

The symphony is like nothing I have ever seen. Six women and seven men in glittering black sit with their instruments, but when the first note—a long, deep pull across a cello—sounds, it is accompanied by a wavering flash of deep blue light. A violin joins, its light dancing up to join the cello's, on and on up to the drunkenly flickering pink hue of the flute. As the song progresses, the lights shift in and out and around each other, a dance as complex as the marriage of notes from so many instruments. A man on the end has a drum beneath his legs, which emits bursts of brilliant white when hit with his foot pedal, and cymbals that crash together and send all the colors popping like Queen's Day fireworks.

Finn leans in close to my ear. "Do you like it?"

"How is it done?"

"They're all royals; Albion does not have a monopoly on magic blood. Though we have far more magical blood, it's also more generally diluted. This concert happens once a year as a sort of demonstration to remind us that other countries are working with the same advantages we are."

"The Hallins." I remember the name from my history text. It's the family that all the Iverian continental countries pull their royalty from.

"Very good. There are only two royal lineages: our ancient Crombergs, and the Hallin line."

"So that's why some of the smaller continental countries will buy royal family members to be their monarchs. I thought it was simply for show, an issue of pride." A few years back some of the more influential families on Melei began talking of pooling our resources to buy a royal family for the island. The notion was quickly dismissed by the magistrates—and deemed treasonous to prevent it from coming up again.

I wonder now if the people behind the idea knew about magic. How would Melei have been different if we had been working with the same advantages as Albion?

Finn continues. "It is all a matter of balance. We have magic, so do they. Though many wars have been fought in the past, the last century has seen an uneasy peace. The two lines do not share secrets or knowledge, and the scales remain relatively even. Crombergs have strength of numbers, but Hallin magic is far more powerful."

"So Albion and the Iverian continental countries can ward each other off. But what of the rest of the world?"

"It is a problem," Finn answers, then leans back, effectively ending the conversation. I try to lose myself in the swirling lights and stirring melodies again, but I keep coming back to that: *it is a problem*. For whom?

The music is over far too soon. Real lights, the electric ones that anyone can see and appreciate, come back on. Sir Rupert's wife startles awake with a tiny snort, and I marvel that this is so mundane in her world.

We walk down a grand, red-carpeted staircase to the main floor where the chairs have already been cleared and servers are making the rounds with trays covered in drinks. Finn takes one for me, but I haven't the stomach for it. It reminds me too much of the gala and what happened afterward.

Several of the visiting royals go out of their way to wish Finn well. There is an odd sort of tension there, like they are not sure how friendly to be with him. One woman kisses his cheeks and murmurs something about his mother, but the room is so loud with conversation that I don't catch most of it. Many of the Albens around us watch Finn's interactions with narrowed eyes.

Other than Finn, the visiting royals seem content to talk

to no one. The atmosphere between them and the Alben gentry is tense, buzzing with the same undercurrent as the lights above us.

Then Lord Downpike enters the room with a woman on his arm.

Eleanor.

She's wearing blue, her hair pulled back to expose the creamy expanse of her neckline, her lips painted dramatic red. She meets my eyes and though her smile does not move, her eyes are screaming with terror.

Twenty-one

"FINN." I SQUEEZE HIS ARM SO TIGHTLY MY FINGERS cramp.

He follows my gaze to where Lord Downpike is smiling at us, Eleanor at his side.

"Spirits take him," Finn curses. "He won't harm her—even he wouldn't dare go so openly against Lord Rupert. He's trying to make a point."

"And what point is that?"

"That he still has options when it comes to hurting us." He sees the look of fear and dread on my face, then pats my hand. "Never mind. I have it under control. Wait here."

He leaves me standing in the middle of the floor, surrounded by glittering strangers. I have never felt so helpless and alone.

I loathe feeling helpless.

I watch Finn stride toward Lord Downpike and Eleanor, Lord Downpike's smile growing bigger and bigger, too big to fit his face, so sharp I wonder that it does not cut his cheeks.

"Are you quite well, Miss Olea?"

I turn to see Lord Rupert's wife looking at me with concern. She's on Ernest's arm, who is watching Lord Downpike and Finn with narrowed eyes.

"I am . . . I am fine, yes, thank you."

She follows our eyes and notes Finn and Lord Downpike having what appears to be a pleasant conversation, but one punctuated by a strange number of hand gestures. Lord Downpike flicks his fingers, Finn taps his cane, Lord Downpike makes a swirling motion as though illustrating a point, Finn slashes his cane through the air.

"Ah, men," Lord Rupert's wife sighs. "From the nursery to the Noble House, they never can stop fighting." She pats my shoulder with stiffly detached sympathy. "They'll sort it out. We needn't worry ourselves over these sorts of things." She yawns behind a gloved hand, covered in rings. "Hmm. Gallen pastries. Excuse me."

She walks past with a whiff of stingingly floral perfume, and I watch her go, aghast. Could she not see the fear in Eleanor's eyes? Does she care so little for the welfare of her own niece? Worst of all, is she really so accustomed to being pushed to the sidelines she no longer sees any evil in it?

"Aren't you going to go help?" I ask Ernest. I turn to him and am surprised to see him watching me with a look of accusation. "What?"

"I advised you to leave Eleanor alone."

"She's my friend."

"You attract trouble. I think you court it. And now you've brought her into it all."

I can feel heat rising in my cheeks as my heart beats even faster, with fear or anger or some unhealthy mix of the two. "I did no such thing. Lord Downpike did this. And you stand here doing *nothing* while your sister is being threatened."

"What would you have me do? Set myself against one of the most powerful men in our country?"

"If it is the right thing to do, then yes!"

"It may be the right thing to do. I would make a glorious stand, denounce him as a cruel and barbarous villain. We could bask in my righteousness. And any hopes I have at attaining a seat in the Noble House would be forever dashed. I would lose my future."

"This isn't about you!"

"Exactly! It isn't about me. And so I will stand by and watch my sister in pain because of your *friendship*. And I will choose to do nothing, knowing that if I play the game right then someday in the near future I will be in a position of actual power, where I can effect real change. Because this isn't about me, Jessamin. It's about my country, and all the people I can help if I don't throw everything away now. I asked you to put my sister's welfare first because I cannot. I have to work toward being able to help all of Albion. Otherwise, the only voices that matter are the warmongers like Downpike."

His words strike painfully. I thought he didn't want me around Eleanor because I am Melenese, not because he was worried for her safety. "None of this is my fault. I'm not even part of this wretched country! I didn't choose any of this!"

Ernest looks pointedly at my dress. "Didn't you?" With a small bow he turns and walks stiffly away.

Trembling with the force of conflicting emotions, I nearly spill my drink. Setting it on the tray of a passing server, I am both relieved and more anxious than ever when Finn rejoins me, Eleanor leaning heavily on his arm. Lord Downpike is nowhere to be seen.

"Are you all right?" I ask.

Her eyelids droop and her face is pale, pinched in pain. "I do not have your strength for resisting spells thrown at me. I'm so sorry, Jessamin, he snatched me as soon as the music was over and . . . I can't remember anything else. I'm so very sorry." Tears pool in her eyes, and I rush forward to take her hands in mine.

"Never mind any of that. All I care about is that you're safe." *No thanks to me.* Ernest's words fling themselves around my head, making me question everything I've done that has brought me here. I didn't choose this, but I stubbornly refused to walk away when I became part of a game I didn't understand.

Eleanor's expression has none of its usual spark. "Think of the gossip—two lords fighting over me at the concert. I am so fortunate."

Finn takes her hand from me and tucks it in his arm so she can lean on him. "I'll call my carriage for you. I think it best if you spend the next few days at your uncle's home."

She nods, and I give her the best smile I can manage.

"Do not move," Finn says to me, his voice stern, and then he walks her out of the grand room.

Eleanor is fine, I reassure myself. But she was put in harm's way because of me. I had no thought for others' welfare when I defied Lord Downpike with that silly attempt for power with his book. I should have known—was warned—that this was all much bigger than me. Much bigger than any book, no matter how much magical knowledge it deprived him of. But I thought myself too clever for it all.

There are more ways to hurt me than I had realized. I think of Jacky Boy and Ma'ati with a sick feeling in my stomach. I'll have to ask Finn to take them on immediately rather than waiting. If they're on his property, they'll be safe. But what will *I* do to make sure no one else is hurt because of me? Not everyone can be carefully shuffled off to other places.

And why should I be a part of any of this? Albion, the continental countries—let them tear each other to pieces. I just want to finish my studies and go home.

I am wilting under the electric lights, coming apart at the edges and unable to hold on to myself or anyone else.

"Drink, milady?"

I reach out without looking, but the same voice says again, this time startled, "Jessa? Is that you?"

Focusing on the servant—had I forgotten to look them in the eyes?—I realize with a shock that he is none other than Kelen.

"What are you doing here?" I gasp, terrified that this, too, is a ploy of Lord Downpike's. If he's found out Kelen was a childhood friend, my first kiss, part of my own island . . .

He gives me an odd look. "I'm working. I could ask what you are doing here, though." He nods down at my dress, raising his eyebrows.

"Oh." I try to wave my hand, but even the gesture fails me. "I—I'm here with—a friend."

"A friend." His flat tone leaves no question as to what he thinks of that. "It appears you've made better friends than me in your short time here. I've been by to see you."

"I know, I'm so sorry. Things have been—well, complicated. Insane, actually."

He nods, one black eyebrow raised in condemnation. "I see."

I can't stand the judgment in his face, not after Ernest's criticisms. "You don't understand, I—"

He holds up his free hand. "No, I understand. I knew our mothers, too, remember?"

"It's not like that!"

"He'll use you up and then throw you away, and there's nothing you can do about it, because in the end you aren't one of them and you never will be. No one here will ever see you as an equal—no matter how many fine dresses you accept."

I can feel tears building, both at his accusations and at the deep-rooted suspicions that he's right.

I take his free hand in mine. "Please, let me explain. Come and see me at the hotel, I'll tell you everything. It's not—" I find myself once again on the verge of saying "*I didn't choose this.*"

But . . . it's a lie. I chose to come here tonight with Finn. I chose to let him into my life. I wanted to, much as I protested otherwise.

"I hope whatever you are getting is worth it." His eyes cut me to the core.

I startle as someone touches the small of my back. "Who is your friend?" Finn asks.

Blushing deeply, I drop my grip on Kelen's hand and stammer, "This is Kelen. We grew up together."

Kelen bows low at the waist, while Finn barely inclines his head. "If you'll excuse me, I must steal Jessamin." He turns, taking me with him, and I crane my neck to watch Kelen, whose face is bathed in stony disappointment as he watches Finn lead me to the other side of the room.

"What is so important? Is it Eleanor?"

"No, no, she's fine. On her way home. I thought you might like something to eat."

He's pulling me along, guiding me with his hand on my back, and I stop. "That's why you had to take me away without bothering to speak with someone I've known for years?"

Finn avoids my gaze. "I didn't think it wise for you to be seen with him."

Anger overpowers shame, flaring hot inside my chest. "Because he's a servant? Because he's not fine enough for this fancy room and these fancy people? Perhaps you haven't noticed, but neither am I!"

Scowling, Finn grabs my hand and pulls me through the crowd as though I am a petulant child. We enter a small side room with furniture draped in protective sheets.

"Why are we in here? Am I embarrassing you?"

"Don't be petty, Jessamin. Of course I don't care that he's a servant."

"Really?"

"Really!"

"Then why the rush to keep me from speaking with him in front of all of your noble peers?"

"I care nothing about them! Forgive me if I'd rather not see you speaking with a handsome man who is clearly interested in you!"

I stop, mouth open. Finn was jealous? That's what this is about? "Kelen is an old friend." Or used to be. I'm not sure he can ever forgive me for what I've become, not after what this country did to his mother.

Finn takes a deep breath, calming his features. "It's not safe. That's all. Lord Downpike could see you chatting and identify Kelen as a potential target. There is a reason I have no close friends, no history with anyone. I can only protect so many people at once, Jessa."

I narrow my eyes at him using my nickname. "So that is what you are doing with Ma'ati and Jacky Boy? Taking them under your protection?"

"Yes, of course."

"And me?"

"Why would I not want to protect you?"

"Yes, taking away my job, putting me in a room I cannot afford on my own, the walks in the park, the meals, constantly hanging around the library and the hotel, dressing me like a spineless Alben lady and parading me around. You are doing precisely what I asked you not to, precisely what I refused to accept when you wanted to hide me away in some country estate. You're trying to control me!" And I've let him. I've pretended to hate it, pretended at resisting it, but here I am. I think back on how happy I was to be on his arm earlier this evening and I cannot understand who I am or what I have done.

I know how I felt when I saw him waiting for me in the hotel. I can't deny that. But I let myself be pulled along in the wake of people with more power than I will ever have. Kelen is right. I will never be an equal here.

Finn's calm demeanor shatters, and he takes a step directly in front of me, forcing me to look up to see his face. "I'm not trying to control you! Spirits below, I'm trying to *court* you! Can you not see the difference?"

I lean back, needing some space between us so I can think, so I can breathe. "But . . . but you don't want—I mean, you're trying to break the shadow connection. I thought you wanted to be free of it. We agreed."

He throws his hands in the air. "I told you how rare it is. I have only known one couple my entire life who shadowed each other."

"Then ask them how to break it!"

His shoulders slump, and he turns away from me. "They're dead. My parents were shadowed from the moment they met, and they loved each other more than anyone I've ever seen. Clearly I was a fool to dream I could have the same thing."

His admission that he wants *me*, a relationship with me, leaves me scrambling to sort out how to respond. I shouldn't be so shocked, but Albens are never so open about how they feel. "I can't—I don't want—I never wanted my mother's life. I don't want to be an Alben's dusky prize."

He recoils as though I've struck him. "For all you think we judge you, I have never *once* cared about the color of your skin or the country of your birth. But it would appear you cannot get past mine." He reaches into his vest pocket and pulls out his deck of cards, letting them drop to the floor. "I will no longer try to be anything more than a burden to you. But don't think for one moment I will stop protecting you."

He moves to storm from the room, then stops, turns toward me, and bows, a cold, detached look on his face like the night of the gala. It hurts far more than I ever thought possible. "Goodbye, Jessamin."

I watch him leave, too stunned to speak. Leaning down, I pick up the top card from the deck strewn on the carpet. It's LOVERS, the edges far more worn than any of the others, as though it had been held and looked at a thousand times over.

Twenty-two

I PACE MY ROOM—NO, NOT MY ROOM, THE ROOM
Finn paid for. It's been a week since I saw him last. I've studied
enough for a lifetime to busy my thoughts, but nothing helps.

Kelen's and Ernest's criticisms fly constantly through my
mind, but still do nothing to push out Finn's final words and
the look on his face.

I can't admit that I was in the wrong with Finn.

But I can't help feeling that perhaps I was.

I do not even have Sir Bird here as a comfort, and I refuse
to write Finn merely about seeing my bird. I sit, defeated, at the
small dressing table and shuffle the deck of cards for the hundredth time. I cut the deck and mix it, my fingers now adept

where seven days ago they fumbled through it. I close my eyes and draw a card at random.

FATE.

I always draw FATE.

But fate is a slippery thing, is it not? After all, had Ma'ati and Jacky Boy not left Melei and traveled separately to a new life here, they never would have met. They would have missed each other and their supreme happiness.

Wouldn't they have? If they're fated to be together and one of them had stayed, would they have ever met? Or would they have found someone else who made them smile on the grayest days?

Consider Kelen. Had we both stayed on the island, we might have continued our summer of fast-beating hearts and stolen kisses. Perhaps we would be engaged now, against Mama's wishes.

I could take it as a sign of fate that, against all odds, we were reunited here.

But Finn. If I had stayed on the thoroughfare that day, not taken the alley, I would never have met him. The thought of never knowing him bothers me, leaves me feeling restless and aching.

I trace my finger down the card, on the length of dark path stretching into the trees. Paths do not only go one way. We choose which direction to take. I refuse to believe that any outside forces can determine the course of my life.

Certainly I have been drawn into something bigger than myself, made a pawn in a game spanning centuries of families unrelated to my own. But I still choose which direction to take, just as Finn chooses, and even that horrible nightmare man Lord Downpike chooses. None of us are without options.´

Ernest is right. I've been making choices, but I haven't been deliberate or thoughtful about them. I've pretended that my actions influence only myself. They don't.

I shuffle one last time. Cut the deck. Close my eyes and spread the cards across the table. I know before I open my eyes which card I have drawn.

FATE.

"Augh!" I knock the cards to the ground. I must get out of this blasted room.

I hurry out and down the servants' stairs. When I get to the back hall I find the way blocked by all the hotel employees, crowding around, trying to see over one another.

"What's going on?" I ask.

One of the chambermaids gives me a pinched and sour glare. "None of your business, *milady*."

I push past her and run into Simon going the other way. His eyes are wide. "It's Ma'ati! She's hurt!"

Heart in my throat, I force my way through, not caring who I step on or elbow until I burst through into Ma'ati's room. She's crying silently, sitting on the edge of her bed while Jacky Boy tenderly cleans her arms. They're covered in cuts and slices like tallies in a ledger. Her face has several long, seeping slits as well.

"What happened?" I kneel at her bedside, grabbing a cloth to help.

"Birds." She closes her eyes, her face pale with shock. "I went out for vegetables and a whole flock of birds flew down at me. I couldn't get away. It was like being caught in a storm—they were all around—"

"Shh." Jacky Boy strokes her hair. "It's all right. Simon's gone for the doctor. I'm here now."

I rock back on my heels, numb and cold with despair. This is my fault, for not choosing a direction. I stood in the middle of the path and threw a tantrum because I did not want to be there. And because of my stubborn denial, first Eleanor and now Ma'ati have been hurt.

"Jacabo." I pull him to the side as he stands to get a clean cloth. "You need to take the position from Lord Ackerly. Immediately. Go tonight, and take Ma'ati with you. It isn't safe here."

He frowns, narrowing his eyes. "What do you know that you aren't telling me?"

"He will be a good employer and you'll be happy and safe. Promise me you'll go."

"He hasn't written for me yet."

"It doesn't matter. He'll understand."

Jacky Boy looks at Ma'ati, his face grave and worried and then nods. "I will. But what about you? I know you're in trouble. I can read it on your face."

I smile sadly and wave my hand. "I'll figure it out. You take care of yourself and Ma'ati."

Leaving her in Jacky Boy's loving and capable hands, I walk in a daze back toward my room. I have two options, I know that now. I can run away, back to Melei the same way I ran here. Let Albion work out its problems without me.

Or I can . . . what? Claim a role in the middle of international strife? Openly face down Lord Downpike? Ernest was right about one thing: some voices don't matter. And I'm afraid mine is one of them. I'm a woman, and a dark-skinned island rat at that. I have no power here.

Feeling bleak and despairing, I write a letter to Finn. No matter how he feels about me, I know he'll help Jacky Boy and Ma'ati. Once they are safe, I'll decide what to do about myself.

Now a matter of habit, as I pass the dressing table I grab the top card and flip it over. I stop, card still unseen in hand, a chill surging through my veins.

I knocked all of the cards to the floor before I left my room.

Trembling, I look down. In my hand, the fate card, but altered. This time in the middle of the path is a large black bird, its single yellow eye fixed on me. I pull another—and another—and another—all the same. There is a small calling card on the table next to the deck.

Little Rabbit,
Your friends are my friends. Thinking of you.
L. D.

Twenty-three

LORD DOWNPIKE WAS IN MY ROOM. COLD WITH terror, I run into the hall to check on Ma'ati again.

"Whoa!"

I stumble straight into someone. Strong arms circle me to keep me upright. Heart racing, I look up to see Kelen.

And immediately burst into tears. "Oh, Kelen." I wrap my arms around him and bury my face in his chest.

"What's wrong? What have they done to you?"

"Nothing, I—they who?"

"These ghost-faced spirit cursers, of course. I knew this would happen. They can't see us without wanting to destroy us. Tell me who hurt you."

I step away, wiping my eyes. "I can't. I don't want you anywhere near this. I won't let you get hurt, too."

"What do you think they can do to me that hasn't already been done?" His dark eyes burn with hatred. "Was it that man? The one you were with at the symphony?"

"Finn? No. He'd never hurt me."

Kelen scoffs. "Listen to yourself, Jessa. There isn't a man on this whole spirit-blasted rock that wouldn't hurt you if given the opportunity. They hate us, they always have, and they always will. We're nothing to them."

I shake my head. I know Finn would never hurt me. Eleanor would do anything to help me, too. "I have friends here."

He laughs. "Friends? You're a novelty to them. A pet. They'll drop you as soon as you fall out of fashion."

"You don't know them."

"I don't *have* to. They're Alben. That's enough."

His words strike straight through me. I would have said the same thing just weeks ago. I would have dismissed an entire country of people just because of their birth, the same way I have always felt dismissed.

"Come on," Kelen says, taking my arm. "Tell me who hurt you and we'll fix them. There's no justice here but what we make for ourselves."

"Kelen, no. You can't."

He grins. "You'd be amazed at what I can do. And then we'll get you on a boat back to Melei, where you'll be safe. Say the word and I'll make it all better. You'll never have to think about this country or anyone in it, ever again."

And in that moment I know a simple truth: *that is not what I want.*

I squeeze Kelen's hand, then step away. "I think I need to fight this one on my own."

His mouth twists wryly. "You always had to be in control, didn't you? Clever Jessa. Never could accept help."

I offer him a regretful smile. "You know me."

"No, I guess I really don't." He sticks his hands in his pockets and, shrugging his shoulders, walks away.

That evening I pace the park, reading passages from my most recent school assignment: one of my father's books, this one about the colonization of Melei. Little reading is done, though, between throwing it in a fit of rage against a tree and picking it up again to repeat the whole process.

I owe Finn an apology. The problem is that I have no idea how to find his front door. I can see the window where I climbed out, as well as the large oak tree that I jumped onto and scrambled down to the ground. But there's no door anywhere on that section of connected town houses. I've already tried ringing the bell at both adjacent properties; neither was Finn's. In fact, neither butler knew that Lord Ackerly lived anywhere in the area.

Nothing to be done for it. Tucking my skirts into my boots, I climb the tree. Mama scolded me, but I always knew the hours I put into perfecting this skill would be useful one day. After scooting down the branch nearest the window, I realize I'll have to throw myself at it. If it's locked I will be in a rather dangerous scrape.

Leaning as far as I can, I grab onto the sill and push the window open just as I lose my balance. I tip forward, falling into the room and landing with a hip-bruising thud on the black tile floor of Finn's washroom.

Graceful, no. But effective.

Fixing my skirts and my blouse, I tuck the book under my arm and walk out of the washroom. The hall has more doors than I remember. I look for the library, but the first room I try is wrong. I back out, then stop, and slowly cross the threshold.

The walls are filled with art. More art than I've ever seen outside of a museum. And not just Alben art, studies of unsmiling people and unmoving fruit, placid and lifeless landscapes. Some of it is clearly Gallen, some Saxxone, and there . . .

I'm standing in front of the largest piece, a huge landscape painted on rough, inexpensive canvas, when Finn says, "Jessamin?" behind me, confusion coloring his voice.

I don't turn around. "He dismisses our art."

"I'm not sure I understand."

I wave the book in my hand without turning around. "My father. He has an entire section on the primitive arts of the Melenese people. He says our finest artists lack technique, lack the ability to translate the real world onto canvas. He can't see that it's not about transferring the world exactly how it is, but rather expressing how it feels."

Finn stands next to me. We look at the painting, a riot of color in green and boldest red, a painting I recognized at once as portraying the fire-petals in full bloom. It is obviously

Melenese, though few of our artists ever sell their work. There is no demand for it, no esteem for something so "primitive."

"I don't know who painted it," he says softly. "My mother had it in her sitting room. When I looked at it, it was everything I wanted the world to feel like. It's the most beautiful thing I have, and I would not change a thing about it."

I nod, finding myself quite unable to speak for a moment. "It's a horrible book," I finally say. "He's a dreadful writer. Pedantic in the extreme and showing a clear inability to see good in any culture other than his own. Patronizing, too, as though my entire island were filled with precious infants in need of learning how to do everything from caring for the sick to learning world history. Did you know that in the dozen years after Melei was colonized, we lost a third of the population to pox? Two of my aunts, half of my mother's cousins. And the children are sent to 'superior' schools learn the history of a culture that is not theirs and does not want them. Many of us are not even fluent in our own language." I sigh heavily. "It's like a song I can't remember all the words to. This is a terrible, terrible book."

"To say nothing of the fact that Milton Miller is a dreadful name."

I snort. "He's the most horrible sort of man. Even the way he blinks his eyes irritates me. And his class is beyond dull."

"He's a fool. Here." Finn takes the book from me and opens to a random passage. "'The women of Melei, though too dark of skin to be truly beautiful, are given to great passion and must be trained in the ways of modesty, morality, and decorum.'"

"From the married man who took a lover while there on a research trip."

"It *is* an odd training method."

I look at the fire-petal painting. "I can't believe someone could come to my island and see only how it could be reshaped as Albion. I don't think this whole country a waste—"

"How kind."

"Shush. It has its own peculiar charms, and admittedly does some things much better than we ever did. But why remake Melei in its image? Why not learn from its brightest parts, share knowledge and resources, and allow Melei to continue to exist as fits it best?"

"Because men are silly, prideful things, and what they love they must possess."

"Not all men," I say softly.

"No. Not all."

"How did Lord Downpike know?"

"About what?"

"About how much you loved this painting. How did he know to dress me like a fire-petal on the evening of the gala?"

"Lord Downpike has never seen this painting, nor does he know how much it meant to me. I will allow him no credit for the vision of beauty you were that night."

I look down, trying to control the smile taking over my face. So be it, Fate, whatever you are. I will stay this course, come what may. "I am deeply sorry. For what I said, and what I assumed about—"

"Never apologize to me. For anything. I'm glad you're here.

Though . . . how did you get in?"

"The bathroom. You really ought to lock your windows, arrogant magician. And don't be too pleased. I'm merely here to ask you to take on Jacky Boy and Ma'ati immediately. And to visit my bird, of course."

Finn stands, no trace of the cat in his smile, only sincere and open happiness. "Of course."

Twenty-four

I SIT IN A SUN-DRENCHED SPOT NEAR THE FLOOR-to-ceiling windows in the library. Finn won't tell me where it looks out to, and the glass is treated so that outside is nothing but bright blurs of color. This is my favorite room in all of Avebury.

Assuming, of course, that the windows actually look out on Avebury. Which I have found is not a safe assumption. *Nothing* is a safe assumption in this house, considering one of the doors next to the bathroom opens into my room at the hotel—an addition Finn insists he made while he was staying there.

After much pestering, Finn admitted he inherited most of the house from his parents. They'd taken the time to craft doors and spell them to open onto several residences through-out the city. One room from a house in Kingston neighborhood, another near the palace, another on the outskirts of the city along the river, so on and so forth. I haven't been in most of them—it makes me nervous to open a door not knowing where it will take me—but it does solve the problem of finding space in a crowded city.

I find myself spending more and more time here. Using a new front door in the park, of course. I made him remove the door that connected to my hotel room. Though it would have been convenient . . .

Finn does not seem to mind my visits. Neither do I.

I watch him, bent over two books, comparing things and taking notes. That's his main occupation. I write essays and study calculus. He copies things from the book that is Sir Bird and tries to puzzle out what the particular spells accomplish. His playful, arrogant face is nowhere to be found. A line takes up residence between his eyebrows, and I find myself wanting to trace it with my fingertip.

He looks up and catches me staring, so I stammer, "I—I thought I told you not to wear the brown tie anymore."

"When did you tell me that?"

"I told your shadow."

He laughs. "I promised you I wasn't an eavesdropper. Any future instructions should be delivered in person." He turns back to the book but I lean forward, wanting to keep him in conversation.

"Are you certain Ma'ati and Jacky Boy are out of harm's way

at your country estate?"

"Yes, of course. No one knows where it is."

"Why did you hire them? I thought you couldn't keep servants."

"You trust them. That was recommendation enough for me. Besides, I've met Jacabo and can't imagine a better man to employ."

"What happens if they go through a closet door and end up on the moon, or wherever else your strange hallways lead?"

"The estate is relatively untouched. They should find nothing out of the ordinary."

"Did you grow up there?"

His face clouds. "No. I was raised in a different house."

I wait for him to offer more information about his childhood, but he is quiet as always on that subject so I let him go back to his studies while I continue mapping differentials, my mind only half on the problems. I am looking forward to finishing up this season of course work and taking more challenging classes, though again I will not be allowed in the advanced mathematics.

Finn slams the book shut, huffing in frustration. It immediately poofs into a mess of feathers, Sir Bird cawing angrily and jabbing his beak at Finn's fingers.

"I'm sorry! I'm sorry! I forget you're both."

"Take better care of my friend," I say, trying not to laugh at their equally grouchy expressions.

"I feel so limited." Finn scowls. "I can't keep tabs on Lord Downpike like I used to."

"Why not?"

"Oh." He gets a look on his face that settles there when he does not wish to tell me something. "I've never employed familiars. They're less than dependable, no offense to present company. Lord Downpike can store magic in them and have them act semi-autonomously, but, as demonstrated by Sir Bird, giving magic to a creature with a mind of its own is not fool-proof. As far as I can tell, when Sir Bird severed the connection, he also cut off Lord Downpike from all these spells. He'll have to start over from scratch on any that he was storing. Which makes me very happy.

"But I digress. No familiars, but my mother taught me to have an unusual degree of control over my shadow. In the past, I've sent my shadow on errands, used it for ears or eyes. Shad-ows can get away with a great deal. No one notices them, and there are so many dim places to hide."

I frown, a memory tickling the back of my head. "The day we first met. When I got back to the hotel, I could have sworn I saw two shadows where only mine should have been."

Finn is suddenly absorbed in looking at his own fingernails. "You asked me not to follow you home, and I didn't. Exactly. But I had to make certain you got back safely." He glances up, face defensive as though he expects me to be angry.

"So that's how you knew where I lived."

"And probably how Lord Downpike discovered you. I hadn't suspected he would be watching me so closely. We've been play-ing political cat and mouse for two years now, and I was too relaxed. But if you noticed my shadow, no doubt he did as well."

"We'd only just met! Why did you care enough to send your shadow?"

He gives me a shoulder shrug of a smile. "You make a first impression."

A clock, buried beneath a pile of books on the mantel, chimes the time and saves me from the blood rushing to my face and demanding I answer him. "Oh, that's me late. I promised to call on Eleanor today. She's been lonely at Lord Rupert's house."

"I will—" He pauses. "Would you like me to come with you?"

I smile and shake my head. "No, you keep up your studies. The sooner you find something to use against Lord Downpike and tip the scales in favor of peace, the sooner we can let poor Sir Bird take up permanent residence in his feathers instead of constantly dwelling as a massive book." I am tired of being on the defensive against Lord Downpike. I can't imagine what Finn must feel like after two years of trying to subvert Downpike's schemes. "Would you show me how it works? When I return, I mean."

"How what works?"

"That." I wave my hand at the bird-book and then sweep it to gesture to the bookshelves. "All of this. I know I can't do it, but I would like to understand how it is done. It is a part of my life now, too, and I refuse to remain ignorant."

When I enter Eleanor's guest chambers, I find her leaning over an ornate desk, expression intent as she holds a flower up to her head.

No, not her head. Her ear. "What are you doing?" I ask.

She straightens with a surprised shriek. "Oh, Jessamin! It's just you. Well. This is embarrassing." She smiles guiltily. "I was eavesdropping on the parlor, actually."

"With . . . a flower."

"My own spell. Don't tell anyone. It's crass to invent new ways to use magic, and everyone would look down on me. But you'll appreciate this! I gave my aunt a lovely potted plant that I recommended she place in the parlor. A very *special* potted plant, that allows me to pick a flower and use it as a conduit through which I can hear conversations. I did not gain my reputation as Avebury's most skilled gossip by chance."

"You have certainly elevated eavesdropping to new and complicated heights. Wouldn't it be simpler to just listen outside the door?"

She leans forward. "Here, on my forehead, feel."

Puzzled, I run my fingers over the spot she indicated. There's a small indentation. "What is that?"

"When I was eleven, I was listening to an argument between my father and uncle. My father stormed out, and the door hit me so hard it knocked me unconscious and left a permanent dent! So I became more creative in the interest of self-preservation."

"You are a wonder."

She beams, lifting the flower again. "I know. Now hush. Uncle is hosting Lord Benton, who has his sights set on a union of the families through Ernest marrying his daughter, Margaret. We hate Margaret, in case you were wondering what our opinion is."

I nod firmly, sitting on a velvet couch to watch as Eleanor reacts to things I can't hear. Much eye rolling follows, along with a few sighs.

"Politics," she mouths, yawning dramatically. But then her eyes narrow and she presses the flower closer to her ear. Her expression changes to one of alarm.

"What is it?"

She shushes me and I wait impatiently until she finally sets down the flower, twisting it distractedly and tearing off the petals. "Well. I do wish I hadn't heard that. It would seem that Lord Benton, who has long been an advocate for peace along with Uncle, is switching allegiances."

"He's supporting Lord Downpike? Why?"

"He didn't say. But he very strongly urged Uncle to either do the same or step to the side and avoid any position at all."

"And what did the earl say? Surely he disagreed."

Eleanor shakes her head sadly. "He said perhaps it was time for him to take my aunt on a long holiday and let things happen however they will."

"So he'll allow Downpike to have his own way. Who else stands against him?"

"Other than Lord Ackerly? Fewer and fewer, I'm afraid." She sits on the couch next to me, and we stare in troubled silence at the tiny flower that delivered such frightening news.

Twenty-five

"SO YOUR CANE FUNCTIONS AS A CONDUIT?" I ASK. We spent the last few days dissecting what Lord Benton's defection might mean, but until Finn can get more information, it's an exercise in madness. He's been teaching me about magic, instead.

"Mmm." Finn nods, checking over the sequence I've copied out of one of his father's books of magical knowledge. I'm beginning to grasp the specific language of magic. It's a lot like mathematics. A shorthand way of expressing much larger concepts. Though I can now look at most of the spells and understand what they accomplish, I can't do any of it. I don't know how to feel about that, but I do enjoy researching and learning.

Though both Finn's and Eleanor's lack of knowledge about the history of magic—where it came from, how it started—annoys me a great deal and makes me reconsider my distaste of studying history. I may have to delve into this instead.

"The cane is a shortcut. I do the work beforehand and funnel it into the cane, and then when I need something quickly I can pull it from there. It is impossible to memorize every spell. I consult my books constantly, with only a handful of spells I can manage without advance preparation. The cane makes me far more capable of pulling up magic at a moment's notice."

"Like tapping a menacing fellow on the head to make him forget he wanted to harass me?"

"Yes, exactly like that."

"I had a knife, you know."

He smiles. "I did know. It was the first thing I liked about you."

"Show me something."

"What would you like to see?"

"Anything. Dazzle me with your boring, practical Alben magic."

Sir Bird preens next to me, tucking feathers into place with a low noise in his throat almost like he's talking to himself. A slow smile spreads across Finn's face as he rubs his knuckles—black and blue with several bruises from Sir Bird's beak.

"Let's see," he says, flipping through his father's book. "Here! I'll need some water in a shallow bowl . . . ink . . . yes, I think this is everything." He gathers the items, then reads over the entry several times, eyebrows knit in concentration. Dipping his pen in the ink, he whispers strange words while writing on the surface of the water. The ink drips down, elongating the form of the symbols that still hover where he wrote them. I recognize one—change. But the rest I haven't learned yet.

Then, without warning, he lifts up the bowl and dumps the whole thing onto Sir Bird.

Only instead of getting wet, as the water washes over his body, Sir Bird's feathers turn . . . blue.

Bright, brilliant, shimmering blue.

Squawking in outrage, Sir Bird hops and flies around the room, frantically shaking his feathers. He lands on the desk with a scrabble of clawed feet, then begins trying to bite off the color.

"Ha!" Finn says, pointing at his knuckles. "Now *you're* black and blue, too!"

I can't help but laugh at my poor, panicking bird. Not to mention the ridiculous pettiness of Finn's magic show. Picking up Sir Bird, I stroke his feathers and speak softly to him. "Hush now. I'll make him fix you. You're still very handsome, but blue isn't your color, is it?"

He caws mournfully, still pulling at his own feathers.

"Finn."

He puts his hands behind his back, trying to look innocent. "What? He deserved it."

"He's a *bird*. You can't really find this much satisfaction in revenge against a bird, can you?"

His voice comes out just a tad petulant. "He started it. Besides, I made it temporary. It'll wear off within the hour."

"There now." I kiss Sir Bird's head and set him on my shoulder. "You'll be back to yourself in no time."

"Tell him to stop pecking at me."

"Perhaps you deserve it. But you're right—magic can be used for things that are petty and ridiculous, instead of just boring."

His smile is soft and sadder than I anticipate. "We used to use that one on each other. My dad would dye my mother's hair pink, then she'd make his green, and I'd pester them until they made mine as red as the flowers in that painting. It's always been one of my favorite tricks." He clears his throat. "It's quite in vogue with society, as well. You'd be hard-pressed to find a noblewoman with her own true hair color."

"I didn't notice much blue at the symphony. Just brown and blond."

"Well, they have to make the spell boring somehow. They are Alben, after all."

I laugh, then lean over to study the spell to see if I can work out how it was all accomplished. "So you could use any ink lying around?"

He nods. "It would have been brighter still if I'd had blue ink, though."

"Interesting. So the quality and type item you use influences it. What about the sugar that Lord Downpike uses? I've been wondering. Could he use any sugar or must he spell it beforehand?"

"He uses it as a reagent to focus and release magic he's stored up. Similar to what I do with my cane, but he keeps the spells in his own body. They lose less potency, but it's a far greater risk should something go wrong. And I can't imagine the strain it must be, nor what it must feel like."

I flex my fingers, noting how much the pins and needles have faded. "He's not a man afraid of pain. But you *do* store some magic in yourself." I gaze significantly at his hair and he smiles.

"I haven't refreshed that in weeks."

"Hmm. I don't quite believe you."

He raises a single eyebrow and both corners of his lips at the same time. "You think I can't be this charming without magical aid?"

I exhale a laugh, steering the conversation from this increasingly large, unspoken *thing* between us. "Maybe he's got the right idea, though. You should expend that energy on a more important spell in case you ever need it. But the magical knowledge of his that we've gathered because of Sir Bird—can't he have just stored the spells before? So it doesn't matter that we have his book."

"Once broken, the connection between Lord Downpike and the spells in this book cannot be restored. If Downpike was storing any of the spells in Sir Bird, he lost them."

"Good boy," I murmur, nuzzling Sir Bird with my cheek. "I won't let nasty Finn dye you ever again."

Finn and Sir Bird exchange jealous glares. Finn breaks eye contact first, returning to the sheet I was working on. "Now, look here." He points to one of the symbols I've copied. "If you shifted that one place to the right, instead of dousing flame with water, you would light water on fire. Change one variable and you change the entire equation."

"Is that why there's so little innovation?" I haven't told him about Eleanor's trick. Finn informed me early on that everyone sticks to the magic they've been instructed in. I've started to wonder about switching things around, though—combining and reimagining some of the more complex spells.

"It's safer. A slight change in any stage could have unintended results. That's why most of the gentry hardly bother with magic at all. They learn the basics as is required of all of us to defend Albion, but other than that they leave it alone."

"Why are you different?"

He sighs, shoulders slipping down as though bearing a greater weight. "Because someone must be paying attention."

"To what?"

"To everything. My parents entrusted me with a great deal of knowledge; they did not do it so I could live a privileged life of ease." His voice gets that heavy distance it always does when referencing his family.

"Mmm, yes, because the homes and wealth and carriages and galas and symphonies are such a burden." I cannot hide my smile, and Finn sits back, noticeably more at ease.

"You've forgotten what a great deal of work it is to be so handsome and charming."

I look pointedly at his hair. "Perhaps you could show me the equation and methodology behind that one. I should very much like to understand how much effort you've put into it."

"It truly was essential when I came to the city without knowing a soul. I had to get invitations to dinner and dances and social engagements somehow. I used to put more stock in its effectiveness, until a certain someone proved resistant."

"Why was it so important? You don't seem to enjoy any of your social engagements."

"I was looking for someone. If no one is willing to talk to you, you can't get much information. Then I caught wind of Lord Downpike's warmongering, and that overtook everything else. I keep a constant watch on the moods of the important families—whether or not they would support aggression against the continental countries and the Hallin line."

"So your charm was a tool."

"Effective enough, until you. You know, I've been reading more of your father's book in an effort to better understand where you come from."

"But he's wrong on—"

"No, no, meaning everything he says I dismiss entirely. But there's one chapter about the Melenese language I found fascinating. Is it true you have fifteen different words for love?" He leans forward, his lips a challenge, like he wants me to ask why he would bring such a thing up.

I refuse to rise to his bait. "Yes. It's much clearer, really. There's a word for the first blush of youthful love free of desire. For longing to be with someone so much you would rather throw yourself to the tides than be without them. For the stale but steady relationship between faithful members of an arranged marriage. For how to feel about someone you thought was everything but ended up never feeling the same way about you. For the poison left over when you love someone and it ends so badly you cannot release the feelings. For the love between a mother and her children, a father and his children, a grand-mother and her progeny, the love between two dear friends, the love that is the first building block of a lifelong affair. There's even a word for a love so devastating nothing before or after is ever seen the same."

"Beautiful," he says. "But I counted only eleven."

"I'm not as fluent in Melenese as I'd like. Alben took even our ability to love from us."

"That is a tragedy beyond expression," he says, and at first I think he is teasing but there is no curve to his lips, no dance to his eyes. The air between us is charged with something unquan-tifiable either in math or magic. I can't look away and I don't want to. But I remind myself that we are unchaperoned, and I am a lady, and there are rules to this sort of thing.

I slap myself in the forehead, startling Finn and Sir Bird, who flaps away to the other end of the room. "What is it?" Finn asks.

"I've just now remembered something very important."

"Yes?"

"I'm not an Alben woman."

He frowns, confused. "You'd forgotten that?"

"A great many people have tried to make me, from the time I was small." I smile, admiring the line of his jaw and the curve of his mouth, and let myself feel whatever I want to feel, even if I cannot remember the exact word for it.

He narrows his eyes. "Is everything all right?"

I throw my arms around his neck and kiss him full on the mouth.

Twenty-six

AS SOON AS MY LIPS FIND HIS, HE BACKS AWAY, nearly falling off his chair. "I didn't make you do that!" His eyes are wide with panic. "Please believe me, I really have not been using any charm spells, and I would never take advantage of—"

I put my finger—from the hand without the glove—over his mouth and trace the soft curve of his bottom lip. "Please stop talking." Hooking the collar of his shirt, I pull him toward me and kiss him again.

This time he does not break away, cradling the back of my head with his hand, his thumb stroking down the side of my neck. His lips are soft and warm and fit mine like the answer to an equation I didn't know I was trying to solve.

Fate is a choice, and I cannot imagine any other choice making me as weightlessly happy as I am in this moment.

We break apart and I beam, unable to contain the giddy warmth spreading inside me. Finn looks the least composed I have ever seen him, a sloppy smile on his face. "That was—you are—"

"You know what they say about Melenese women. We are given to great passion and must be trained in the Alben ways of modesty and decorum."

"I would much rather be trained in your ways."

"I suspect you'd be a quick study."

He leans his forehead against mine. "What now?" he whispers.

"Now," I say, angling in as though I would kiss him again, "I am going to visit Eleanor." I stand, laughing at the frustrated scowl that takes over his face. "We cannot have too many lessons in one day. You must practice and perfect what you've already learned before moving forward."

"I'll endeavor to be your best pupil."

I turn to leave but he catches my hand in his. He looks up at me with dark eyes open and sincere. "Thank you for giving me another chance."

"Thank you for deserving one."

I practically skip toward Eleanor's uncle's town house. It's a few blocks away from the Greenhaven Park door, but I relish the time to myself to consider what just happened. I'm not sure what it means, to me at least, but I don't have to be sure. Whatever happens between Finn and me, I care for him right now more than I knew I could ever care for anyone.

The future will take care of itself. In the meantime, I see nothing wrong with kissing. Kissing is *wonderful*.

Lord Rupert's butler shows me in, saying that Eleanor will see me in her private sitting room. She hasn't been feeling well lately, still not recovered from her nerves after the symphony.

"I have decided," she says from the couch where she's tucked up beneath a quilt, "that I never again want to be the center of gossip. Gossip is much better observed and spread than lived."

My dreamy haze collapses when I see her. She looks as though she's lost weight even in the three days since last I called. I sit next to her, putting my hand to her forehead, which is cold and clammy.

"Have you been seen by a doctor?"

"I'm fine. Just tired. But you look like a sparrow in springtime. What has you all bright eyed and blushing?"

I laugh. "You haven't given Finn a plant, now, have you?"

"I don't need to spy to tell something is different. Tell me."

"I kissed Finn."

"Lord Ackerly? Kissed you? No—*you* kissed *him*?" She sits straight, eyes as round as children's marbles. "You are the single best thing that has ever happened to me. I thought Moira Chapel's flirtation with the gardener was the best story I had heard this year, but this tops all. Has he proposed, then?"

"No, and I wouldn't accept if he did. Not yet. I'm perfectly happy to figure out just how much I adore him without committing to adoring him forever."

"You have a strange idea of marriage if you think that's what it is about. I expect an engagement before the end of the month. Untouchable Lord Ackerly indeed. Promise to tell no one but me first. I'll have to book every waking hour with calls to see as many looks on as many faces as possible when they hear."

I laugh. "Who else would I tell?"

She settles back down, resting her head against the sofa with a cat-in-the-cream smile. "Of course, it would make sense that Lord Ackerly would find the most ridiculous match possible. Oh, pardon, I don't mean it to be rude."

I wave my hand. "Doubtless our whole relationship is viewed as a lapse of sanity on his part. But why does it make sense?"

"On account of his parents. He's told you about them?"

"Only that they shadowed each other." I blush, realizing that, though I've only now opened myself to my feelings for Finn, he threw his soul to me with reckless abandon. I wonder if what is a thrilling, unexpected romance to me is actually a massive relief to him after how I've dismissed his shadow and even demanded its removal.

Eleanor huffs. "That man is hopeless. Here he was sitting on one of the great forbidden romances of the century, and he didn't bother to tell you? I must do everything around here. He'll have told you about the two magical lines, correct?"

I nod, remembering the symphony. "Albion has all the descendants of the Crombergs, and the rest are Hallins, spread through the continent."

"No one knows exactly when the split happened, but it was as deep and unbridgeable as any divide in history. The Hallins, being smaller, guard their magical knowledge with deadly fierceness. Crombergs have been killed for merely asking the wrong questions while traveling abroad. We don't have to be so vigilant about our magic, since our strength is in numbers, not skill. But for ages it's been mandatory to keep the two lines of magic completely separate. So imagine the scandal when the youngest daughter of the king of Saxxone fell in love and eloped with a certain Lord Ackerly the elder."

"Finn's mother was from Saxxone?"

"A princess. Please do not leave that part out, it makes it ever so much more romantic. Anyone else would have been killed, but the king of Saxxone is the most powerful man alive, and the story is that she was always his favorite daughter. So he forbade anyone from doing them harm, but banished them both from the continental countries forever. Lord Ackerly was shunned in Alben society, but as he had already inherited—and those laws are ironclad—there was not much anyone could take from him. They moved to his country estate, removed from everyone and utterly unconcerned, so in love they were with each other."

"What happened then?"

She smiles sadly. "No one knows. They were more or less forgotten. I hadn't even heard of them until two years ago when the young Lord Ackerly descended on the finest social circles of the city, charming and handsome and rumored to be downright deadly with his magical knowledge. Everyone called on him, trying to find out whether he had learned Hallin magic. He never demonstrated anything but the most proficient wielding of Cromberg skill since Lord Downpike, whom many consider to be the most powerful man in Albion.

"Lord Downpike was, of course, obsessed with finding out what he knew. According to rumor, he's been planting spies for years all over the Iverian continent—in Gallen, Saxxone, even the smaller countries like Ruma. Nothing worked. Lord Ackerly was a new, easier target. If Lord Downpike could get your Finn on his side, he thought he could access the elusive Hallin magical knowledge. Downpike tried everything—bribery, threats, even theft—to get to Lord Ackerly, but nothing worked. Lord Ackerly was unconnected to everything and everyone, acquaintance of all and friend to none. He only stepped in when he thought someone was leaning too close to encouraging war. There was nothing for Lord Downpike to do, no advantage for him to secure. Until . . ." She trails off with a pointed smile.

"Until me."

"Until you."

"But Finn has said nothing of having extra magic."

"I've tested him myself—oh, don't tell him! His magic is pure Cromberg. There was nothing strange in it."

I nod. "And the things I've studied from Lord Downpike's and Finn's books function in the same way and contain the same relative information."

"You're studying magic now? But I thought—can you do anything?"

"No, no. My father may be Alben but he is not noble in any sense of the word. I simply nurture a scholarly curiosity."

She laughs. "You probably know more than I do now."

"I'll admit I find it odd that you have access to all of this information and power and you choose to ignore most of it."

Her smile becomes sly. "Dear Jessamin, I ignore nothing."

"But what of the history? I want to know how it happened, where it came from. Who were the original Hallins and Crombergs? How did they discover the magic? What happened to divide them?"

Her look grows serious. "Don't ask too many questions there. Some history has been lost to time. Other histories have been deliberately hidden. You're not supposed to know any of this to begin with, and—" She shifts into a hollow, rattling cough. She pulls a handkerchief out to cover her mouth.

"Are you sure you're feeling well?"

She's coughing too hard to answer me, so I pour a glass of water and take it to her. When the cough finally passes, she puts the handkerchief down. We both stare.

It's spotted with blood, seeping as we watch to form the familiar silhouette of a large bird.

"Oh," Eleanor says, a soft exhalation of surprise. "That can't be good."

I stand, then sit, then stand again. "Where is your uncle? He won't stand for Lord Downpike threatening you!"

Eleanor continues to stare at the handkerchief, her pallor gray. "My uncle left for a month-long holiday yesterday."

"I'm sending the butler for a doctor immediately. Where is Ernest? Can he stay with you while I run to fetch Finn? Finn can fix this. I know he can."

Eleanor nods, eyes glassy and unfocused. "Hattie, the maid, she'll fetch Ernest." She looks up, her lip trembling. "Jessamin, I'm scared."

I pull her to me, kiss her forehead. "I will take care of you. You'll be fine. I promise."

I wait until the butler is dispatched and Hattie is helping Eleanor into bed before rushing down the stairs. Ernest passes me, his look frantic.

"Jessamin, I—"

"Neither of us can afford to stand idly by anymore, Ernest. I'm sorry for whatever part I play in this, but it is not my fault. It is Lord Downpike's doing entirely. And until the people with power in this country are willing to openly stand against his vicious bullying to further his cause, everyone is at risk."

He doesn't have time to respond before I am out the front door. Finn can fix this. He will. And then—I don't know. I don't know how long we can play this game, run around dousing the flames Lord Downpike is sending to lick at our heels.

As I turn a corner at a run, someone grabs my wrist, spinning me to a stop against his chest. I look up into Lord Downpike's falsely handsome face.

"Such a hurry, little rabbit. It's as though someone has died. Or is dying, perhaps?"

"You can't. You won't. The earl would destroy you."

Lord Downpike's hand encircles my wrist in a viselike grip. I try to pull away but he shakes his head. "Careful now. That special glove of yours might come off if you struggle much more. Walk with me like a civilized person, not some rampaging *savage*." Keeping his bruising hold, he tucks my hand in the crook of his elbow, walking at a leisurely pace I am forced to match.

"Now, never mind about the earl. I certainly don't. If his

niece were to succumb to a sudden wasting disease, who could blame me? I have nothing but the girl's best interest at heart. After all, it is my job to protect Cromberg lines, to advance them. But I do think I have seen this particular curse—I mean, illness—before. Very fast-acting. She will not last the night."

"I will kill you myself." My voice is hoarse with hatred for him and fear for Eleanor.

"Such threats! A fierce little thing for being the helpless pet of Lord Ackerly. But we are all in luck! I know the precise magic to restore her to full health."

I clench my jaw, hating him, wishing I could do anything but accept whatever terms he offers. "What do you want?"

"Nothing that is not already mine. Return the book you stole. It holds the exact process I need for your Eleanor. Once it is safely in my hands, I will perform the magic necessary to save her life."

"I don't believe you. You know how to reverse the spell."

"Do I? Will you really risk Eleanor's life? You could ask your dear Lord Ackerly to find the spell, but it's such a large volume and she has so very few hours left. Ah, here we are." He stops in the park, shielded by trees but with a view of the door to Finn's home. "Do hurry. I can almost hear her desperate coughing from here."

He releases my hand, and I stumble forward on leaden feet.

I cannot give back the book without losing the only insurance I have against another attack, but I cannot allow Eleanor to suffer and even die for my sake. I burst through the door, screaming for Finn. He'll know what to do. He'll fix Eleanor, turn Lord Downpike's evil plan on its head.

There is no answer, so I run through the hall to the library. A note is tacked to the door.

> *Urgent summons from the queen. Stay in the house until I return. Please.*
>
> *Yours,*
>
> *Finn*

Twenty-seven

I DON'T KNOW WHICH I DREAD MORE—THAT Sir Bird will be in bird form when I enter the library, or that he won't, and I will never get to say good-bye. I push open the door to find him perched on the edge of a chair, completely back to his normal black, arranging a pile of shiny coins and buttons.

"I—" My voice catches. Sir Bird looks at me, extending and retracting his wings nervously. "I have to give you back to him. Lord Downpike. If I don't, Eleanor will die. Do you understand?"

Sir Bird is very still and then slowly bobs his head once.

"I already owe you my own life. And if you don't want to do this, I won't make you. I'll open the door and you can fly away and I'll try to find some other way to save Eleanor."

He hops with a flap of his wings and lands on my shoulder and then nudges my cheek with his beak. He's giving me permission, and it breaks my heart.

"Will he hurt you?"

Sir Bird shakes his whole body from crown to tail, puffing up his feathers, then caws in his most dismissive tone.

"You are the finest, bravest creature on the whole planet." I take a deep breath, and then have a thought. It's a gamble at best, probably pointless, and at worst will bring down more pain and trouble on all of us. I'm already allowing Sir Bird to be sacrificed. Eleanor is dying. Can I risk it?

Is it even possible?

"If I were to write a few pages, could I put them in the book? Could you make them a part of yourself?"

He lets out an uncertain squawking sound and then hops to the table. I kiss his feathered head and stroke the length of his back. "Thank you," I whisper, then he turns into a book.

Sabotage, sabotage. If, like Finn, Lord Downpike has to renew spells every time he uses them, then maybe I have a chance to mess with his abilities. Opening, I search frantically for anything I recognize. I cannot risk damaging a spell that might be the one Eleanor needs. If it's even in this book. Finding pages we'd looked at earlier, I rip them out as carefully as I can, hoping Sir Bird cannot feel it. I line them up with a blank sheet of parchment and transcribe the sequences nearly identically, mimicking the pen strokes as best I can. But I make subtle changes, substitute the wrong elements, the wrong words. Fire for water, confusion for clarity, darkness for light. I alter the parts of the equations I can understand. If I had more time, if I'd been able to plan . . . But this is the best I can do.

Then I tuck the papers back into the crease and hold my breath. A series of black sparks dance along the spine, and when I pull lightly on the pages, they stay affixed.

Lord Downpike wins this round, and I only hope that he has nothing further planned right now. I pick up the book to take it out to the nightmare man, but it trembles and then pops back into Sir Bird's form.

"You should stay a book. It seems safer for you."

Sir Bird pecks my hand.

"All right! Your way is best. I won't argue."

I walk down the hall with a heavy heart, already mourning the loss of Sir Bird. Something inside me is shaking loose, rattling around and making it hard to breathe. I push aside my own fear for what will happen when I hand the book to Lord Downpike. I'll have no more insurance against physical harm.

It does not bear thinking about. There are no other options. I will not sacrifice Eleanor for myself.

Taking a deep breath to steady myself, I wipe under my eyes. Lord Downpike will not see me a tearful, fearful mess. Sir Bird nips my ear softly, and I nod. "I'm glad of your company, dear friend."

I open the door. Twilight has cloaked the park in shadow, but I can see Lord Downpike standing at the edge of the trees. Before I can cross the threshold of the house, Sir Bird takes off from my shoulder with a loud series of caws. "Oh!" I reach out for him, then drop my hands, resolved. He took the offered escape. I'm not sorry. At least one of us has freedom.

So be it. I will throw myself at whatever semblance of mercy a man like Lord Downpike has. I lift my foot to step onto the porch, when I look up and see Sir Bird land in front of Lord Downpike. Downpike reaches down, takes Sir Bird around the neck, and twists his head with a quick, snapping motion.

"No!" I scream, but it's too late. In his hands is nothing but a book. I slump against the door frame, hands over my mouth, silently shaking my head as though I can undo what he's done.

"Not coming out to play?" he calls, tucking the book under his arm and strolling closer. "Clever, sending the poor birdie out so you could stay safe in Lord Ackerly's home. I am impressed."

That was why Sir Bird changed. So I wouldn't have to leave the protection of the house. I owe him my life again, and he . . . oh, Sir Bird.

"Are you *crying* for my unfaithful familiar? Women are such strange creatures. I suppose you kept up your end of the deal, though I had hoped to take a stroll, maybe have tea together."

I narrow my eyes, Lord Downpike blurred by the tears there. "Fix Eleanor. Now."

"As you like. What was that countercurse . . ." He flips through the book then snaps it shut. My stomach tightens. If he noticed I altered spells, I've lost any hope of gaining an advantage and Sir Bird's sacrifice is wasted. "That's right. I left it in a sugar bowl in her silver tea service. Make sure she takes a cup with two scoops and she'll be fine."

"You didn't need the book," I whisper.

"I *did* need the book. But not to fix Eleanor. Would you like a ride in my motor to her home?" He smiles, and again I see a hint of what is underneath his strange face that doesn't move quite like it should as he talks.

"She would not." Finn stands behind Lord Downpike, his cane gripped tightly.

Lord Downpike doesn't take his eyes off of me. "His now," he whispers. "Bought and paid for. You aren't nearly as interesting as I'd hoped, little rabbit. Until we meet again." He nods, tipping his hat at me, then walks past Finn without so much as acknowledging him.

Finn rushes up the steps and pulls me back inside, closing the door. "I should have known it was a trick to get me away from the house. When I got to the palace and they had no record of sending for me, I . . . but you didn't leave. He couldn't take you, not across the threshold."

"Sir Bird." I break into sobs. Finn takes me into his arms and I let him, resting my face on his shoulder, his hands rubbing gentle circles on my back.

"Why did you give him the book?"

"Eleanor. Eleanor! We have to get to her. He cursed her, she's dying. She needs two scoops of sugar from the silver tea service."

"It's not safe for you, not now that we have nothing physical to threaten him with. Stay here. I'll take care of her and be back as soon as possible."

I nod into his shoulder, wanting him to stay and hold me.

Then I pull away and wrap my arms around myself. "Go."

He opens the door and runs out. I watch him disappear into the trees as he cuts straight through on the most direct route to Sir Rupert's house. In the tops of the trees, a dozen yellow eyes stare at me from soulless black faces.

Twenty-eight

I WALK ACROSS THE SMOOTH BLACK SAND OF Melei's northernmost beach, a day's journey from my village. The breeze off the ocean whips my hair to the side, and I have to keep pulling it away from my eyes. A slight chill cuts through the humid summer air. I ought to be perfectly content but something is off.

I look around for Mama but she isn't with me. I'm never at this beach alone. We come for summer holiday, Mama and I and Nani and even sometimes Henry and his family. But as far as I can see, there's no one here.

The wind cuts colder, and I rub my hands over my bare arms. The filmy skirts of the red dress are trailing out away from me on the wind, reminding me of the scarlet ribbon spelling out LOVERS on the card I drew from Finn.

Why am I in the red dress? I don't want to be in this dress, I hate this dress. I threw it away. I turn around to hurry back the way I came, but the beach stretches on infinitely. I look down and see Sir Bird's lifeless body on the sand. "No," I whisper, but when I reach to pick him up he disappears.

A nameless fear surrounds me, chokes me, and I turn to run back when I notice something ahead of me. I walk toward it, my terror growing, but I must go that direction. There are no other options.

On the beach is a table, rich dark wood, laid with a familiar tea service.

I try to run the other way but the table is behind me now, and this time Lord Downpike sits at it, wearing a suit and top hat, black feathered wings tucked behind him. "Do sit down," he says, giving me his sharp smile.

I sit across from him.

This isn't real, it can't be real, but I can taste the salt air and feel the stomach-turning terror as I smell the tea.

"It's not real," I whisper.

"Of course not." He says it with a condescending laugh and the wind dies, leaving us in a vacuum on the soundless, motionless dead beach. The smell of the tea is overwhelming and I put my hand to my nose to try and block it.

"Oh," I cry out. My hand is a mess of broken, splintered bones and ghastly bruises. "No. No, Finn fixed it."

Lord Downpike pours the tea, stirring in scoop after scoop

of sugar. "But you still remember the pain. He couldn't take that away, could he? He couldn't make you forget what you've already been through. Put your hand on the table."

I stare at my hand, fingers splayed out, unmoving on the tabletop. "Wake up, Jessamin. Wake up, wake up."

"Not until I say so. Tell me, are you enjoying your time with your dashing Alben lord? Is he taking good care of you? You make a lovely pet."

My brain screams at my hand to move, but it doesn't. It should hurt, the state it's in. "I can't feel my fingers."

"I can change that. What is Finn doing? Has he shown you any magic? Told you about his mother?" Lord Downpike picks up a hammer, idly waving it from side to side as though testing the balance.

I seal my lips shut. I will not engage this dream. I will not. *I'm fine, I'm asleep, I know I am, I know I am.*

Lord Downpike sighs. "Very well, then. Your mind already knows exactly what this will feel like. I don't have to do a thing." He brings the hammer down on my hand, and I scream.

"Jessamin!" Finn says. He's not on the beach. Where is he? I'm screaming, screaming, my hand—the pain is too much, I cannot—"Jessamin, *wake up.*"

I sit up, gasping, my hair tangled around my face. "My hand!" I clutch it to my chest, stare at it in the dim candlelight. Nothing but the black glove, the cold tingling sensation overlaying the sharp, bright aftertaste of pain still lingering.

"That's the third time tonight." Eleanor leans against my doorway in her white nightdress. Her hair is in a long braid down her shoulder, and she looks exhausted.

"I'm . . . I'm so sorry. I was . . ." I cannot tell them, cannot get the words out. I know my hand is fine, *I know it*, but the pain! I close my eyes, unable to get rid of the smell of tea lodged in my sinuses.

"It's perfectly understandable," Finn says, rising from where he was sitting on the edge of the bed next to me. "You've been through so much." He doesn't sound tired like Eleanor. He sounds weighted down, sad.

"I am beginning to regret agreeing to stay here with the two of you." Eleanor walks into the room and sits in a chair beside my bed with a heavy sigh. "I thought I'd be watching your rooms closely at night for far more lurid and interesting goings-on than screaming night terrors."

"I don't know what's come over me." I shift, embarrassed, kicking my feet free from where they're tangled in the sheets. Finn has taken us both in, now that we know Eleanor isn't safe and we no longer have possession of Lord Downpike's book.

Oh, Sir Bird, I am sorry.

I thought—heavy with grief for Sir Bird—that I would sleep heavily. Instead, my mind is plagued with horrors.

"Give it some time." Finn pats my hand. "Everyone has nightmares."

"They've never bothered me like this. They feel so real, so out of my control."

Eleanor frowns thoughtfully, then runs out of the room and comes back in, carrying her snuffbox.

"Isn't it an odd time for that?" Finn asks.

"Oh, hush. You aren't the only one here with magic, and if there is one thing I am good at . . ." She pulls out a pinch, and I barely have time to close my eyes before she blows it right in my face.

She cackles. "If there is one thing I am good at, dear friends, it is detecting the presence of magic. I can *always* find it."

I open my eyes. Particles of dust glow, swirling in a slow pattern around my head. Eleanor takes me by my shoulder and pulls my head forward. "They're originating from back here." She touches a spot on the back of my skull. "Anything happen there?"

"No, I—yes! My ribbon, and some hairs. Lord Downpike has them. I'd forgotten all about it."

Finn stands, eyes blazing with fury in the dim light. "How dare he." He storms from the bedroom. Eleanor climbs into bed next to me, scooting me to the side and putting her cold feet on mine. It's a great comfort to have her next to me, sealing me off from the remnants of the dream and anchoring me here.

Finn comes back and I finally notice he's wearing a thin, white nightshirt with breeches hastily pulled on underneath. I can see his collarbones.

What is it with me and that boy's collarbones? I blush and then smile to myself. At least this is a better thing to dwell on than the fact that Lord Downpike apparently has unlimited access to my dreams.

Finn clears the nightstand next to the bed, setting down one of his heavy, handwritten books already open to a page. He has several other things—a burning candle, a pair of delicate scissors, and some powdered substance.

I examine the book, trying to decipher both the method and end result of the spell. Near as I can tell, he needs a clipping of my hair—the conduit, already being used by Lord Downpike—powdered poppy seeds, the gateway to sleep, and wax to be used to seal off Lord Downpike's pathway.

I tap my finger thoughtfully as Finn asks permission with a look, and I nod for him to cut a small strand of my hair. He takes it back to the dresser.

"I think we could change it," I say.

"Beg pardon?" Finn looks up from where he's copying down the necessary symbols.

"Isn't there a spell to turn something back onto the attacker? Using a mirror? Couldn't we substitute a mirror for the wax, so instead of sealing my dreams from him, we turn it around and allow me to be in control when he tries to enter?"

Finn frowns. "Why would we do that?"

"Is it possible?"

"I suppose it would be, in theory. But why risk it when I'm certain we can block him?"

"He has more of my hair. Strands he took from the comb. What's to stop him from repeating the spell?"

"If he does, we block it. Again. As many times as we need to."

"That's not enough. I already have to hide from him during my waking hours. I don't want to go to sleep at night worrying that he'll find his way in again."

"But what good will it do you to be able to control things, if he can still enter your sleeping mind?"

I smile grimly. "I intend to make it a place he'll want to stay very far away from."

Eleanor giggles beside me. "You are mad."

Finn's frown deepens. "I don't think we should risk it. Theoretically, it would work, but I'm far more comfortable using a spell I know."

I stand, leaving the warm comfort of my sheets, and go to my bathroom to retrieve a small, gilt mirror. I set it down next to Finn's materials and look him full in the eyes. "I agreed to stay here because it was safest for everyone. But you must let me respond to threats in the way I see best."

There's a moment, a hardening behind his eyes, where I think he will disagree with me, force me to go with his plan. And he could. I'm in his home, under his protection. Lord Downpike's words whisper mockingly: *Is he taking good care of you?*

And then, to my surprise, Finn nods. "But I insist on staying the night with you so that if anything goes wrong, I can wake you immediately."

I beam, flush with victory, and then suddenly cold with second thoughts. Perhaps this was a battle best left unwon. As I watch Finn preparing the spell, I nearly stop him several times. But no. I will not run and hide any more than I must.

When all is said and done, the process is anticlimactic. He writes the symbols on the mirror, drops the powder onto it, and then sets it by my bed.

Eleanor sits up with a start. "Spirits below, I fell asleep. Magic is so dull. Now, if you two think I will sit in a chair and chaperone, you're quite wrong. I'll leave your door open and mine as well, but I am far too tired for gossip, so please do nothing interesting." She kisses my cheek and then stumbles out of the room, still half asleep.

I sit on the edge of my bed, nervously eyeing the mirror. "Do you think it worked?"

Finn nods, but the smile on his face is betrayed by the line between his eyebrows. He hovers beside me and nods at the bed. "It would help if you went back to sleep."

"Oh. Right. Of course." I climb back under the covers and lie down, feeling awkward and exposed. Finn sits in the chair next to the bed, watching me.

"I will never get to sleep like this." I scowl at him, but the truth is I'm terrified. My hand aches with remembered pain, and I don't think I can face it happening another time. I remember hiding in Eleanor's armoire with Finn, how much I wanted to lean against him and let him hold me.

He has made a concession tonight. I can do the same.

I scoot over, leaving enough room for a Finn-sized body. I give him a look.

His eyebrows disappear beneath his golden hair. "Beg pardon?"

"I promise not to take advantage of you." I try for a lighthearted laugh, but it falls flat. I switch to honesty. "I only want you beside me. I need to know—to feel—I'm not alone when I face him."

He smiles, and I am relieved that it's gentle and soft, a safe smile. He eases himself onto the bed, lying flat on his back, not touching me. I close the distance and lift his arm over me, resting my head on his shoulder. His hand comes down lightly on the curve of my waist.

"Thank you," I whisper. I feel safer than I have in weeks.

"Don't think I provide this service for just anyone," he whispers back.

It doesn't take long until I find myself on the black sand beach. I'm aware this time, none of the odd dream-forgetfulness of before, and my gut reaction is panic. But no. I am in control. I change my dress from the awful red one into one of my plain skirts and tops. The skirt has a pocket, and I push my hand into it.

I smile.

Lord Downpike is waiting for me at the table. I take my time and stroll toward him. A flicker of confusion shifts his face into something else, but it settles before I can process what it was.

"Do sit," he says with his sharp smile.

I return it with one of my own, pull the knife out of my pocket, and slam it onto his hand, pinning it to the table. His wings spasm then disappear, and he looks down at his hand with shock and pain before bowing his head. I expect him to wail with anguish, but he looks up at me with a wry smile. "Very clever."

"I'm a clever girl."

"But it's not enough, is it? It will never be enough. You can be as clever as the sun is bright. You can best all your peers in school. You can try and try and it—*you*—will never be enough. How does that feel, little rabbit? Knowing you will never truly be in control, never truly have power, simply because of who you are?"

"I think you underestimate me," I say, but it comes out more timid than I want.

"I think you know I'm right. This isn't your world, and it never will be."

I look around at the beach. We're in my dream. "Actually, right now this is *entirely* my world." I pull a large meat cleaver out of my skirts. "You should leave."

He laughs, hand still pinned to the table and then gives me a look I can only describe as . . . affectionate. "Well done."

And then he is gone, and the dream is just a dream.

Twenty-nine

Dearest Mama,

I hope this letter finds you well. I am sorry not to have written sooner, but I was not sure what to say, nor did I want to have to tell you unless I was certain that it could not be avoided.

I have left the school. Circumstances rendered me unable to attend classes, and though it breaks my heart to have my months of hard work and studying count for naught, rest assured that I am continuing my studies on my own in a more rigorous structure than my professors instituted.

I know that you were against the idea of me

attending school here. I had hoped to prove you wrong by excelling there and

I am sorry, the ink on this page seems to be running. What I mean to say is, I am grateful for all of the love and support you have given me, even when we did not agree. I hope to make you proud. I am staying at a new address, which is enclosed, at the home of a dear friend. Eleanor, who was recently ill, is staying with us as well and we spend our evenings in happy companionship.

The world is a much more complicated place than I used to think. I am trying to find my place in it. I miss you very much and wish you were here to chide me on my clothing choices and help me know what to do.

Your loving daughter,

Jessamin

P.S. I am delighted to tell you that Jacabo and Ma'ati, a lovely girl from the island, were married. They have found employment at the country estate of a wealthy lord and are happily settling in. Please congratulate his mother for me.

"Dashingly handsome," Finn says.

"Beg pardon?" I blow on the paper to hasten the drying of the ink.

"You forgot 'dashingly handsome.' Dear friend is nice but hardly covers the extent of my qualities."

Eleanor looks up from her own letter writing. "How did she describe me? Because I have always preferred my eyes to be referred to as the 'color of a storm-tossed sea.' If either of you were wondering."

"You did not fare much better. In fact, I think I am ahead. I am a '*dear* friend,' and you are merely 'recently ill.'"

I push the letter aside and face him. "Reading private correspondence is in poor taste, Lord Ackerly."

"Unless it is terribly interesting," Eleanor says, "which Jessamin's letters are not. Mine, however, are lurid tales of my near-death experience and subsequent sequestering against my will in the home of the mysterious and brooding Lord Ackerly. I fear I may have given you a tragic past and a deadly secret or two."

"Are we staying in a decaying Gothic abbey?" I ask.

"Naturally. When I'm finished, there won't be a person in all the city who isn't writhing with jealousy over the heart-pounding drama of my life." She pauses, tapping her pen thoughtfully against her chin. "I don't suppose you have a cousin? I could very much use a romantic foil."

Finn shakes his head. "Sorry to disappoint."

"Alas. As long as I'm not the friend who meets a tragic end that brings you two together forever through shared grief." Her line meets dead silence, and a sly grin splits her face. "Oh wait, I nearly was."

"Horrible girl." I tug her ear as I walk past. She yawns, though she has only been awake a couple of hours. She writes more letters than anyone I know, and it seems to exhaust her.

I, however, am well-rested. Several times Finn has asked after my dreams, which have remained free from cameos by Lord Downpike for the last two nights. I think he is not one to pursue something when he no longer has every advantage. I suspect Finn's inquiries have more to do with the fact that he no longer has an excuse to stay in my room at night.

Perhaps I could make up more bad dreams.

No. I need to get some air. I need to do something—anything—away from here. Even three days trapped inside has been too many. Finn is in and out all the time, making appearances at various social engagements, keeping up connections, trying to keep the scales tipped toward peace, but Eleanor and I are utterly homebound.

It reminds me of a game all the children on the island played: Fox and Rabbits. There was a free area, the rabbit hole, where you could hide and be safe from the prowling child playing the fox. I never used it, no matter how many times I was caught. I loathed, even then, to pretend at hiding rather than running free and taking my chances.

I pick up today's newspaper and leave the library and its perpetual sunshine. I am in the mood for a bit of drab gray. The washroom suits my craving for privacy and I sit in a chair next to the window, idly scanning the paper.

An article referencing Melei catches my eye. I frown, skimming, and then read the whole thing start to finish. It is written by none other than my father, a fanciful and horridly false account of the glorious era Alben colonization has ushered in for the poor, downtrodden, dirt-ridden natives.

"In closing, I would posit that, given the vast benefits seen in every aspect of life on this primitive island, the effects of an Alben system of government and oversight cannot be overestimated. Consider the colonies a case study. If such a savage people can be so improved, the patriotic Alben cannot help but envision what our impact could be on civilized countries' fertile grounds."

Practically blind with fury, I storm back into the library and throw the newspaper onto the table. "Have you seen this?" I remember now the girl in my class referencing his newspaper articles. I'd never bothered to look them up.

Eleanor glances down and then goes back to her letter. "Oh, that? He's written a whole series on it. Terribly dull. Read the Society section instead."

Finn picks up the paper and reads the article, the frown line deepening between his eyebrows. "A series?"

"Hmm?" Eleanor sets down her pen. "Yes. Most of the time he picks a specific negative aspect of native culture that the colonization was able to correct, and then compares it to a continental country and what could be done to improve their social systems or methods of government. I only know because Uncle insists on reading them aloud to Lady Agatha and then asking her opinion, which is always the same: 'I think I will order a new hat.'"

I pace in a rage. "Of all the self-righteous, culture-blind, arrogant twaddle! I have half a mind to go to his office and box his ears!"

"Jessa." Finn's voice is soft, lacking all of my indignation.

"What?"

"I think we ought to call on your father."

Eleanor drops her pen, leaning in eagerly. "To ask his permission? I have a list of requirements for the colors you may use at the wedding. My complexion ought to be taken into account. It's only fair."

"For spirits' sake, Eleanor, I would not give my father the honor of asking his permission for anything. We're going to box his ears! Yes?"

Finn doesn't smile. "I'm concerned about the tone of these articles. I would like to ask your father about them."

"I can think of any number of things I would rather do on my first trip from the house, but if it gets me out, I suppose it is enough." The idea of going back to the school fills my chest with an ache. It was often awful, but it gave me purpose. I don't like being caged, don't like the sense that by sitting here being *safe*, we still are doing nothing to remove ourselves from Downpike's claws.

Finn takes his cane and puts on a hat. It emphasizes the dark curves of his brow, the line of his chin, and I suppose that being locked in a house near him has not been all bad. Indeed, I think it a good thing Eleanor is here as a nontraditional chaperone. Finn catches my look and a secret smile pulls his lips.

I glance to the side, trying to hide my own smile, trying not to think about his collarbone hidden just under his shirt.

"I would also like to state for the record that I am happy to be godmother to your children, but they must address me as Miss Eleanor. None of those silly nicknames."

"I don't know what you are on about," I say.

"Oh, please. Get out of here and into some fresh air before you two spontaneously combust."

"Would you like to come?" Finn asks.

"No, unlike the pacing wonder that is Jessamin, I am content to sit inside all day, reading and writing letters and napping. I'm quite suited to a life of protective custody. Besides, Ernest might call later."

We leave her with a promise to bring back a surprise, which she dictates should be fresh flowers, but not daisies or mums. Finn chooses a door that opens from the long, dark hall to a narrow alley crossing a street filled with vendors.

"How many doors do you have?" I ask.

"Right now, fifteen. Several are permanent, the others rotate."

I nod, trying to remember the specific combination of symbols and elements needed to create a door between areas. I know I read it in one of his books.

"You're talking to yourself," he says. "Are you nervous?"

"To see my father? Goodness, no. I'm working out a puzzle. Hush."

He's quiet, watchful as we merge into the crowds of people traversing the sidewalk, men and women shouting and competing for attention over their wares. I feel safe here, far safer than I ever did at the symphony or gala. It's easy to be invisible among so many people. Even I don't stand out with my skin and hair amidst so many other transplants converging on this street. It smells of fish and wheat, and for some reason things feel easier here. Maybe because everyone is on equal terms. No one haggling has enough money. There are no manners, no formality. A woman has a baby at her breast, sitting on the steps to a money-exchanging house. A man and his girl lean against a lamppost, finding a private moment amidst such a public place to share a passionate kiss.

I suppose mathematically it makes sense. With a large enough number, a single digit will not have any impact. It's when you isolate the numbers, set them apart, that they become important on their own.

Back to doorways. I *know* I remember how they are formed. And thinking about doorways distracts me from looking over my shoulder for bird spies. Must keep my mind busy.

Finn is still talking. "It is not a matter for your father, but I have been meaning to ask. Would you—I mean, when this is over—"

The symbol for earth, and the one for air, and a third for . . . movement. Yes. The door functions as a transfer point, a focus for the magic. Like the quadratic formula. A stable base for all of the different variables to function around.

"Are you listening to me?" Finn asks.

"Running water."

"What?"

"When we were escaping from Lord Downpike's home. The symbol was under running water, and you said it helped. There was no door there."

"Oh, right." Finn looks disappointed to be discussing doors. "It's a trickier matter to move without physically moving between thresholds. Takes a good deal more power. Using the earth and natural elements helps. That's why I put that transport point underground."

"Were you planning on spending much time running through the sewers and needing a quick escape when you came to the city?" I shake my head at the woman aggressively shoving ribbons at me.

Finn is quiet, then says, "Yes. I was. I didn't come here for the fine society and opportunities to dine with lords and ladies."

"Why did you come after so long of avoiding it all?"

He lets out a long, sad breath. "I came to find my parents' murderer."

I stop, blocking the flow of foot traffic. "They were—oh, Finn." I suppose I should have realized, or at least suspected, but he only told me they were dead. Suddenly, the fact that Finn appeared in the city out of nowhere, striving to make connections and immersing himself in magical society without forming any real friendships makes perfect sense.

"Have you . . . do you have any idea who did it?"

His eyes darken like a cloud passing over the sun. "No. I thought for a time it was Lord Downpike, but his alibi is airtight."

"How?"

"He was in jail that evening. Picked a fight in a tavern and nearly killed two men."

"But a man of his skills, surely—"

"They have special cells for the nobility. There is no way he could have been out that night."

"But with magic, maybe he set something up? Did it . . . long distance?"

"It was . . . messy. Whoever did it took his time, and he did not use magic. Not for the end. It was personal for him. As near as I could tell, my father was killed first, and then my mother . . ." He passes a hand over his eyes. "It was not the work of someone uninvested in the outcome."

"Finn, I . . ."

He looks down the sidewalk. His face is once again composed and carelessly handsome. "This isn't our concern right now. It will keep. I can't be focused on it when other things hang in the balance. I never found the information I sought, but I find enough else to trouble me."

Before he can resume walking, I circle his waist with my arms and pull him close, nuzzling my face into his neck. Here I was, bemoaning my fate for being drawn into a conflict for a country I don't love. Finn has given up something deeply personal and tragic to protect others. He's noble in the sense of the word that matters. "I am so sorry."

His back muscles loosen, and he pushes his face against my hair, breathing deeply. "Thank you."

A woman passing us clears her throat and whistles approvingly. Sharing a small, sad smile, we resume walking, nearly to the school grounds.

"She would have loved you," Finn says. "They both would have."

"I wish I could have met them. And I'm sorry you have to meet my father."

We enter the building, the smell of ancient wood and dust and leather making me homesick for my cozy library carrel.

Outside Professor Miller's office door, Finn taps his cane against the frame.

"Yes, yes, sorry, I am nearly done, just a moment, I have it right here for you, Lord—" The door opens, and my father's squinted and puffy eyes open wider in surprise. "Oh. Hello."

"Lord who?"

Professor Miller wipes his forehead nervously, a sheath of papers clutched to his chest. "What?"

"Which lord were you expecting?" Finn snatches the papers. I remember how his assertive airs used to infuriate me, but today I am grateful for how they cow my father. "This is another of your articles extolling the benefits of imposing Albion on the continent. Who are you giving it to?"

"I . . . we haven't been introduced. Jessamin?"

Finn walks forward, forcing my father to stumble back into his office. Without asking, he crosses to the other side of the desk and begins opening drawers, looking through them. "I have no desire to be introduced to you. You don't deserve your daughter, and I won't do you the courtesy of pretending to be polite."

Professor Miller stutters. "That's private. You can't be in here."

Finn pulls on a drawer, but it won't budge. He taps it with his cane, muttering a single word, and it pops open.

"Hey! How . . . you can't, and I . . . I'm calling for the guards." I let him walk past me. I don't care enough to stop him.

"Interesting." Finn pulls out a small pistol and lays it on the desk. "And more interesting." In his hands is a bundled stack of envelopes. He pulls off the top one and hands it to me. In the corner, where a return address goes, is stamped: THE OFFICE OF HIS LORDSHIP, THE MINISTER OF DEFENSE.

"What does it mean?" I ask.

Finn looks exhausted. "It means we know who is commissioning those news articles from your father trying to sway public opinion and make them view expansion in a positive light." He puts the gun back in the drawer and closes it.

I feel it settle into place in my head. The attempts to win public opinion via positive examples. The criticism of other countries. The delicate balance that exists between Albion and the Iverian continental countries to prevent any one country from becoming more powerful than the rest.

The balance that hinges on both sides having their own magic.

"He wants to invade," I say.

"And all he needs to ensure victory is access to Hallin magic."

Thirty

I WATCH THE DOOR IN FEAR. "WE NEED TO LEAVE."

"I want to speak with Professor Miller," Finn says. He's still searching through the letters.

"He's expecting a *lord*. Lord Downpike. Do you want to face him here?" I hate that I'm scared, but I am. It's one thing for Finn to face Downpike on equal ground, but if I'm here, I give Downpike an automatic advantage. Finn will try to protect me over anything else.

Finn tucks the letters into the jacket of his three-piece suit, and we hurry into the hall.

"Hey!" Professor Miller shouts from where he's turned the corner in a shuffling, unsure run toward us. "Stop! The guards are coming! Stay where you are."

"Never mind that." I tug Finn's arm. We turn back around but then stop dead. Lord Downpike stands in the center of the hall. He looks from us to my father, a smile creeping across his features.

Finn raises his cane defensively.

"By all means, don't let me hinder your flight." Lord Downpike bows and sweeps an arm out to let us by.

I look at Finn, confused. His eyes are narrow, posture wary, but he walks ahead, keeping himself as a shield to me the whole time. When we come to the doors, I burst through and we hit the sidewalk at a run, passing through the gawking crowds, my breath catching painfully in my chest by the time we reach the portal back to Finn's house.

"What happened?" I gasp, leaning against the wall in Finn's dim hallway. "Why did he let us go like that?"

"I don't know."

I sit down on the floor, my skirts pooled beneath me. "Lord Downpike can't really think a few newspaper articles will help his cause. No one would agree to trying to colonize the entire Iverian continent. Or even a single country like Gallen or Saxxone. It would mean war for certain."

"He has been trying to sway public opinion in that direction for some time now. And it is not such a stretch to think they would approve. Not if Lord Downpike holds all the power and can guarantee an easy victory." Finn slides down the wall to sit next to me, his shoulder against mine. "We have to stop him." He takes my hand, staring at the way our fingers connect.

I lift our hands and brush my lips across his knuckles. "He depends on accessing Hallin magic to overthrow the balance of power, yes?"

"Yes."

"And he hasn't been able to get it from any of the Hallin lines."

"They're too smart, too careful. Cromberg knowledge is dispersed and diluted—even if they took dozens of our nobles, it wouldn't matter. We rely on strength of number. But Hallin magical knowledge is concentrated, a vast and depthless pool that only a few can draw from. He'll never get it from them."

"Which is why he has been so focused on you." I don't want to ask, but I must. "Do you have it? The information he needs?"

"There are no books of Hallin magic in this country."

I narrow my eyes. That wasn't a direct answer to my question. I wonder if he's seen the magic Lord Downpike wants, or if he knows how to get it. "You're not telling me everything."

"No, I'm not. I'm sorry. I think my parents died because of this, and I won't put you in any more danger than I already have. Bringing you into all this is the greatest guilt in my life. And still, selfishly, I'm glad for it."

I put my hand on his cheek and turn his face to look me in the eyes. "I did not choose to start on this path, but I chose to stay."

"I don't suppose, then, that you will accept my offer to send you somewhere safer than here."

I laugh. "As always, no. I am precisely where I want to be."

"If something happens to me . . ." His face is grave and so

serious I realize that he thinks it a strong possibility.

"Do not even speak of it. That's nonsense and I will not have it."

He leans forward and kisses me, his lips gentle and tender against mine. Something slides over my gloved ring finger and I draw back to look down. Finn's ring with the family crest of two trees intertwined sits, heavy and gleaming, over the black satin.

"Finn, I—"

"It's a promise," he says. "From me to you. You needn't promise me anything back, not yet." His sly smile sneaks into place. "Though soon would be nice."

I push my fingers through his hair, matching his smile. "You will need a good deal more charm to persuade me."

He stands so abruptly I nearly fall on my side.

"What is it? What's wrong?"

"I find myself in sudden dire need to increase the potency of my charm spelling."

I laugh, and he offers me a hand to help me stand. We walk, arm in arm, back to the library, where Eleanor startles and tries to act as though she hadn't been leaning against the door, listening.

"I thought you'd given up listening at doors. Do we need to update you, or have you heard enough?" I ask, sitting next to her with a smile.

"I haven't any idea what you are referring to, Jessamin. I was merely checking for a nasty draft. You may feel free to tell me all about Lord Downpike's plan for an aggressive military take-over of the entire continent, aided by the Hallin magic he thinks

Lord Ackerly has, but that Lord Ackerly insists he does not. I will be *very* surprised to hear it. And then you can add to my shock by taking me aside and whispering that Lord Ackerly has given you his golden ring with the family crest, and I can promise you that it means much more than you think it does, and he is being sneaky by pretending it is merely a promise."

"Eleanor," Finn says, a single eyebrow raised. "Would you be a dear and check the pantry to see whether we need to order more groceries?"

"Oh, fie on you, Lord Ackerly." She flounces to a love seat, lying on her stomach with her chin on her hands. "I will do no such thing. You two are going to discuss your plans to defeat Lord Downpike's nefarious machinations, and spirits take me if I will be anywhere but here."

"You can start with some of your marvelous letter-writing skills," I say. "Ask whether it is worth the risk to make a power grab on the continent, implying heavily that you have information it's in the works. Ponder what will happen when those of you with less magical ability are called upon by the queen to go on the offensive against vastly more skilled Hallin practitioners. And then comment on the ghastly new dress that Arabella Crawford was seen in, just for good measure. You can check the pulse of noble opinion and see what direction they are leaning—whether there is a real risk of their following Lord Downpike down this mad path."

"You are the cleverest girl I know." She stands and goes to her writing desk, dumping off a stack of books without ceremony. "I'm so pleased my lifelong cultivation of gossiping skills will be essential in saving the world. And to think, my mother said it would get me in trouble."

"Do you have everything you need for the spellwork?" Finn asks.

Eleanor stops, pen poised midair. "Whatever do you mean?"

"I mean the way you're so drained after writing. I know what it feels like to expend a great deal of energy on magic, Eleanor. Your letters are not ordinary missives."

She turns and smiles demurely at us. "I have no idea what you are speaking of."

"Hmm," Finn says. "I think you do. And I find myself very, very glad you are on our side. You frighten me."

"A well-wielded pen is a woman's best weapon." Laughing to herself, she turns back to her letter writing. I look at Finn but he shrugs.

"And as for us," I ask, "what should we do?"

He shakes his head. "I really can't say. Everything I think of is either too dangerous or too inadequate. If I outright attack Downpike, someone will end up dead. I fear we'll have to spread the word and wait for it to settle, see who falls on which side. I know how much you hate being locked up in here, but this is a political game, and until—"

A bell rings, and Finn frowns.

"What is it?"

"The door chime for my official front door. No one ever calls on me."

It rings again, insistent pealing as though someone is doing nothing but tugging on the line. Taking his cane, Finn walks out into the hall. I follow. He opens a door I haven't been through, which leads us to a gleaming foyer, marble floors, and white pillars around a large oaken door.

"Stay behind me." He opens the door.

The porch is crowded with purple-uniformed guards. "Lord Finley Ackerly?"

"Yes."

"You are under arrest for the murder of Milton Miller and the attempted murder of Lord Downpike, minister of defense, as well as high treason against Her Majesty, the Queen."

Thirty-one

THE GUARD NEAREST THE FRONT, A BRICK WALL OF
a man, frowns. "If you do not come willingly, we'll use force."

"This is insane!" I step forward, trying to put myself between
Finn and the guards. I don't know if they can enter his home.
I hope not. "He hasn't murdered anyone! I was with him all
afternoon. Milton Miller is alive. I'm his daughter," I add, desperately grasping for some sort of authority.

The guard's stony gray eyes do not shift from their stern,
impassive glance. "I am sorry to inform you, miss, that Professor
Miller was shot to death in his office. We have witnesses."

"Then they will tell you that I was in his office, too, and
when we left my father was alive!"

The guards share a look, a silent nod passing between the two nearest me. They take out a second pair of wrist irons. "We'll have to take you in as well, on suspicion of being an accomplice."

"No." The voice chills my blood, and the guards part to let Lord Downpike through to the front. His suit is artfully disheveled, a single plum-colored bruise standing in dark contrast on his forehead. "I will vouch for the girl. When Lord Ackerly attacked she was clearly under a heavy charm. She stood in the corner as though seeing nothing. No reason to let him take her down with him."

Finn shakes his head, as cool as the marble beneath our feet. "You will not get away with this, Downpike."

"With bringing you to justice? Of course I will. Officer, when you search his jacket you will find a series of confidential letters I wrote to Professor Miller answering his scholarly questions about the nature of our defenses against continental attacks. Lord Ackerly, you have finally been exposed for the Saxxone spy that you are. By queen and country, I will see you hanged."

"No! It's him, it's always been him!" I point to Lord Downpike, who smiles with false pity.

"Lord Ackerly, please release your hold on this poor child's emotions or we will be forced to lock her up as well."

Finn puts a hand on my shoulder, forcing me to look at him. He's calm, too calm, and I cannot handle it, my heart will not take it. "Tell them! Tell them it's all lies, that Lord Downpike is behind everything! He must have killed my father after we left.

They will find his . . ." I pause. The fingerprints. Finn took his gun out of the drawer. And he still has the letters in his jacket. "Please," I whisper. "Let's run."

Finn tucks a loose strand of hair behind my ear, letting his fingers linger on my neck, then leans forward and presses his lips to my forehead. "I cannot allow them to break the barrier on the house. If Downpike has enough help he can do it. Don't leave. Don't allow anyone in."

He turns from me, and I grab his hand. "No! Finn, please!"

He whispers a word and taps his cane against the ground and I find myself fighting through the air as though it were a solid thing, unable to follow him.

He has rendered me powerless to help him, and I cannot forgive that.

Lord Downpike exhales softly when Finn crosses the line of the door and then smiles at me, his pale eyes flashing black. "Break his cane."

A soldier takes it from Finn, snapping it across his knee. There's a hollow, popping sound and all the soldiers wiggle their jaws to clear their ears. I fall forward onto my knees as I'm released. I expect to see a physical change in Finn, but if anything he stands taller, prouder. The soldiers cuff his wrists behind him, and he doesn't turn around as they walk him away.

Lord Downpike hangs back, standing just outside the threshold of the door. I want to throw myself out, to run and take Finn back, but he blocks my way.

My voice trembles with rage. "The truth will come out. Besides, you need him alive."

"For such a noble principle, truth is a fragile, malleable thing. As for needing *him*, you underestimate yourself in this equation."

I laugh hollowly. "If you think I have any information you will be sorely disappointed. I can't reveal something he never told me."

"Then come with me and we'll discover the truth together. If you're as worthless as you claim, you can be finished with this whole game. I'll let you run free, little rabbit. I can be merciful."

I narrow my eyes, gripping the door handle. "When I destroy you—and I *will* destroy you—please believe I will offer no such mercy." I slam the door in his face.

"Is there nothing your uncle can do? What about someone else? Surely among all the nobles there's someone who can stand up and cut through the web of lies!" I throw the paper down on the table, the headline LORD ACKERLY: SAXXONE SPY AND MURDERER, CROWDS CALL FOR IMMEDIATE HANGING carving a hole in my chest from where it leers at me.

"I'm trying." Eleanor's voice is tight with strain. "Uncle will not get involved."

"Have you had a letter back from him, then?" Ernest asks.

She bites her lip, raising her eyebrows. Then, with a cagey shrug, she says, "He has received my letter and that's enough for me to know his mind. I have also tried Lord Haight and Sir Cartwright, but they won't respond. The problem is that Lord Ackerly made no friends! He had many admirers and made no enemies, but no one knew what his agenda was. All he did was ask questions and encourage people to avoid any aggression toward the continental countries. So, given his parentage, when he is painted as a Hallin spy in such a full picture, everyone is inclined to believe Lord Downpike."

I turn to Ernest, who is pacing in front of the library windows. "What about you? Can't you do anything?"

"I have far fewer connections than Eleanor."

"But you're a lord, nephew and heir to an earl. You could go directly to the queen, appeal on a higher level than we can."

He grimaces, no doubt weighing what it would cost his future. "I can try to get an appointment, but I'm not sure it will do any good."

"We have to at least try." I cradle my face in my hands. "It has been three days, and all we have to show for it is mounting false evidence against Finn." I stand and scream, sweeping my arm across a stack of books on a table and knocking them to the floor. "Curse him, what was he thinking? That we would sit in this house, safe and isolated, until he dangles from the end of a rope?"

"Jessamin," Eleanor says.

"Spirits below, he is an arrogant fool, and I will not stand by while he nobly accepts a fate he does not deserve! I think he saw this all as a solution. If he dies, Lord Downpike cannot get the Hallin magic. If Finn even had it to begin with! I hate—I hate—"

Eleanor pulls me into a hug, and I cry into her shoulder. We're interrupted by an urgent knocking sound.

"What is that?" I ask, pulling out a handkerchief to wipe my face.

"Knocking."

I roll my eyes and smile at her. "Yes, obviously. But from where?"

I go into the hall, listening at the doors until I come to the door that opens onto the park near Eleanor's house, the one Ernest comes and goes through. We knew Ernest was safe because Finn had allowed him in before—plus, we desperately needed someone to bring us food and supplies.

But Ernest is already here. A cold chill sweeps through me. I hesitate. Finn said not to leave and not to let anyone else in. But I can open a door at the very least.

I am greeted by a dark and cloudy afternoon. I don't know whom I expected on the porch, but it was not Kelen. He stands, hunched, looking nervously over his shoulder, hand still raised to continue his urgent knocking.

"What are you doing here?" I ask.

He turns to me, and his face is covered with the same cuts and slashes I saw on Ma'ati's when she was attacked by the birds. "Jessa?"

"Oh, Kelen! What happened?" What a stupid question. I know what happened. And I know why. I should never have spoken with him at the symphony. Will Lord Downpike leave no connection unharmed? I'm so glad Mama is far outside his grasp.

"There was a man. He stopped me on the street and asked me to deliver a letter to you. I said I hadn't seen you and didn't know where you lived now. Then I asked how he knew that I knew you, because it seemed strange." A birdsong drifts past us on the bitter breeze, and he flinches, looking back over his shoulder. "He told me you had business. I didn't like the looks of him so I told him where he could get off, and then a great flock of demon birds swooped down out of nowhere, pecking and scratching and—then they were gone, and he handed me the letter and told me to deliver it myself or he would know." He holds out a thin envelope, crinkled in the corner where his fingers are clenched around it.

"I'm so sorry," I say. "So very sorry. I never thought . . ."

"Can I come in?" he asks, and I recognize the wild look in his eyes of someone on the verge of losing their composure. It is the same look I carry with me all the time since Finn was taken.

"Of course you can—" I stop, closing my eyes and taking a deep breath. "No. I can't explain why. I want nothing more than to have you in and clean you up, but this is not my home, and I can't let you past the door. If you'll wait right here, I'll bring a cloth and a basin of water."

"What are you involved in, Jessa?" His eyes with their almond corners narrow in concern. "You should have let me get you out."

"Please wait. I'll be right back, I promise." I run to the wash-room and fill a basin with water, then grab several hand towels. When I come back out he's sitting on the porch, arms around his knees and eyes trained on the sky.

"Here." I set the basin on the porch step next to him, along with the towels. Only my hand crosses the threshold.

He frowns and then holds out the letter again. I take it, sick to my stomach but oddly hopeful. Perhaps Lord Downpike has given up. Perhaps he realized that Finn hanging accomplishes nothing.

Perhaps I have been declared queen of Albion. It is just as likely.

I break the seal and pull out a single sheet filled with elegant writing. A card drops down, but I do not pick it up. The fate card, once again decorated with the gleaming yellow-eyed bird. This time, the bird has its beak open wide around the letters, swallowing them whole.

Kelen cleans his wounds, muttering about killing the man if he ever sees him again, while I read the contents of the letter.

Little Rabbit,

Lord Acherly will go to his grave without giving me what I want, but I suspect you will be more accommodating. Please do not bother protesting that you do not have the information. Let us not pretend you are anything other than clever. I say this not to flatter you, but because many lives depend upon it.

It took two years of waiting for your Finn to have a weakness, but you bring all the tender compassion of a woman to the bargaining table.

I have recently had disturbing reports of violent rebellious rumblings on the island of Melei. Whole stacks of reports, written and sealed by the ministry of defense. I can think of no option but to brutally smash this rebellion and all associated with it. I fear no one will escape unscathed by the demands of restoring order.

The letter commanding the occupying soldiers to show no mercy in burning the village at the epicenter—I believe it is the same village you are from—will be posted tomorrow.

Unless you deliver to me what I need: a book of Hallin magic. You do have a flair for returning books to me. I hope for the sake of those poor, primitive colony rats that you do not fail.

As a friendly gesture, I may even be inclined to find evidence clearing your Finn's name. Make me happy, little rabbit. Many lives depend upon it.

Tender regards,

L.D.

"No," I whisper.

"What's wrong? You look as though someone has died. Oh, no, someone has, haven't they?"

I shake my head, hollow with dread and hopelessness. "Not yet. But they will. So many will. He will destroy Melei."

"*What?* Who?"

I close my eyes, cradling my head in my hands. "The man you met, Lord Downpike. He thinks I have access to something that he wants, and if he doesn't get it he will order the slaughter of our entire village."

"But he can't!"

"He can."

"Why would he do that?"

"Because I took a path I had no business being on, and now I must pay the price." We sit in a vacuum of silence, both lost in our own worlds of fear and confusion.

"Can you find it?" Kelen's voice is soft, unsure. All the fight has gone out of him. "The thing he wants?"

"I honestly don't know."

"Would it be so bad if you did?"

"It would mean war. Alben domination of the Iverian continent. Doing to other countries what they've already done to Melei, on a grander scale."

"Who cares?"

I look up into Kelen's black eyes, surprised. "What?"

"Who cares? Let these arrogant spirit cursers fight their own battles. This is nothing to do with you. If you have a way to protect Melei from being ravaged any more than it already has, then take it. The wars of these ghost-faced monsters are their own fault."

"But it's wrong to give in to him. Lives will be lost."

"Do you value Alben lives, continental lives more than the lives of your own people? Are you that far lost to this poisonous country that you'd put their safety above the safety of your own village? Your own mother?" His words have no venom, but I can see the disappointment in his eyes.

I shake my head. "I don't know what to do."

Kelen stands, dropping the cloth now spotted with his blood. "I wish I could help, but seeing as I'm not allowed into a fine lord's house, I suppose I can't. You've already shown you don't accept help, anyway. I hope you make the right choice. I really do."

He walks away, taking with him one of the paths I didn't choose. I wonder what would have happened, what would have been different, had I given up Finn at the start.

I look down at the letter in my hand, feeling the weight of

lives in my palm. I want to sit here forever and never move, never make a decision. But that is not an option, and I am better than that.

I stand.

First things first, to see if I can actually find the magic Lord Downpike wants. Then I'll decide what to do with it.

Thirty-two

ELEANOR COLLAPSES ONTO THE COUCH, THE entire library a labyrinth of madly strewn books. Most of them aren't even magic. There are history volumes, philosophy, even a full section of gothic novels.

"It's useless. This whole place is positively drenched in magic. I couldn't isolate a single item if our lives depended . . . well. I can't."

While Eleanor has been following magic trails, I've physically checked everywhere. The kitchen, the art gallery, the guest bedrooms Eleanor and I have been staying in. I searched everywhere in Finn's room, the absence of him so physical it was a sharp pain in my stomach. I even checked for loose floorboards, hidden panels, everything.

I briefly wondered if he would have hidden something at his country estate, but considering that was where he wanted to send me for safety, I can't imagine he would risk that.

No. The library is where he studied, where he worked, where he spent nearly all his time.

"If he didn't want anyone to find something, I doubt we'll be able to." Ernest scowls, then tightens his tie. "I'll—I've got to be off. I'll call on you both tomorrow." He twitches nervously, and I fear he's given up on us entirely.

Eleanor waves good-bye to him, then turns to me. "I'm so sorry. We tried."

I nod, throat tight. Ernest is right. Even *if* Finn had a book of Hallin magic to begin with, if he wanted the book hidden forever, we have no chance. I wish I could visit him, talk to him. He would know what to do. But I can't leave the house, and the prison returns all the letters I've sent him, unopened. Eleanor's, too, which is an even greater loss, since she can apparently know things just by her letters being read.

"You can go," I say, defeated. "There's no reason to stay here now. Downpike knows he has me. I can't imagine he'd bother hurting you."

"A blessing of unimportance. I'll stay until tomorrow, though. If you need me I'll be in my room, spying on the letters I've sent. Something might turn up." She squeezes my shoulder as she walks by. "Maybe he's bluffing."

I touch my glove, the pins and needles nearly gone. I do not doubt Lord Downpike's vicious sincerity.

Alone now, I sit and stare blankly at the setting sun beyond the windows. The sun won't set here for another hour or two, and again I wonder where this library is. I pick up one of the books next to me, a gothic romance, and open it.

Edeline Annaliese Hallin is written in slanted, feminine cursive in the front. I pick up another of the novels. The same. And another. The same.

Finn's mother. It has to be. I had never heard her name before.

Finn mentioned that parts of this house were his parents'. I know now why this was Finn's favorite room, why he spent so much time here: it was his mother's library.

And then I remember something he said out in the hall with a smile of a secret humor: *No book of Hallin magic is in this country.*

I rush to the windows, pushing against them, trying to find any that slide or open. I must get out, must see what's beyond this room. Grabbing a chair, I slam it into the window as hard as I can. I'm thrown against the floor for my effort, the window not so much as cracked. Desperate, I start at the far end of the window wall, searching for a hint of an opening. I miss it the first time, but doubling back I notice a small, round indentation in one of the vertical lead seams between glass panes.

I lean in closer, tracing it. Finn's heavy golden seal ring glints in the dull light, and I'm unsure if I should shout for joy or cry out in despair. Is it better for me to find the book or to fail? I cannot tell. But now curiosity has taken over, and I must see this through. I turn the ring around on my finger and put my palm flat against the glass so the raised circular top of the ring fits into the indentation.

The pane in front of me shimmers and disappears. I walk through into a balmy twilight, on a balcony overlooking a mirror-clear lake surrounded by deep green pines. There are mountains in the distance, carefully groomed gardens immediately beneath me. I turn and look to the side to see a turret jutting out, the flag on top bearing the crest of Saxxone royalty.

The castle. His mother's library in the castle where she grew up, the one she had to leave forever. I lean against the carved stone railing of the narrow balcony, missing Finn and missing his parents for him. Feeling sorry for a woman I never met who had to leave behind everything she loved and knew, because she could not give up the man her shadow chose.

I smile, knowing at least she got to keep a segment of her old life, a library and a balcony blocked off from everything else. But still home. I wonder if I could choose only one part of Melei to keep with me always, if I knew I could never go back, what I would pick.

I think it would be the sun-spackled glen next to a waterfall hidden deep in the mountain hills behind my village. I should very much like a door that opens there.

There's a bench in the corner of the balcony. I want to sit on it and think, but then I notice something beneath.

I kneel on the stone floor and duck my head down. There's a chest, wood carved with the family seal I wear on my finger. My heart racing, I pull it out and find the same lock that kept the window-door closed. The ring fits, and it pops open with a *click*.

I reach in to find a sheet of stiff parchment on top.

Last Will and Testament of Lord Finley Rainer Ackerly,
son of Lord Thomas Ackerly and her Royal Highness Edeline
Hallin. Being of sound mind and judgment, I hereby bequeath
all my earthly possessions and inheritances to my betrothed, Miss
Jessamin Olea of Melei.

   Signed this day in front of witnesses,
   Lord Finley Ackerly

I sit on the hard floor, stunned and angry. I don't know what bothers me more—that he claims me as his fiancée, or that he thought the odds of his death were high enough that he had to find one last way to try and take care of me.

"Fie on you, Finn Ackerly, if you think I'm going to let you die."

I set aside the will with a scowl and return to the chest. Sitting snug in the bottom is a thick volume of deep green, an unfamiliar crest stamped into the cover. I pull it out, brush off a layer of dust, and crack it open.

Inside are symbols and directions, crammed in tiny writing, page after page after page. I don't have to be able to use any of it to know that in this book is all of the Hallin line magical knowledge.

I hold in my hands the fate of Melei, the fate of the continents, the fate of Albion. The fate of my Finn.

I have never known such a heavy book.

Thirty-three

IT'S LONG PAST FULL DARK WHEN I FINALLY carry the book back inside the library. The windowpane reappears, sealing itself shut behind me, and the room is pitch black. I feel my way to the desk against the wall where I know I'll find a small glass kerosene lantern. Fumbling, I pull a match from the drawer and light the wick.

The soft, warm glow throws the room into shadows, and I sit with my back to it, looking at my own shadow. These past days with Finn gone, I've spent more time than I care to admit watching my shadow, waiting for glimpses of his, wondering if he's watching or listening, if he even can from a prison designed for magic practitioners.

"I don't know if you can hear me," I say. "And I know you can't answer. But I'm lost, Finn, and I wish you were here. I have to make a decision, and whichever way I choose, lives will be lost. It won't be my fault, it will be the actions of an evil man, but he makes me complicit. I don't know that I can live with the results of my choice no matter what it is." My shadows flicker, probably in response to the unsteady light behind me.

"I think you would caution me to do whatever I must in order to keep myself safe." I smile. "I think you also know me well enough by now to know that I will certainly not listen to your advice on that matter. I'm lost no matter what happens tonight. I wish . . . I wish many things, but I wish I had been able to tell you that I love you, in so many more ways than that word can convey in Alben, and I'm sorry for how things look like they will end. I would have liked the chance to yell at you for claiming me as your betrothed without my consent."

I pause.

"I would have liked the chance to let you wait in agony and then, maybe someday, accept an offer of marriage."

The lines of the shadows grow a bit stronger and I smile. "Well, if wishes were water I'd have a well, as Mama liked to say. And since you are not here to tell me what to do so I can decide to do the opposite, I'll have to make up my own mind."

I stand, carrying the lamp with me, unwilling to turn on the electric lights and illuminate the empty house I don't expect to return to. The lamp is elegant, all glass, the bottom globe holding the fuel with a wick going up to the top globe where the flame gleams. It feels fragile, personal.

I go to my bedroom to change, buttoning a dark overcoat on top of my white blouse and long skirts as rain patters against the windows.

If the independent input of fate is the line of my derivative equation, it most likely ends in my death at the hands of Lord Downpike. But how can I shift the other variables around that line to save the highest number of people? Which variable do I sacrifice? X, being the Iverian continent, has a vastly higher proportion of people. Y, being Melei, has a vastly higher proportion of personal importance. Z, being Finn, seems to be so tied to my line I cannot imagine a way to extract him from my same fate.

And is Lord Downpike a variable, or is he the chart on which all other variables are plotted?

No. I will not give him that power. I may not be able to write him out of the equation of my fate, but I can eliminate his variable.

I smile, and whether it is the prospect of my impending doom or the realization that, one way or another, everything will be decided soon, I feel light and disconnected, unweighted by the worries of the world.

I pick up the worn umbrella from the kind woman in the park. It seems like a lifetime ago I accepted it from her. There is goodness everywhere, more than enough to combat the Lord Downpikes of the world. I tuck the book beneath my arm, take up the lantern, and walk down the hall.

"Good-bye, Eleanor," I whisper.

I open the door to the park and am unsurprised to find my porch lined with big black birds. "Go tell your stupid master I have what he wants. I will be waiting in the park." I walk past them, missing Sir Bird terribly. I would have liked his company tonight.

The rain patters loudly on my umbrella and drowns out any other night sounds. It's an actual downpour, more ambitious than Avebury's usual attempts, and I feel sealed off from the night beneath the curve of my protection. The gravel path is puddling in lower areas, water streaming into more water, which will seep down into the tunnels beneath the city where I first rested my head in the hollow of Finn's neck.

So much water.

I think of Sir Bird, and a tiny flame inside of me dares to hope.

I make my way to the center of the park, lantern light turning the rain around me into golden drops. When I leave the path, the earth squelches under my feet, already saturated. Overhanging branches drop heavy collections of water in staccato bursts onto my umbrella.

I wait.

Before long, a figure in a dark suit materializes like a shadow from between trees, staying just outside the ring of my light. He has no umbrella, merely a hat set back on his head. He seems unaware of the soaking rain, smiling at me as though we were dear friends meeting under the sun.

"Well done, little rabbit."

"I want Finn freed. Now."

"Oh." He says it as a sigh, a false note of sympathy behind his voice. "Finn made a rash decision just a few minutes ago.

Thanks to Eleanor's industrious brother, Finn was being delivered to the courts to have an audience with the prime minister when the guards reported he stopped and did not respond to anything they said, as though he were listening to something they couldn't hear."

The shadow. He *was* listening. A cold dread fills my stomach.

"After a moment he went mad, throwing off his guards and running for the bridge. They had no choice but to shoot him."

Pain washes over me like the pounding of the tide. "No," I whisper.

"It's very disappointing. I had further plans for him."

"He's not dead."

"The royal guards are excellent marksmen, and without his cane he had no magic stored. They're recovering his body from the river now. Such a pity."

"You're lying."

"Stupid girl, if I wanted to lie, I would tell you he was alive and well and you were doing the right thing to secure his freedom. I would feed you hope. But you know how this ends. You've already made the decision to sacrifice everything in order to protect your precious island home. I was worried for a while, that you'd been so seduced by the pale, glittering wealth of this country, by their fine manners and dead eyes and simpering customs, that you might actually be willing to let me burn the village."

Finn. My Finn. I want to collapse to the ground, to sink into it. This grief would consume me like a moth in a flame, and I want to let it. I want to hand over the book and be done with it right now. But then I would not be the woman Finn gave his shadow to. I refuse to be anything less than what I am.

"You won't win."

"I will. And after I've exterminated the Hallin line, I'll be the most powerful man in the world. But you don't need to worry about that. You've done your part."

"How do I know you will not still punish Melei?"

He shakes his head. "You really are daft, aren't you? Everyone always thought you were so smart, but you can't see *anything*. I was so happy when I found you again that first time. I meant what I said, that I would have kept you for my own. You would have been happy. Maybe I still will keep you."

"All the magic in the world couldn't make me love a man like you."

"Really?" He steps closer, into the soft pool of light around me. His face is covered with glimmering droplets of water. "But you'd kiss me."

"You're mad."

Laughing, he pulls out a handkerchief from his waistcoat pocket. "Am I?" He wipes his face. Along with the water droplets, his very skin is taken off, revealing a darker one beneath with the sharp smile and sharp eyes that I caught glimpses of all along.

"Kelen," I whisper.

Thirty-four

KELEN'S GRIN SPREADS ACROSS HIS FACE. "IN THE
flesh. Well, in someone else's flesh. Most of the time."

"You're working for Lord Downpike?" I feel dizzy, unbalanced, disconnected from reality.

"I *am* Lord Downpike."

"You can't be. It's impossible. You only left the island three
years ago."

"Don't insult me by assuming Lord Downpike could have
done all this, set it all in motion. He was so blind he could not
recognize his own son when he hired me on as a servant. You
weren't the only one of us with Alben blood. Lord Downpike's
blood just happened to be more useful than pathetic Milton

Miller's. Not so precious as your mama treated you, now, are you?"

"You killed my father."

"We bastard children have to look out for one another." He smiles, and I cringe, trying to sink into myself and get away from him, get away from the new light this rewrites our history in. "I spent a year working for Downpike, watching him, studying his books and his magic when he was asleep. But I was the lowly colony rat servant, and he never thought for a moment I was anything more than that."

"But how did you—you *became* him."

"It was his idea, really. He was so paranoid about Hallin magic that he'd have done anything for it. He needed an alibi no one could question. So he called me into his study—powerless, faithful servant me—and cast a spell to make me look like him. I was to go and get myself jailed for the evening, which I did."

"Finn's parents. He killed them, then." I wish I could tell Finn, could answer this question for him. Oh, Finn. I close my eyes against the rush of grief. Too dangerous to lose myself now. I force myself to look at Kelen.

He waves his hand, the gesture a knife in my heart. "Downpike came back, as pale as beach sand and shaking, covered in blood. He asked me to help him get the blood out of his clothes. I answered by choking the life out of him. It was no challenge at all to replace him. After I let the servants go, no one noticed a thing. These nobles do not take care of their own."

"But why? Why any of this? Why would you want to extend Albion's power, continue your father's legacy?"

"Spirits below, you are obtuse. My only interest is securing so much power that I control everything. If you are not the most powerful person in the room, you are nothing. And when the Alben gentry is decimated in the coming conflict, well, that is no great loss. I'll eliminate them all in the end, anyway. I will never be at another's mercy again."

I shake my head, unable, unwilling to process all of this. "You hurt me. We were friends, and you hurt me."

"I *am* sorry about that, little rabbit." This time he uses the Melenese word for rabbit, and I remember how he used to be the fox, every time we played Fox and Rabbit—how could I not have realized? "I never meant for you to get involved. I saw you the first day you met Ackerly and began watching you out of tender care. Then you gave me an opening with Ackerly, a chance to finally manipulate him. And I wanted to punish your Finn for thinking he could have you, for thinking he could claim one of my people for himself just as his country claimed my entire island. I was going to make you forget. You wouldn't have remembered the pain, and you would have been so happy to be reunited with me. I would have protected you, Jessa. I would have kept you free from all this. He couldn't do that for you, could he?"

"I wouldn't let him."

"Think of all the pain you could have avoided if you hadn't chosen him. But I'm in a forgiving mood. I may yet take away your memories and let you fall in love with me." His smile cuts through the night, blacker and colder. "And then I'll give them back and let you lose Finn all over again. Over, and over, and over, for the rest of your life, as punishment for choosing him."

He takes off his hat, pouring water out of the brim, and then puts it back on his head. "Now then. My book. Hand it over like a good rabbit, and I won't destroy Melei."

"You wouldn't."

"I wouldn't let soldiers kill the people who stepped aside and let our entire culture be stomped underfoot? I wouldn't let them harm the people who let a visiting noble rape and abandon my mother? I wouldn't let them destroy the people so infuriatingly weak they cannot even take care of their own? I would. I will. Give me the book."

I look into his eyes, a dead black that reflect no light, not even a flash from the lantern. "You threatened everyone that I love. You killed my bird. And you took Finn from me."

I drop the book on the ground, raise the lantern, and smash it down. The glass shatters, spilling kerosene, which immediately catches fire. The whole book is consumed.

"No!" Kelen screams, shoving me aside. He stomps on the flames but the oil won't be smothered, the choking harsh scent of the smoke overpowering the wet earth around us.

Cursing desperately, Kelen reaches into his pocket and pulls out a handful of sugar. He whispers a word and flings the sugar outward. It hits the book and the flames eat higher.

An inarticulate howl of rage tears from Kelen's lips. He throws both hands in the air and screams a single word, releasing all his power, trying to turn flame into water using a stored-up spell.

One of the spells I changed in Sir Bird's book.

The rain pouring down ignites in droplets of fire, and as they connect with more water, the magic spreads. The puddles around us shoot up in crackling, hungry flames, and Kelen's sodden clothes turn into an inferno.

He screams, dropping to the ground and rolling, but the water around him lights on fire, fire and more fire, devouring him alive, a bright and burning beacon in the night.

My umbrella catches, and I throw it to the side, the wet hem of my skirt igniting. I turn in a desperate circle, but there is nowhere to run. I am surrounded by flames and will meet the same fate as Kelen.

A spurt flares up next to me, and I cringe back, bracing myself for the burn, when darkness rises in front of me like a shield, blocking the flames. I gasp as Finn's shadow wraps itself around me, covering me with the cold pins-and-needles sensation.

If Finn is dead, how can his shadow still protect me?

I run from the flames, my skirts smoldering beneath Finn's shadow, and do not stop until I am well out of the fire's range. I kick off my outer skirt, and then look down at where an extra layer of shadow lies on my skin.

"Thank you," I whisper, but the shadow dissolves as I watch. I grasp at it, desperate to keep it—*him*—here with me, but I cannot hold on to anything.

The flames eat higher, the sizzling and popping of water meeting heat a discordant night chorus. I sit on the ground and watch. Another Melenese custom we were forced to abandon was the funeral pyre. Kelen does not deserve the last rites of a warrior. But I think he deserves this death.

I won.

And I lost.

And I cannot find it in me to feel anything but dead. That is one of the words for love I forgot. The word that means a connection so strong that when your love dies, your body goes on but your soul sinks into the ground after them.

I stay there as the local constables come and put out the flames. I stay there as Eleanor rushes out with a blanket to wrap around my shoulders while I numbly repeat my statement that Lord Downpike perished in flames of his own making in an effort to cover up his crimes. I stay there until morning when the sun breaks through the clouds, and I can see—once and for all—that I have only one shadow.

Thirty-five

"BUT WHY A SCHOOL IN GALLEN? SURELY THE ONE here will have you back." Eleanor's voice has a distinct note of whine in it.

I set down my pen from where I am writing a letter to Mama about my plans to attend school in the capital of Gallen. I have suggested that, as she no longer has payments from Milton Miller—a man I have not been able to spare tears for, though I do not think he deserved to die—she ought to come live with me and give me the chance to take care of her as she always took such excellent care of me. I hope she accepts. I would like to build a new relationship with her as an adult.

I feel very old these days.

I shake my head at Eleanor. "Gallen is much more liberal in their acceptance of women scholars. I haven't the energy to fight that battle here anymore. You should join me. I hear there is drama to be had where Gallen men are involved."

She laughs and sits on the desk next to my letter. "I already cannot keep up with all of the invitations for visits and tea times. Everyone wants to hear about Lord Downpike's secret, evil plots. I never thought I would say this, but I think I am tired of being Avebury's most prestigious gossip."

"Spirits' blessings." I smile but avoid her eyes. It feels false letting her spread details of Lord Downpike's death when I know that the real one died years ago. I wonder often whether I did the right thing in concealing Kelen's role in it all. But I wanted Melei left out of this entirely. It was never our fight, though Kelen and I managed to become the central figures.

Perhaps it was selfish, but I cannot bear to have my country sullied by one crazed man's actions. Lord Downpike was already a murderer, after all. Kelen's secrets died with him, and that must be good enough for me. I saved Melei, and I probably saved Albion and the continental countries as well. But I did not manage to save the person that made the world shine for me.

Eleanor must see the shift in my expression, because she puts a hand on my shoulder. "Finn's memorial was well-attended. The prime minister himself came, along with the Saxxone ambassador. It was a nice ceremony."

I close my eyes and nod. "I would not have entrusted it to anyone else. I'm certain you did beautifully by it. I'm sorry I didn't come, but I find . . . well, there is so much packing and planning to be done, and I knew none of his friends, anyway, and . . ."

"It's all right, Jessamin." She hugs me. The doorbell rings and she stands. "That will be Ernest."

"Please give him my thanks once again. For trying to help with getting Finn to the prime minister."

"I will. As for me, I'm ready for tea. A tea all alone where I do not have to regale anyone with my lurid tales of intrigue and heroism." She pauses. "I will miss this house. It'll be lonely returning to my big, empty place without you. I think I'll convince you to live with me yet. I'm very persuasive."

I wave my hand with a small smile. She walks out, closing the door softly behind her.

I pick up my things and move to another chair, away from the square of late afternoon sunlight streaming in through the library window. I spent the last two weeks staring at my shadow, willing it to be more than just mine, willing it to show me some hint, any hint of Finn. I drove myself near mad with grief, and after spending his memorial yesterday standing by the window staring at my shadow until I could not see anymore, I vowed never to watch for it again.

Last night I dreamt of the tree-arched path of Fate. It was dark, and I was alone, and I did not know how to move forward anymore. Even now the pain of missing him threatens to well up and drown me. But I will not dishonor his memory by devoting my life to mourning him. He wouldn't approve, and it would go against the things I think he loved about me.

I wish I had told him everything I loved about him. *Love* about him. I can hold on to those, at least. I twist the heavy gold ring on my hand. I took the glove off yesterday, when the last of the sensations had finally faded. Another gift from Finn I will keep forever—my hand whole and unblemished, with his ring on my index finger.

I hear the door open again behind me. "Honestly, Eleanor, I will not move in with you. You're welcome to come to Gallen. I'm certain we could find something for you to study."

A voice that is not Eleanor's answers me. "I plan on studying history scholars, actually."

All the grief I have neatly packed and stored in the shadows of my soul springs up, rising into my throat and choking me. I stand, unable to turn, unable to draw a breath for fear of being mistaken, my eyes glued to the floor. A fine pair of shoes enters the narrow range of my vision.

They cast no shadow.

"You're dead," I whisper, still not daring to look up.

"Nearly," Finn answers, his voice the soft song of my dreams. I look up, barely able to see him through tears. He's thinner, with the pale and drawn look of someone who has been sick for a long time but is on the mend. "It's a tricky thing, trying to use a transport spell stored in your body while being pulled down a river bleeding to death. You will have to excuse me for getting lost and taking so long to get back to you."

"I will excuse no such thing." I throw my arms around his neck and bury my face in his shoulder. "You are not excused, you will never be excused, and you will spend the rest of your life making it up to me."

He laughs. "I had planned on nothing less."

My lips meet his, and I do not resign myself to this fate. I claim it as my own. Forever.

Acknowledgments

FIRST, ALWAYS, THANKS GO TO NOAH. MY SHADOW may stay put, but my heart couldn't help but jump to you. Thanks for treasuring it.

Elena, Jonah, and Ezra, you create magic simply by existing, and I'm so grateful to have you in my life.

Michelle Wolfson, there is no one I'd rather build a career with. Thanks for always being there for me.

Erica Sussman, you deserve endless credit for never knowing what I'm going to give you next, but always knowing just what to do with it.

Natalie Whipple and Stephanie Perkins, you always enable my crazy in the best possible ways. What would I do without you? (Don't answer that. It's a post-apocalyptic scenario and you know I don't like those kinds of stories.)

The team at HarperTeen—Christina Colangelo, Casey McIntyre, Stephanie Stein, Michelle Taormina, Alison Donalty, Jessica Berg—you are all a joy to work with, and I'm so grateful for your collective talents.

Mom and Dad, thanks for giving me the books that supplied the magic junior high and high school were, shockingly enough, lacking.

Erin White Goodsell, without you my teenage years would have entirely missed an awareness of feminism and post-colonialism. And Lindsey White Bench, thank you for weirding out your husband by crushing so hard on Finn. It was the encouragement I needed. Lauren White Hansen and Matt White, guess you both should have done something more remarkable to make it into this acknowledgments section. (Wait, guess you did anyway.)

Special thanks to Jane Austen, Susanna Clarke, Diana Wynne Jones, and Hayao Miyazaki for telling stories that inspire me.

Finally, to my readers. You are exceptional. Never let anyone make you feel like you aren't enough.

A story of humor, romance, family . . . and chaos.

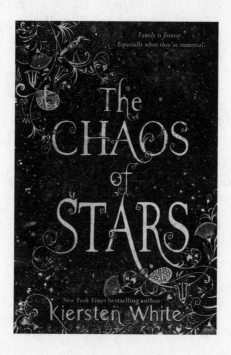

Read on for an excerpt!

When I was a little girl, I still believed I was part of the world's secret magic.

Mother wrapped her hair elegantly in white cloth. I begged and pleaded until she did mine as well. At the river, Mother gathered pebbles and sand, small plants, sun-bleached bones. I splashed along the banks, or rode on female hippos if Taweret, my aunt and the goddess of childbirth, was with us.

But my favorite place to be, even more than in the brilliant sun reflecting off the water of the Nile, was with my father. When I was old enough to navigate the steep, worn steps by myself, I was there every minute Mother allowed. As soon as I finished my morning worship, I'd skip straight down. Coloring on the floor next to Father's knees as he nodded and watched things I couldn't see. Giggling as I ran between Ammit's unmoving lion and hippo legs. Memorizing the pictures along the walls, making up stories for the people portrayed there.

Mother gave me my very own paints, and Father proudly gave me a room. I'd never been happier. Countless hours down there I painted, sketched, planned. I drew the stories of my life on those walls, filled them with the people and places I loved. My mom, beautiful and strong. My dad, serene and kind. Grandma Nut stretching across the sky to watch us all. They were my family; they were my story.

My cat, cranky old Ubesti, came down with me sometimes, though she much preferred the warm, sunlit stones under the skylights in our house. One morning when I was barely thirteen, I decided I needed a live model for her newest portrait on my walls. She was in her usual spot, mangy fur dull and matted even in the light. I went to pick her up, expecting a yowl of protest, but was met instead with a limp, lifeless body.

My mother immediately knew something was wrong and came into the room to find me crying. She consoled me with a hug that soothed my hiccupping sobs, and a kiss that made my head stop hurting from the tears.

"Don't worry, Little Heart," she said. "How would you like Ubesti to be yours forever?"

I nodded, desperate. I'd seen my mother heal sick locals, witnessed her save a baby others had given up for dead. She was *magic*. Surely bringing my elderly cat back from death would be no problem—after all, she'd resurrected my father. Death was not a barrier for Isis.

She took Ubesti's body from my arms and told me to meet her downstairs in my room. I nearly tripped in my haste to get there, pacing with nervous excitement. Even after all the potions and amulets I'd helped her with, she'd never done actual spells for me, and at that moment I loved her even more than I knew possible.

My father came in, smiling his soft, distant smile, and my mother followed him, beaming and carrying a large jar in her hands. It was carved with glyphs, the lid shaped like a cat's head, all made in precious alabaster.

"What's that?" I asked, eager to see what resurrection required.

"This is the vessel that will carry Ubesti to the other side, where she will wait for you." Osiris nodded solemnly as my mother handed him the jar and he placed it on the large block of stone that I used as a table in the middle of the room.

"Wait—other side? What other side?"

"The afterlife," my father said, looking at me with pride in his eyes. "I am pleased you chose her as a companion for your journey through death."

I staggered back, staring in horror at the jar I now realized contained my cat. "You—she's not coming back to life?"

"No, Little Heart, not to this life."

The world shifted. My childhood rewrote itself, everything changing as I realized what this room was, what the person-sized, rectangular stone box was. "This is a tomb. This is *my* tomb." I could barely see my parents through my tears, but their smiles hadn't changed.

"Of course," my mother said.

"I'm going to *die*?"

"Everything dies." My mother took a few steps toward me, but I held up my hands, blocking her.

"You don't die! He doesn't die!"

"No, Little Heart, but you—"

"You're going to just let me die? And put me in there, all by myself, forever?"

"You won't be alone. You'll be with your father and all your brothers and sisters who have gone before you."

"But I won't be *here*!"

"No."

"You don't care? That doesn't make you sad? You're not going to do anything to stop it?"

Finally my mother caught on, and her expression softened. "Oh, Isadora, when you understand—"

I ran out of that horrible room. For the first time in my life I *did* understand. All of the stories, the histories I'd been raised on? I had no part in them. My parents brought me into the world to die. They didn't love me enough to keep me forever—they didn't even pretend like they did. My entire childhood of warmth and love was a drawing in the sand—impermanent and fragile and gone in a breath of wind.

Just like me.

Nut, the sky goddess, had disobeyed Amun-Re, god of the sun. She'd taken the god of the earth as a lover. Amun-Re feared that introducing more gods into the world would create an imbalance of power.

Amun-Re put a curse on her that she could not give birth on any day of the year. But Amun-Re did not account for Thoth, gentle god of wisdom and writing. Thoth challenged the Moon herself to a game, and won enough light to create new days. Because those days were not cursed, Nut was able to give birth to Osiris, Isis, Set, and Nephthys.

Osiris, Isis, Set, and Nephthys went on to commit theft, adultery, fratricide, and even attempted murder and extortion against the sun god himself. In retrospect, Amun-Re was probably on to something with that whole "more gods, more chaos" thing.

I FORGET TO ACCOUNT FOR THE TIME OF YEAR when I turn on the sink to scrub the charred remains of the lamb skewers I'm cooking. A torrent of water shoots out, bouncing off the pan and soaking me.

"Chaos!" I shout, furious. I shouldn't even be making dinner. We're having family over, so Mother wants everything to be nice. If she wants it to be nice, *she* should cook. But no. It's summertime. Every summer Isis mourns the death of her beloved husband, and the Nile overflows with her tears. Used to be the whole country would flood, but then they went ahead and dammed the dang thing. That, combined with the lack of worshippers, means now when my mother enters her period of mourning, the only difference you can tell is a substantial increase in water pressure. Awesome for showers, but otherwise pointless.

Still, she uses it as an excuse for everything. Yesterday I asked what was for dinner, and all I heard back were wails for the death of her husband.

Made even more awkward by Father, sitting at the dining room table in his robe and mummy wrappings, reading the paper. Because sure, he was murdered, it sucked, but guess what? Not dead anymore!

I slam the pan back onto the stove and throw new skewers on it. This kitchen was supposed to be ornamental. When I was designing it last year, I never thought I'd actually have to use it. I don't even know how half the state-of-the-art appliances work. They were picked based on color scheme.

Despite a second try, the skewers come out more charred than browned—my mother's efforts to domesticate me foiled yet again.

I throw everything together and balance it on my hip as

I walk out of the kitchen (eggplant walls, shiny black granite counters, sleek black fridge, apparently useless black stove set flat in the counter) and into the dining room. This room is butter yellow with white wood paneling, and a black table to pull in the color theme from the kitchen. The table is perfect: sleek, modern lines, not a scratch on it, one of my best buys ever. It's also occupied by two of my least favorite relatives—Horus, my nightmare know-it-all of an oldest brother, and Hathor, his drunken floozy of a wife.

I slam the platter of charcoal, sauce, and garnishes down in the middle of the table and then sit for dinner. Mother clears her throat primly. She looks strange. Normally she barely gets out of bed during her mourning period, but other than the occasional freakout like yesterday, she's been downright perky.

"Did you pray?" she asks.

"For the last time," I say, narrowing my kohl-lined black eyes at her, "I refuse to pray to my own parents. It's ridiculous."

"Osiris?" My mother looks at him as though he might, for once, step in.

My father slowly turns to the next page of his newspaper. This one's in Tagalog. The whole family is blessed with the gift of tongues (even me), and my father's hobby is reading every newspaper he can find in every language imaginable. No doubt he realizes that newspapers are a dying form. He sympathizes with all things obsolescing and dead. He is the god of the underworld, after all.

I smirk at Mother, knowing that the second she appealed to him I won the argument.

"Very well." She cuts a dainty bite of the blackened mess and chews it, a very nonseasonal smile gradually pulling at her mouth. My mother is beautiful, in a warm, comforting sort of way. Wide hips, full lips, and a bust that inspired art for thousands of years. I'd prefer not to have inherited that from her, but in the grand scheme of things it's not something to complain about. I'm also rocking her same thick, jet-black hair and large almond eyes, though I have heavy bangs that skim my eyelashes and layers that obscure my jawline, strong like Osiris's. Still, no one's making any statues of me.

And no one ever will.

Hathor takes one bite and gags, washing it down with her glass of beer that magically refills itself. She's the *goddess* of beer. And sex. My mother's favorite son married an eternal lush. It'd be funnier if Hathor weren't always slinking around, touching everyone and giving long, lingering looks to anything that moves.

Her dramatic, cat-eye-lined gaze fixes on me. "Essa!" she coos. "This is wonderful."

"It's Isadora."

"Of course!" She laughs, low and intimate. "After all this time I can't keep track anymore! If only your mother would branch out a bit."

Sometimes it hurts to be forgotten while I'm still alive. But she has a point. Every single one of my mother's hundreds of offspring have had variations of her name or my father's. Hathor and Horus (and pretty much everyone else) don't even bother trying to remember my name.

"Nice as always to visit." Hathor smiles at my mother. Or bares her teeth, really.

"It's such a pleasant surprise when I invite my son to a family dinner and you tag along, too." My mother's smile has even more teeth.

After a few tense moments between the two of them, Mother imperiously breaks eye contact. Then she beams at us, clearing her throat over and over again until Osiris finally sets down the paper and looks at her.

"I asked you here for dinner because I have an announcement. I'm pregnant!"

Father blinks slowly, his eyes as black as his skin, then picks the paper back up. "A bit ahead of schedule. What about this one?" He nods in my general direction. I'm too shocked for the *this one* to sting. I'm sixteen. She has a baby every twenty years. Twenty. Not sixteen. Of all of the traditions the goddess of motherhood and fertility could throw out the window, this is the one she picks?

Isis shrugs, trying to look guilty behind her delighted smile. "I thought we could shake things up a bit. Besides, Isadora's getting so big."

"What, I had a growth spurt so now I'm expendable?"

9

I can't believe she's replacing me already! She could at least pretend I matter even though she didn't care enough to make me last forever like stupid Horus.

I'm so mad about this—I *am*—I'm furious. The only reason there are tears in my eyes is because I used too many onions in dinner. "Besides," I say, trying not to sniffle, "you're the one who's always going on about schedules and traditions and doing things the same way all the time so that chaos can't creep in and mess things up!"

"I think it's wonderful," Horus says, eating with gusto. "Keep the family line going."

I glare at him, knowing exactly what he gets from my mother having more babies. What they all get. I won't pretend otherwise. "Are the batteries running low? Time to pop out a new little worshipper who will be more obedient?"

Mother's glare silences me with a familiar burst of pain. She shakes her head, and the pain eases a bit. "Don't be dramatic, Isadora. You can help me with the baby! It'll be good practice for when you have your own in a few years!"

Oh, death, anything but that. There are enough statues of her nursing miniature pharaohs everywhere I turn that I vowed long ago never to have kids of my own. No squealing babies sucking on my girls *ever*, thankyouverymuch. I quickly wipe under my eyes. Stupid onions.

"You'll be a great help to Mother," Horus says, flashing his falcon-bright eyes at me in a cold smile.

"Gee, thanks, Whore-us." He can't hear how I spell it, but it makes me feel better just knowing.

"When's the new one due to arrive?" he asks our mother, and she beams back, practically glowing now that she is in full maternal-glory mode.

"Two months."

I choke. "Two months? Aren't babies supposed to take, like, four times that long?" I lean back and look at her stomach. Now that I stare, there's a definite bulge. And she's been wearing her flowiest ceremonial robes lately. I hadn't thought anything of it.

"I waited for the right time to tell you. I didn't want to upset you."

"Bang-up job on that one."

"Isadora . . ."

I hold up my hands in surrender. "Fine. Awesome. Two months."

"Another thing," Isis says, her voice getting distant and tight.

I groan. "If you say it's twins, I'm going to stab myself in the eye with this fork."

"I wanted to ask if anyone has had any dreams lately."

The gods all shake their heads, then everyone turns to me.

"Loads of them," I say. "Every night, in fact. It's amazing." Isis's eyes begin narrowing, and I hold up my hands. "Sorry! You'll have to be more specific."

Worry clouds her face. "Dreams of darkness. Dreams of danger."

I shrug. "Nope. Nothing but sunshine and frolicking in the Nile with a herd of purple hippos."

"Purple. Hmm." Her face is way too thoughtful. Never underestimate the ancient Egyptian emphasis on the ability of dreams to portend the future. As far as I'm concerned, a dream is a dream is a dream.

Osiris uses my mother's distraction to stand and drift back to the underworld section of the house, as the others continue talking about the baby news.

I feel a wave of bleak sadness, a desperate, gasping sort of terror. This new life coming to our house forces me to face my own impermanence in a way I try to avoid at all costs. I'm replaceable. Utterly, completely replaceable.

A STORY OF HUMOR, ROMANCE, FAMILY . . . AND CHAOS

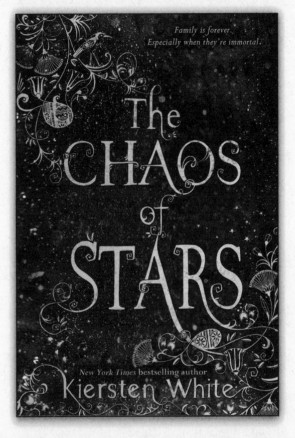

Family is forever.
Especially when they're immortal.

The CHAOS *of* STARS

New York Times bestselling author
Kiersten White

Isadora's family is seriously screwed up—which comes with the territory when you're the human daughter of the ancient Egyptian gods Isis and Osiris.

When Isadora gets the chance to move to California, she jumps on it. But she quickly learns there's no such thing as a clean break from family.